CURSE OF BLOOD AND SIGHT

AMY PROKOPIS

Amy Prokopis

For Jill, who reads it all first.
You're the best.

DISCLAIMER

This book discusses mental health, sexual assault, and contains on-page sexual content. The sexual scenes in this book include bondage and dominance.

CHAPTER 1
ANGEL

The box truck squeaked and rattled around me as it bumped down the alleyway. I've had three vehicles since arriving in New Orleans, one of which was actually mine, and this truck was by far my least favorite. All this space behind me had been empty since I stole it, space that would've been useful when I first transported my victims. I would have preferred something more comfortable and less noisy, but we were in an industrial part of town and utility vehicles and half-dressed people staggering along the sidewalk didn't raise any eyebrows.

Finally, I arrived at the warehouse. I parked next to the door and climbed out of the truck, locking the cab before fishing the padlock key from my pocket. The warehouse door was rusted around the hinges, but still sturdy enough to contain what I needed it to. The building was soundproofed to maintain privacy —not that screaming would be unusual in this neighborhood. A man covered in blood would raise suspicions though, which is why I had a change of clothes stuffed in my backpack.

I unlocked the door, slipped inside, and locked it from the inside. Already I could feel the tension, smell the fear mixed with the salt of their sweat. I turned from the door to face the first of two rooms. This one had a section just a few feet from the alley door with showerheads and hoses mounted along the wall. From the looks of it, the entire place had been gutted long ago, but there were still enough rigging and plumbing to suggest that meat or fish had been processed here at one time.

I slipped off my backpack and hung it on the door handle, keeping it an entire room away from the mess to come. I removed my shoes and sat them by the wall before going to the door to the next room, the largest space in the warehouse. The door opened with the grating sound of metal on metal. I didn't need the light to see them across the concrete floor, but I wanted them to see every bit of me, to know what was coming. I flipped on the lights along the wall, and they came on with a loud buzz that died out as the fluorescent lights flickered before flooding the room with light.

"Welcome back," Paul Saxon said with a laugh. Anyone else would've thought he'd gone insane from the days he'd spent with his arms suspended by the rigging along the ceiling. I knew Paul though and I knew men like him. He relished these games, basked in watching the way his torture exhausted me. He knew I was disgusted by the act and rather than taunt me with the memories of the past few months, he knew egging on my nature hurt far worse.

He had no concerns about his sister, Olivia, who was strung up several feet from him. She appeared unbothered each time I returned, but the anxiety clung to her skin and would glimmer in her eye whenever I stopped in front of her. No matter the thoughts I focused on, the hurt they did to Lily, I couldn't bring myself to touch Olivia. Even now, seeing how thin she looked, knowing that I'd already let her starve once only to be brought back to life by her guardian immortality ...

"Are you out of ideas already?" Paul smirked. "Or maybe you're rethinking how much more you can stand."

I forced myself to step into the room, shutting the door behind me with that awful squeal, and went to the rolling table I'd left along the wall. It held an assortment of weapons I'd found around the warehouse and a few that I had brought for the task. I pushed that table across the room until I was just a few feet from Olivia and Paul. I pulled the tarp from over the table and let it fall in a heap behind me.

Paul's smile only grew wider. "I think what's left of the man inside knows how twisted this is, but the monster can't stay away. You may hate me, but I can't die and the monster needs that daily fix."

My hand shook as I reached for the first weapon on the table, a serrated knife. I gripped the handle, but didn't raise it from the table. I was close enough now that I could hear the blood in their veins, not to mention the smell of it. There was a moment every time I came here, when I stood just like this before the blood spilled, that I felt like an alcoholic in a bar. I knew I should be done with this, but I felt so much more in control after each visit. It was like waking from a long night of sleep and completing a marathon all in one. It dulled my senses enough that I almost felt human among the crowds of New Orleans.

"You will pay for what you did to Lily," I said, keeping my eyes on the knife. I knew if I looked at him that I would see nothing but amusement. Knowing that made my body tremble with anger, but seeing it ...

"Over and over, I know," Paul laughed. "You've told me."

"It will never be enough," Olivia said. She hadn't spoken so directly since I brought them here. I looked at her and for once there was emotion in her expression, almost a plea in her eyes. "He took from her what can't be repaired. She may heal, but that won't change what happened."

It happened so fast, that darkness within me overwhelming me until I was gripping that knife and standing a foot from his deranged, smiling face. My knife sliced across Paul's chest and blood splattered across Olivia, adding color to her pale face. Paul gritted his teeth against the pain for just a moment before that deranged smile returned and he let out a whoop.

"I knew he was in there," he said, leaning forward as far as his restraints would allow.

I felt a chill against my back where my T-shirt had ripped apart as my wings emerged. They were spread wide, and I'd risen almost a foot above Paul. There was a fire in his eyes that only made it harder to cling to my humanity, my thoughts of Lily the only reason I hadn't ripped out his throat with my teeth. He knew it. Each time I came it got harder to resist, easier to give in to the anger and accept the kill.

"Look at me," Olivia said, briefly pulling my eyes away from Paul's smirk.

"My sister has never had a taste for violence the way we do," Paul said.

"Don't look at him! Look at me!"

Lily. I thought about Lily and the way her blue eyes went wide and her cheeks flushed whenever I touched her. God, I could practically feel her soft skin against my own and it was like a glass of cool water to the fire that threatened to burn me alive from the inside out.

"You and I both know that he's deranged," Olivia continued, her voice trembling now. "My brother was unhinged before we woke, before we became guardians. He's been unrecognizable ever since."

She turned her face away from me as a tear spilled onto her cheek. Paul let out a deep sigh and I made the mistake of looking at him again. He was annoyed. When he caught me staring, he grimaced, and it wasn't until a line of blood dribbled down his chin that I understood what he was doing, that he'd bitten part of his own tongue off. He spat a mouthful of the blood at me that landed at the corner of my mouth. The taste was on my tongue before I could think to resist and a second later, I was inches from his face, fighting the desire. I was so close that if I stuck out my tongue the blood dripping from his mouth would fall into mine. I pushed away the thought and stabbed the knife into his shoulder instead, closing my eyes and listening to his scream echo around us, letting it ground me in reality, making my skin crawl, and reminding me how destined for hell I was.

"You want to be free of him the same way I do," Olivia said, once again gaining my attention. Her expression was firm, angry even despite the tears that slipped down her face. "What he did, his entire existence, will haunt you as long as he's here, but he doesn't have to be immortal here."

That caught my attention, pulled me out of my instincts enough that I could move away from Paul to stand in front of her. "What do you mean he doesn't have to be immortal here?"

Relief flooded her dark eyes, and she tipped her head back to look at me, her red hair falling down her back as she breathed in a sigh.

"Come on, Olivia," Paul said gently, as though he might tease her back into playing another round of the game. This was all like Monopoly to him; power and control.

"We've been guardians a long time, long enough that I know where a few of the gates are along the east coast," Olivia said.

"Gates?" I asked, ignoring the urge to use the knife in my hand again.

"They are gates to the Shadowlands, a direct entrance to the supernatural world. It's how demons come into ours. Guardians defend it and kill whatever evil crawls out, but we can't survive in the Shadowlands, not without a match, a soulmate that would make us mortal again. Without that, going into the Shadowlands means walking in a kind of purgatory as an immortal forever. You toss Paul through a gate and he won't be able to come back out."

Purgatory. Immortal and stuck between the mortal world and the supernatural one. My muscles relaxed as a new smell permeated the air.

Fear. Male.

"Where's the nearest gate?" I asked.

"Not far from New Orleans," she said, eyes alight with excitement. "I'll take you."

"You'll tell me."

"I'll *take* you," she repeated, ignoring the fact that I'd raised the knife so that the point brushed the soft skin beneath her chin. "Because I have no intention of going with him and keeping me alive comes with a benefit you'd be stupid to pass up."

I hesitated. The last few months taught me that neither Saxon was worthy of life. The last few weeks taught me that Olivia might be even more dangerous than Paul. He was demented and no risk was too great if there was a reward of any kind, but Olivia Saxon was smart, and her moves were much more calculated than her brother's.

The worst horrors in this world are not always the bloodiest.

"That's not how this works, sister," Paul said with a laugh and then turned his gaze to me. "I'll tell you exactly where that gate is because I'm not afraid to live among the demons for eternity. She is though."

There it was, that fear that stole the dim light from Olivia's eyes and gave away her only ticket to freedom. She was not innocent. She helped Paul capture Lily. She allowed him to hold her hostage, watched him torment her, knew what he had done to her ...

I was on Paul in a second, my claws digging into the skin at his shoulders and my teeth sinking into his neck. I allowed myself to take a couple of strong pulls, hearing his heart beat faster and feeling the way his pulse fluttered against my lips before I forced myself to back away. Paul laughed, this time the sound filling the room.

"The gate is in a swamp, Maurepas Swamp," Paul said with a satisfied smile despite the twinge of pain I saw in his eyes. "You can get rid of us there, never to step a foot in the mortal world again. You won't do that though because it means going back to the hunt. You will have to kill again."

"I'll take you to the gate and we can toss Paul in, but keep me for yourself!" Olivia shouted over her brother. "Keep me so you don't have to kill. I stay alive. You feed from me, knowing that if you drain me I'll just heal again. I'll be an immortal blood bag."

I hated the relief that flooded my body. It was possible, made sense even. It's part of why I felt so good now. I never had to worry about keeping fed or losing control. It meant letting Olivia go unpunished for her part in this though, or at least it felt like it. I wanted them both gone. I wanted to take a piece of them back to Lily, be able to promise her that this chapter of her life was over in hopes that it would provide her some closure. I believed Paul when he told me where the gate was. He'd never go down without a fight or without leaving behind some kind of destruction. He'd never let his own sister be his downfall.

"Maurepas," I said and drove the knife into Paul's chest, stilling the thumping of his heart and watching as his body hung limp from the restraints. I turned to Olivia next, the relief in her expression fading as I approached her.

"I made you an offer you can't refuse," she said, pulling against her chains.

"Did you?" I asked as I stepped closer. My lips were pressed to her throat a second later, teeth sinking into her skin. My muscles relaxed as the warm blood flowed over my tongue and I allowed instinct to take over, holding her against my chest until she went limp in my arms.

All that room in that box truck would come in handy after all.

CHAPTER 2

Two plaques on the wall, one silver and the other gold. They were the only decoration on the far wall of what used to be Anne's room, now filled with a new cello, a violin, a viola, sound mixing equipment, and enough lights and camera tripods to make anyone suspicious about what I was filming in my free time. I couldn't bring myself to decorate the space, not even motivated by the opportunity the space provided for video backdrops. Instead, it was filled with the instruments, filming equipment, and two YouTube Play Buttons. Aside from the stool I used to practice cello, there wasn't even any furniture in the room.

Angel called every day. We still had half of July to go before classes started again. I caught myself anxiously waiting for his calls each day, nearly thrown into panic attacks if he was late. He could tell that I was anxious each time I got on the phone with him, and he reassured me that he was safe and would call each day. Still, it wasn't healthy, and I knew it. He knew it. He made me promise that I was taking care of myself, and I'd somehow convinced him I was. I wasn't sure when I got to be such a good liar, because the reality was that I was starting to have visions outside of my dreams now and they made me afraid that he was lying too.

They would come in flashes. I'd see Angel looking over his shoulder as he walked down a dark sidewalk. He'd stopped outside a building that had a small courtyard behind an elegant wrought-iron gate and a pair of bright-red double doors at the end of the path that entered into ... something. I never saw what the building was. I knew it was a vision because Angel looked rough. He'd cut his hair, no longer sporting his signature topknot, and he looked as though he'd been wearing the same clothes for a few days from the look of them.

The only thing that kept me from spiraling into a pit of anxiety was keeping busy. I did that by using my free time to finish songs I'd been working on, produce them all, film faceless videos, and post them to my YouTube channel. Wilted Rose Strings had exploded after the release of "Lion Inside" and each video I posted after that only did better. I had so many likes and comments that it was overwhelming and impossible to keep up with, and what had gone from being a side gig that paid for my grocery run suddenly paid for my apartment, bills, and left me with enough to stash in a savings account. I didn't tell my parents about it until my mom noticed I'd switched accounts so that my rent was coming from mine and not theirs.

All the cautious encouragement they'd given me about my YouTube career had been blown out of the water and they were regularly bragging about me to their friends and around the country club now. My only request was that they keep the name of my channel secret. I wasn't ready for people to know that yet. I couldn't imagine ever being ready for any real publicity, but some influential musicians and YouTubers had made videos talking about my songs or mentioned my channel online. My Spotify was another shock I was still processing. The number of people listening to what I'd recorded in my makeshift studio ...

My followers were calling this an album, but I was just recording and releasing music. I didn't realize there was a pattern to it until they started pointing it out in the comment sections. It hurt a little when I realized they were right. All the songs I spent day and night working on were so angsty. They performed well, better even than "Lion Inside," but I could tell they were a reflection of my anxiety and frustration about my visions and not having Angel nearby.

I was pulled out of my worries when my phone vibrated in my pocket.

"You're early," I said in a sigh of relief.

"I'm glad that so-called lecture taught you to lock the balcony door, but I need you to open it for me now, Mouse."

Everything inside me came to a screeching halt and I felt my eyes burn when I realized what he meant. I laid my cello on the floor with my phone and ran from the room. I shoved the curtain back from the sliding door and burst into tears at the sight of Angel standing on the balcony. I hurried to unlock the door, and the air swirled around us. My arms were wrapped around his neck and my legs around his hips, my face buried into the crook of his neck. We were in the kitchen when I looked up, the sliding door still open across the room.

"I'm home, Mouse," he said in my ear, holding me tight until I let out a breath. He sat me on one of the barstools and wiped the moisture from my face. I held on to the front of his shirt. All my anger at him for being gone so long vanished as I looked over him. He was clean, smelled like his usual floral self, and still had his long hair pulled into a bun at the crown of his head. It was almost like he'd been gone for a weekend or a work trip and not for some dangerous vampire business like he had told me. He told me he might not be home before the fall semester started.

"I thought you needed more time. I thought you would be gone so much longer," I said, a tear slipping down my face. He didn't brush this one away. Something in his expression changed, like he had some news and his hands on my waist tensed for a moment before he pulled them away entirely.

"Anne called me," he said.

I looked down at his hands, now resting on my thighs until he used one to lift my chin so I was looking at his serious expression.

It made my stomach twist. I knew I was a terrible liar—at least I had thought I was. I don't know how I'd manage to sound so confident over the phone, but I knew I wouldn't be able to manage it in person. Again, he didn't brush away the next tear that fell.

"I haven't talked to Anne in weeks," I said. It was the truth.

"She told me she picked up her stuff a few weeks ago and you weren't the same. She also told me that she left a few things behind as an excuse to come back, and that when she came back last week things were worse."

Damn it, Anne.

"I've been really busy. I've been working like crazy to release new music so I would have a new album out for the fall semester of classes when things with YouTube will need to slow down."

Angel looked away from me and let out a frustrated sigh. "I don't want to sound like a creep." He massaged the spot between his brows before looking back at me with that serious expression again. "Do you remember sharing your location with me, that I can see where you are?"

We both shared our locations. I could see where he was, and he could see where I was. We turned on that feature on our phones when we were still in the hospital after Paul and Olivia had held us hostage. It had all been so terrifying that we both felt a little better having that information if something were to happen again. I'd never thought that the information might tell him anything was wrong until now. I still didn't understand what it told him.

"Yes," I said.

"After Anne called me, I started checking your location a few times a day and I felt like an obsessive boyfriend doing that at first, but then I noticed that you don't go out. Lily, you never leave this apartment."

"You know I'm a homebody and besides, I've been absorbed in my work. I'm enjoying it. I'm getting a lot done."

"I've seen it. I also see that the kitchen looks untouched and what's worse, Anne is the least observant person I've ever met and for her to notice that something is off with you and for her to put her ego aside enough to call me asking for help ... I came home because I was worried about you, Lily."

"No one should be worried about me."

"Do you worry about *me*?"

His words were enough to give me pause, and I could see in his expression that he knew why. He knew he'd made his point. I knew he was right, and it felt like I'd been punched in the gut. I felt the moisture leak onto my cheeks again and I wanted to bury my face in his chest, but when I tried, he held my shoulders firm. God, the way he looked at me, like he could read it all on my face ...

"I worry about you when you aren't here," I said, hating how small the words sounded.

"Do you trust me?"

Ouch.

"Yes. I do trust you. It's not that," I said, my heart speeding up in my chest. The vision didn't seem like anything special. It was just Angel walking along a street and then to the door of a building. It wasn't particularly noteworthy, but it invaded my dreams enough that it had to be important.

"Then why didn't you tell me you were struggling? I would've come home."

"That's the thing, I didn't want you here. I mean, I do want you here, but I know it was important to you to go on this trip. You asked me to trust you and I did, I've been waiting."

"But you weren't honest with me," Angel said, his tone gentle but firm enough that it made my stomach knot. I could barely look at him and he must've sensed it because he lifted my gaze with a finger under my chin. "This trip is important, but you are far more important to me, Mouse. I ask how you're feeling every day. I told you I would be home in hours if you needed me."

"And I told you that I'm fine," I said, my heart leaping in my chest at how assured my tone was. I wasn't one to engage in conflict. I hated it. I avoided it whenever I could, but I knew he wouldn't judge me or put me down for whatever I said. Thinking about that fact now only made the guilt in my gut twist more because I *had* lied to him and the truth was that I was spending all my time on my YouTube channel to avoid dealing with the stress I felt from the vision and my worries about what might happen to him. I hadn't been honest with him, but even worse was how I'd been lying to myself.

"What have you eaten today?" he asked, brushing my hair behind my ear.

God. It was three o'clock in the afternoon and I realized now that the last thing I ate was a croissant after I woke up from the vision at two this morning. The truth must've been evident because he let out a deep breath and I saw his jaw tighten.

"Have you at least been drinking water?" His eyes landed on the half-empty mug of coffee on the counter.

"There's water in coffee," I said, not fully committing to the joke. He wouldn't have found it funny anyway. "You're mad."

"I'm not mad," he said, his eyes returning to mine. It felt like there were snakes in my stomach and the hard lines of his jaw only made that worse. He straightened up with a sigh, a hand going to the back of his head and the other pressing a spot between his brows. "Okay. Maybe a little mad."

"I know I should've told you. I've been getting a lot done for YouTube, but I realize now that maybe that was just me trying to avoid dealing with my emotions. And you know that my appetite is funky when I'm anxious," I said. The tension eased when he stepped between my legs, his expression softening, and pressed a kiss to my forehead.

"I know. I understand why you didn't tell me everything," he said and cupped the side of my face, using his thumb to pull my lower lip free from between my teeth.

"You're right. I wasn't totally honest, and I should've told you. I just—I don't know—I wanted to figure out what I was feeling before I explained it all to you."

"You don't need to have it all figured out, Mouse. You don't need to know what's wrong. We can figure that part out together, but I can't help at all if you don't tell me how you feel."

I leaned in to kiss him. It was a relief to press my lips to his, to feel his chest beneath my fingers as I held the front of his shirt. He pulled away before the kiss could grew any deeper, taking my hands from his chest and pressing a kiss to my knuckles.

"I told you that I wouldn't let anyone hurt you, even if that person is you, Mouse," he told me, that knowing look reminding me of the last time he called me out for risking my safety. Warmth flooded my core, and I pressed my thighs together. "I think that you should go take a long shower, maybe do a face mask or whatever you like to do for a bit of self-care. I'll make any meal you want after."

"You could probably use a shower after a day of travel," I said, feeling my face heat.

Angel smirked and let go of me. He moved a hand to my right leg, sliding it so his fingers grazed the skin between my thighs as he leaned in close.

"Not until after you've eaten and had a lot more water. You have a whole day to make up for, Mouse." He laughed, but I could tell from the look in his eyes that he was serious.

Damn him.

I pouted as I slipped off the barstool and he landed a playful swat on the seat of my sweatpants as I walked toward my room.

CHAPTER 3

I was aware of every sound as I showered, a part of me hoping he would give in and come join me. He didn't and I instead let my mind imagine what would happen if he did. I washed my hair, even used what was left of a hair mask that Anne left behind after she moved out. I made sure to shave. Then, I dried my hair and changed into the cutest pajama set I owned, a satin tank top with a matching pair of shorts. It was this or another pair of sweats and after pulling the shorts on, inspiration stuck.

If he was going to make me wait until after I ate and took care of myself like a big girl, then I was going to make it just as difficult for him.

I turned to the side in the mirror, adjusting the shorts until they sat high enough on my hips to better reveal the curve of my butt. I didn't wear a lot of makeup most days, especially when I was just lounging around the house, not even if Angel was with me. I worried about being too obvious. My heart skipped in my chest at the idea of being caught in my little game, so I settled on just a little mascara and used my straightener to add a bit more polish to my look.

My stomach rumbled when I left my bathroom and smelled the eggs and peppers. Of course, he'd make my favorite. I left my bedroom for the kitchen. He'd stripped down too, his jacket lying over the back of the couch and his shoes sitting on the floor beneath it. He stood in his jeans and black shirt in front of the stove, barefoot as he moved the contents of the skillet to a plate on the bar.

"First thing tomorrow, we are restocking the pantry. You can't live on toaster pastries and cereal," he said and looked up from the plate. He hesitated for a moment, just long enough to look over me before he straightened up with a smile and turned to the stove again.

"You cooked. I'll clean," I told him, reaching across him for the pan on the stove.

"Let me," he said as I turned to set the pan in the sink. "Go eat before it gets cold."

"I will. I just want to wash this first," I said and turned on the faucet. I held the skillet down in the sink, leaning over it in a way I knew made my satin shorts rise higher. He let out a deep sigh and it felt like electricity shot through my body as his arms slunk around me. He pressed a kiss to my temple as his hands moved to mine, pulling the pan free and then turning off the water.

"If you wait any longer, I'll make sure you eat standing up." He whispered the words in my ear and a shiver of anticipation ran over my skin. His arms were gone, and he was on the other side of the counter now, that smile telling me that he had no intention of participating in my little ploy.

I groaned. "You don't play fair."

He laughed. "Fair? I told you that you needed to take care of yourself first. Shower. Eat a good meal. Drink some water. You're the one who came out here in those tiny shorts and that thin top."

Ugh. Was the omelet the meal, or was I?

"Yes, but you aren't playing by the rules," I giggled and leaned on the counter. The way my top slipped lower was unintended, but his eyes took notice, which was a bonus.

"Oh, you wanted there to be rules," he teased and leaned his elbows on the counter between us. We were close enough that I could hear him as he lowered his voice to a whisper. "I can set rules, Mouse."

I was slowly burning from the inside out, barely able to stand still as I stared back at him.

"Some rules are meant to be broken," I said in a whisper, barely able to find the words thanks to the pounding of my heart.

He smirked and reached out to push my hair behind my ear. "You be a good girl and sit down and eat your meal, and I will enjoy mine once you're finished. I can promise that it will be mutually beneficial."

Oh.

It took a moment to regain control, ignore my racing heart and the heat that pooled between my legs. Angel scoffed and sat back, pulling out the barstool next to him. The anticipation was eating me alive as I rounded the counter to sit next to him, my cheeks only warming more as he laughed.

"I have to admit," he said and pivoted in his chair to face me. "I like this side of you, when you initiate, go for what you want. You seem powerful."

That first bit of eggs reminded me how hungry I was and eased a little of the hunger for other things. "It makes me feel powerful. And I do go after what I want. At least, I do now more than before I met you. I mean, I have YouTube and it's doing well and I'm putting my music out there more. That's what I've been throwing myself into while you were gone."

"Yes, but no one knows that it's you," he said gently. I knew he didn't mean it as criticism so much as encouragement. "I don't want you to do anything that makes you uncomfortable, so tell me if I'm being an ass. I just know that from the way you talk about it and all the work you've put into music ... Tell me if I'm wrong, but it doesn't seem like you're fully happy being Wilted Rose Strings when you could be Lily Thompson."

It hurt a little, but he was right. I created Wilted Rose Strings so I could write the music I felt called to write without worrying about failure or critique. The name was a shield and as time went on and things happened with Paul, it became a shield for more than just my career. It was a little ironic now to think about how I'd been using my music to avoid how anxious I've been feeling since Angel left. Maybe the anonymity only enabled me to hide from other things, an excuse to not put my name to things that might be empowering and fulfilling.

"If I'm wrong—"

"No," I cut him off before he could further soften the blow. "I know what you mean and you aren't wrong. I think it was easier to put myself out there and write the music I want to write when I didn't have to worry about what other people thought about me. I thought having Wilted Rose Strings would add a layer of separation, but all it's really done is ..." I groaned. I wasn't doing that great of a job explaining myself. I turned from my plate to face him. "I feel like my solution for anxiety and not disappointing my parents and the people who've helped me as a cellist was to just avoid how I've been feeling. Creating Wilted Rose Strings was me indulging in this totally different music to scratch an itch I've had forever without needing to claim it. Now that it's grown so much and my parents are on board I think I've just been letting myself down this whole time instead."

Angel smiled encouragingly. "You don't have to out yourself as the creator or anything to claim it, Mouse. But I'm sure there are opportunities out there you haven't embraced and could."

That was true. I'd gotten a few inquiries to appear on podcasts. A few other musicians on YouTube had emailed me about doing collaborations and I already knew exactly what that would look like. There was one particular singer I would have loved to work with and her email still sat unread in my inbox.

I turned back to my plate and continued to eat, telling him about the singer. He asked me what the vision for the collaboration was and as I told him my idea, I felt myself relax. The eggs were cold when I returned to the last few bites after detailing the entire piece. I hadn't written the song yet because I was holding on to that dream collaboration and just couldn't bring myself to email her knowing that it would mean a video chat and then an in-person meeting. It made me anxious, but not in the way I was used to. This was exciting.

"I've missed you," I said and exhaled, pushing away my empty plate and turning toward him.

He smiled, but it didn't touch his eyes the way it had before. It was almost a somber look, and I thought maybe he was reflecting on our time apart like I was, except that something told me this was different. He looked down at his hands and licked his lower lip.

"Come here," he said and stood up. I followed him to the couch and sat down, waiting for him to sit next to me. Instead, he sat on the coffee table in front of me so that our knees brushed. He took my hands in his and let out a deep breath. "I didn't want to leave you here, especially after what happened, but I couldn't have you anywhere near this. I won't risk losing you again, but I do owe you an explanation. All I told you is that I had to leave, that I would be back, and that I needed you to trust me."

I nodded. It was the only thing he told me. I could've checked his location on my phone, but I hadn't thought to do that. I just trusted him and not because he asked, but because I did. The fact that he was sitting across from me to discuss this now, looking so serious, was the first time I felt nervous about it all. I was starting to worry that he was leaving me again and that he was trying to distance himself from me because he was a vampire.

"I tracked down Paul and Olivia Saxon," he said.

My entire body went cold. I had to replay the words in my head to understand the implication. He tracked them. He found them. He was back now, which only meant one thing.

"You found them? So, they're ..."

Angel nodded and held my hands tighter. "Yes. They were heading south. I captured them and drove them to New Orleans. I was figuring out how to kill them when Olivia told me about a gate there. Guardians can go through the gate to the Shadow-lands, but they can only come back out into our world if they have a match, a soulmate that makes them both mortal again. Olivia told me she would take me there to toss Paul in. Neither of them have a match. She tried making a deal to save herself, but I already had everything I needed."

Tears had already spilled onto my cheeks. Thinking about what had happened, Paul's arms around me, the sound of his voice in my ear, and the way he'd locked me away in that estate. That man didn't exist anymore. Not even a piece of him was left in this world. A sob broke past my lips.

"So, he's gone?"

"He's dead, Mouse, for good. It's all over," Angel said and the moment he reached for me I folded into his chest. He held me tight, probably expecting a full panic attack that never came. I felt more relaxed than I had imagined, relieved, tears calmly flowing down my face as I took deep, sobering breaths against his chest.

"I have something for you," he said. I pulled away, rising from his knee so he could go to his luggage near the balcony. He pulled something small from the front pocket before turning to face me. "It's not what it looks like."

"Um, okay," I said tentatively, twisting my fingers around a strand of my hair. "You didn't have to get me anything. Going after Paul was enough. More than enough."

He smiled and lifted a small velvet box. "You're mine, as long as you want to be, and no one touches what's mine." The lid opened on a hinge, revealing a simple square ruby hanging from a thin gold chain.

I gasped. "Wow. That's—Angel, you don't have to give me things like this."

I could tell he knew exactly what I meant. He was living in a barely furnished apartment in a questionable part of New York City. He lived under the radar and hadn't had a job for a long time. This necklace must have set him back a lot, but he only smiled wider like he knew something I didn't. That's when it came to me where he likely got his money. The killers he hunted wouldn't need it anymore.

"Like I said before, you're mine. I take care of what's mine," Angel said and removed the necklace from the box. I turned my back to him, pulling my hair away from my neck so he could fasten the chain there. He let out a deep breath that tickled my ear and after the necklace was safely clasped, his hands slid down my hips. He brushed his fingers just beneath the hem of my satin shorts and kissed a spot just beneath my ear before whispering, "Now that you've eaten, it's my turn."

CHAPTER 4

Angel scooped me into his arms and with vampire speed he took me to the bedroom. The purple lights hanging around the perimeter of the room were on, casting dim light around the room. I was glad I'd made the bed this morning as he sat me on the edge. He pulled off his shirt in a single motion, tossed it aside, and gave me a look that immediately made my face heat. He took my hands in his, guiding me to my feet so he could pull me closer.

"I've definitely missed this," I said and pressed my hands to his chest, sliding my fingers along the curve of his muscles.

He chuckled and pulled me closer by my hips, close enough that I could feel just how much he wanted me too. "Immortality isn't worth it if I can't spend it worshiping you this way."

Oh.

My heart was still recovering from the little dance it had done in response when he lifted my eyes to his with a finger under my chin. He smiled deviously, licking his lower lip before I was distracted by his hand sliding along the waistband of my shorts.

"You thought you could tease me with these, didn't you?" he asked, his finger dipping just past the waistband, taunting me as he brushed that finger from one hip to the other. "Use your words, Mouse. I'd like an answer."

Ugh, the way my body ached for more.

"Yes," I said, biting down on my lower lip. He freed it with the pad of his thumb before using it to raise my chin again, forcing my eyes to meet his dark gaze.

"Keep your eyes on me, Mouse," he said. Finally, that hand slid past the satin of my shorts and over the most sensitive part of me. It was like a zap of electricity, easing into slow strokes as I moved to kiss him. He resisted, his hand still there beneath my chin keeping my eyes focused on his as those strokes slowed to a torturous pace.

"Angel," I started, ready to ask for more when that wicked smirk returned to his face.

"Ah, you wanted rules, Mouse," he said with a laugh, brushing a thumb along my cheek. "Keep your eyes on me or I'll stop. I want to watch you when you come undone around my fingers."

I gasped when I felt those fingers. I didn't understand how he could do so much with just that single hand, slow and steady, almost too slow. Angel brushed a tear from my face, and I let out a whimper, eliciting a groan from him that sent me over the edge. He smiled wider as I pressed against him.

"Eyes on me," he reminded when I closed my eyes, forcing them open again as I rode out the last of the wave with deep breaths. Just as the tide receded, he lifted me into his arms. He laid me on the bed, kissing me hard as he slid my underwear from my hips. He straightened up, sliding them the rest of the way off before he lowered himself to his knees.

Oh no. I couldn't.

Before I could form any thoughts, he tugged me to the edge of the bed. He knelt between my knees, pressing soft kisses along the inside of my thigh.

"I-I thought you said it was your turn," I told him, reminding him of the words he'd said that started this whole thing.

"I said I'd eat after you did," he said, lifting his head just far enough to flash an onery smile my way. "And I will."

God. Damn him. Damn him and those talented fingers and that dirty mouth.

My eyes were on those lights above us as soon as his mouth found my center. It took just a few soft touches for it all to crash down again, my hand pressed to my mouth to keep from alerting the neighbors.

Angel was above me now, pulling my hand from my mouth. I kissed him, tasting the salt of my tears on my tongue as it met his. I gasped when I felt him between my thighs. I moved my hands to his hips, pulling him deeper until his body was flush against mine. Angel moved my hands away one at a time until he had both pinned above me on the bed in one of his, the other hand sliding between us until I felt my body tensing again in response.

"Angel," I moaned. "I don't ... I can't."

"Good things come in threes, Mouse," he said and tightened his grip on my wrists. "And you are such a good girl."

Again, I was sent over the edge, lost among so many sensations that I was sure I would be exhausted by them. He rolled his hips, taking me deep as I recovered from the bliss to watch as his expression changed above me. His mouth parted, muscles flexing. He'd eased his grip on me enough that I pulled my hands free so I could feel those muscles. He groaned in response, a sound that seemed to echo in his throat as he picked up pace. I could feel my body heating in response, and I wasn't sure I could endure another round.

I whimpered and dug my nails into his back and his groan turned into something darker, more primal. He held me tighter, my back arching against the sharp sting of his nails along my shoulder blades. He let out a loud moan, a deep breath following before I felt the cool air against my skin.

He was gone. I looked away from the ceiling, seeing now why the room had gone dark. Angel stood near the bathroom, naked and with bat-like wings stretched from one wall to the other. He was panting heavily, his eyes going from his wings to my face. The last bit of pleasure that warmed my skin cooled at the fear in his eyes. His wings began to recede as he looked at his hands.

"Shit," he said, sitting next to me on the bed a moment later.

"I'm fine, Angel," I told him, turning to face him when he reached to my shoulder. I could feel the cuts, scratches more like it. They didn't hurt. At least, they didn't hurt in a bad way, and I felt my face flush in response to the thought.

"Lily, please," he said, scooting across the mattress so he could look at my back. He groaned. "I let my guard down. I should never have—"

"I like it when you're rough," I said, standing up. I went to the bathroom, watching in the reflection as he followed after me with a hand fisted in his hair. I turned enough so I could look at my shoulder, see the shallow scrapes there.

"Yes, but not enough that I leave marks," he groaned, stopping behind me. I tried to turn to face him, but he held me in place by my hips. He pressed a soft kiss to my neck. "Please, let me take care of these."

My first instinct was to refuse and do it myself, but I realized a moment later what he meant. He wanted to use his vampire powers to heal the scrapes. They'd be gone within the hour, and he wouldn't have to worry about me feeling them. It didn't hurt more than a little papercut. They were more like a reminder of the night to me, but I knew that he wouldn't view them that way.

"Okay," I said.

He let out a sigh and I saw him relax in the reflection of the mirror. He pushed my hair over my right shoulder and set to work, kissing the scrapes and brushing his tongue along the marks to heal them. Once he was finished, they were no more than faint pink lines on my skin.

"Come with me," Angel said and kissed my cheek. He led me by the hand back into my bedroom. He lay down on the bed, propped up by the headboard. I snuggled to his side, resting my head against his chest while he ran his fingers through my hair.

"I've missed you," he said.

I raised my head to look at him. "Me too. You have a lot of time to make up for."

He laughed when I reached for the button of his pants, letting him take my hand and kiss my knuckles.

"You're a greedy little thing," he said.

"I'm just glad you're back."

"Me too, Mouse," he said as I lay back down, sleeping pulling me under within minutes.

CHAPTER 5

I woke up to the smell of coffee. I felt surprisingly well-rested, the best I'd felt in weeks. Angel wasn't next to me anymore. I sat up in bed, noticing the time on my phone when I unplugged it and stood up. It was nine o'clock. I'd slept in.

I was in a daze as I made my way to the kitchen, still reeling from my dreamless sleep. Angel saw me coming and pulled a mug down from the cabinet above the coffee maker. His expression fell as he poured the coffee.

"What's wrong?" he asked, setting the full mug on the counter and replacing the carafe.

I took a seat on one of the bar stools. "Last night was the first time I've slept through the night since you left."

I saw the worried look cross his face, the same one he wore when he told me about Anne's concerns. Thankfully, it softened after a moment, and he turned to the fridge for a bottle of cream. The guilt that had settled in my gut didn't fade with his concern though.

Angel added a bit of cream to my coffee and mixed it, looking up at me again. He sat the spoon aside and let out a heavy sigh. "Tell me," he said gently. "Let me in."

"I've been having visions. I know, I should've told you sooner—"

"What kind of visions?"

I took the mug between my hands as he scooted it across the counter to me. "Well, you. They're of you. *It's* of you. It's been the same vision every night when I go to sleep. They started after you left."

"What am I doing in them?" he asked, leaning his elbows on the counter.

"You're walking down a sidewalk. I just assumed you're in New Orleans, because the vision started after you left to go there. You walk down a sidewalk and go to this old building. The entrance is behind a wrought-iron gate. There's a kind of court-yard there with bushes and a bright red door with a knocker in the shape of a star."

"What does the knocker look like?" Angel asked.

I opened my mouth to repeat what I'd just said before I saw how serious his expression was. He wasn't just concerned by my vision. It was like he was taking notes and not just because I could predict the future. I thought about his trip. If he'd left me to hunt down the Saxons and he found them not far down the East Coast, why did he need to take them all the way to New Orleans? It seemed strange that it would be the only place where there was a gate to the Shadowlands to toss them into. They'd lived in New York, surely that meant there was a gate closer.

"Angel, why did you go to New Orleans?" I asked. I could see in his eyes that I'd asked the right question.

"I told you after we got home from the hospital that I've been looking for the cure for vampirism," he said, moving to his luggage still sitting in the living room.

"Yeah," I started as I followed him, taking a seat on the couch armrest and watching as he picked through the main compart-ment of his suitcase. "You said you'd been gathering the things you needed. You showed me the guardian blood. You said there were more things you needed ... something about a witch telling you what to do."

He nodded and stood up with an envelope in his hand. "I need to find the witch."

"She's in New Orleans?"

He opened the envelope and pulled out a photograph. "I paid a witch here in New York City to do a little research. She found out her coven is in New Orleans. The witch I need is in this photo, the long-haired one."

I took the picture from him. In the photo, three people sat outside around a table. There was a man with dark hair who was passing a baby bottle to a woman with a short bob sitting across from him. She held a small baby in her lap. Between the couple was a Black woman with long hair; beautiful curls framed her face. Unlike her friends, who were in the middle of a conversation, her eyes looked straight ahead at the photographer.

"Did you take this?" I asked and looked up from the photo.

"A long time ago," he said and let out a deep sigh. "I'd already been looking for a witch or warlock who knew how to reverse this curse. The covens of Europe are very old, and they keep connected enough that it didn't take long to exhaust them as an option. That's how I ended up in the U.S. and after more searching, I found her."

"All these things you have to gather, like the blood, are they part of a spell that this witch can do? Is that what this is?" I asked, watching as he fidgeted with the spot beneath his shirt where he wore a glass vial containing the soil from his home in Spain.

"She was so different from any of the witches and warlocks I'd ever met. She left her coven, for one. She said she was on her own adventure of discovery. I found her in Virginia, but that's not the first place she'd ventured to. I didn't know where she was from or much about her coven at all. She must've known I was different too because she approached me after I took that photo. It was the first time we spoke after I'd been stalking her," he said and held the envelope to me. "She was smarter than most people, maybe even the smartest person I'd ever met. She was a strong witch who didn't take her power lightly. She didn't like to use it, but I convinced her. She said she knew a spell to help and that I'd have to find some items first."

"What kind of items? You told me about the blood of a guardian."

He shrugged. "She only told me the first. She said to come find her after I had the blood."

I turned the envelope between my hands, finally opening it. I placed the photo back inside and removed a folded piece of paper. It was a printout of a webpage. My skin went cold and I felt a strange tingle. It was the first time I recognized the sensation. I'd always been so preoccupied by the vision that followed that I didn't notice how it felt before. The vision flashed through my mind in double-time and I noticed details I hadn't before thanks to the piece of paper.

"This symbol," I said and pointed to a drawing in the corner of the page. It was a crescent moon with an owl perched in the middle. "This was on the gate in front of the building." Not just any building. It was an apartment building. That's what this website said—a single-page website from the look of it. Beneath the familiar brick wall at the top of the page was a button to click for more information. Someone had written a series of numbers on the paper beneath that button.

"I searched when I was down there, I couldn't find anything. I couldn't even find this website online. It's like it doesn't exist. I think the witch here in New York had to go to the dark web to find it," Angel said. It was a little surprising that he didn't know how to get to the dark web, but I didn't press him about the website. Another detail came to me as I replayed the vision. It ended through the courtyard with that bright red door. I originally thought it was a star knocker. I could tell now that it was a fleur-de-lis.

An owl was sitting on a crescent moon on the wrought-iron gate. The path was cobblestone. There were large green bushes obscuring the courtyard. The entrance had a large red door with a fleur-de-lis knocker and there was a keypad on the doorknob. I wasn't sure if the vision continued or if it was just wishful thinking, but I could see myself typing the numbers from that piece of paper into the keypad. The door swung open, revealing a lobby lit only by sconces along the wall. Along the left wall were gold mailboxes, and hanging from the wall just above was a large gold bell with the words *Night Owl Apartments: Please Ring for Service* engraved on it.

"Night Owl Apartments. These numbers are a code to get into the building," I said and looked up from the paper. I handed it back to him, surprised by how quickly the images faded. It was enlightening though. "I don't know how to summon my visions, but certain things can trigger them. It's like a game of association, like you showed up with a box of random puzzle pieces and I already knew what the image was supposed to be once they were all together. It made it easier to get a clear picture of the vision."

Angel let out a laugh of disbelief and moved closer to me. "You are amazing."

I felt the blush warm my cheeks. "So, what's next? We go back to New Orleans, right?"

His smile faded a little. "I don't know, Mouse. You've already been through a lot in the last few months."

"I think that's one reason why you *should* take me with you," I told him and gently slapped my hands against his chest. "I survived one of the worst experiences a person could face and I'm coping with it."

My stomach twisted at the look on his face. Was I coping? I already knew what he was thinking. I wasn't eating regularly. I kept to myself. I worked all the time. I was so dedicated to my music and education, but I wasn't prepared for classes to start again.

"What's the other reason?" Angel asked, pulling me closer to him by my hips.

"Well," I started, a little rattled still from the concern in his expression. It took me a moment to gather my thoughts. "I was able to figure what you're looking for once you gave me more things to work with. The vision expanded. Maybe I can get better at this and going with you is more than just finding a witch. Maybe I can finally feel control."

Control. I hadn't thought that's what this was, but the words flew from my mouth so easily that my subconscious must've been screaming it at me for a while. It was what usually made me anxious—feeling unsafe or out of control. The visions made me anxious. I couldn't summon them and I had no idea when the next would strike. If I could learn to control them, maybe the anxiety would lessen too.

Angel let out a deep breath and I saw the answer in his somber eyes. "No."

"Angel—"

"I won't put you in an environment like that where danger could find you."

"I won't be left here wondering if you're okay again," I said, gripping the front of his shirt. "I can help. In the last few months, I've had visions before something bad has happened. They are getting more accurate too. It only makes sense to have me with you."

"Lily," he sighed. He opened his mouth to argue but stopped. I could see his brain working to find a rebuttal. It made my heart leap in my chest, excited that maybe I wouldn't be left here after all. Being alone to have visions about him while I was in the middle of class or walking down an aisle at the grocery store sounded unbearable. I didn't want him to endure his struggles alone in finding the cure any more than he wanted me to endure mine.

"I can help. You asked me to trust you when you left. Trust me when I say that I can help," I told him.

He let out a sigh and nodded, his expression pained. "That night when I saved you at the club and brought you home, put you to bed, and you said my name in your sleep ... I knew I needed you to find the cure. But the way I need you most is so different, and I wouldn't survive another day let alone another century if something happened to you."

I brushed his cheek, and he leaned into my touch, taking another deep breath before he pulled away.

"But you're right," he finally said. "Your powers as a seer are exactly what I need and having you with me will make the coven more welcoming to me."

The tension in my chest eased and I wrapped my arms around him. He didn't indulge me as long as I wanted and he pulled back, a serious expression holding my attention.

"Are you going to be ready for your classes if you go? The semester isn't that far away. We should be back before it starts, but I don't want you stressing about it if we get back close to the first day."

I forced a smile. I'd registered for classes before I brought him home to meet my parents. I'd since changed all my classes once, moving to different sections and dropping a few altogether so that I barely remembered what state my enrollment was in. None of it seemed to fit after I met Angel and especially not after my YouTube channel exploded. Getting my degree was important to me, but I just didn't know what that looked like anymore.

"I'm all set," I told him and stood on my toes to kiss his nose, glad to see that it brought a smile to his face.

"Then start packing, Mouse," Angel said with a laugh. "We leave now, if you don't need to do anything first."

"No. I'm ready," I said, already halfway to my bedroom.

CHAPTER 6

Angel didn't need to sleep or eat or stop at a gross gas station restroom the way I did, making him the perfect chauffer for a trip all the way to New Orleans. I sat in the passenger seat of his black SUV and he made me tell him about what I'd been doing since he was gone. The truth was that I hadn't done much, so I told him about my YouTube plans instead and I played all the songs I'd already recorded. He was the most supportive boyfriend a girl could ask for and only encouraged my ideas and helped me flesh out the ones I was unsure about. As the sunlight faded, I crawled into the backseat and fell asleep along the bench seat.

Aside from a few stops for the necessities, Angel drove through the day and night, and we were driving into the New Orleans before I realized how far we'd come. The humidity hit me first and I worried about whether I had packed light enough clothes to fit the weather. Angel promised that we could stop to shop if we needed.

"All of these balconies," I said as we drew closer to the French Quarter. Nearly every building was at least two stories and had intricate wrought-iron balconies. It all reminded me of buildings I'd seen on a few of my family's trips to Europe.

"There is a lot of history here," Angel noted as we slowed thanks to the thickening traffic.

"I can feel it," I said, the words more than just a metaphor. I really did feel that strange tingle along my skin like I might have a vision, but one never came. We pulled into the port-cochère awning of a lavish hotel. A valet immediately approached Angel's window, and a bellboy waited with a cart for our luggage by the passenger door.

"Reservation under Ramírez," Angel told the man as he checked the tablet in his hands. Once he found what he was looking for, he offered to park the car. I climbed out of the SUV, my legs feeling like Jell-O after sitting for so long. How I could possibly be ready to sink into a hotel bed for a nap after the hours of sitting in his car, I wasn't sure.

Angel took my hand and we followed the bellboy into the large lobby, soft jazz music greeting us as I took in all the details of the space. It was a mix of old world and new, the French inspiration there at every turn. I was pulled from the detailed ceiling as Angel led me to the front desk to check in.

"When did you book this?" I asked, more surprised that he was able to get a room at a place like this on such a short notice.

He smirked as the woman at the counter took his ID and credit card. "While you were packing. I wanted to stay somewhere nice while we search the city."

The woman returned, pulling Angel's attention from me so he could finish approving the details. We had a suite with a king-size bed. There was a balcony, the information pulling my interest away from a group of women dressed in short cocktail dresses on their way through the glass doors on the other side of the large lobby. The room the women had entered was the hotel restaurant and the concierge told us that it was worth visiting at least once during our stay. As though on cue, my stomach growled. It wasn't loud, but I saw the corner of Angel's lip twitch upward as we finished getting the welcome spiel and took our keys.

"I can have food brought to our room if you would rather," he said as we approached the elevator. The longer I moved around, the more my body woke up from the long drive. I wasn't sure I wanted to sit down just yet.

"I think we should clean up a little and try that restaurant," I said as the silver doors of the elevator slid apart. "We've been stuck in the car for so long that just being around other people might be nice."

Angel laughed as he followed me into the elevator, pressing the button for our floor before sliding his arms around me from behind. "Sick of me already?"

"You know what I mean," I said, feeling my face warm.

He pressed a kiss to my cheek and gave me a gentle squeeze around my middle that made my heart take flight before the doors slid apart again. He held my hand and rolled our luggage behind us, letting go of me to pull his keycard free to unlock our room.

"Do you want to shower first?" I asked as I walked into the room. "It will take me longer to get ready."

The suite was cute. It had a king-size bed pressed to the left wall and photos of historical sites across the city hanging along the wall above the desk to the right. The TV flashed all the usual touristy spots. I immediately went to the French doors to inspect the balcony. It was a street view, nothing super extravagant, but I couldn't help but stand transfixed for a moment by the surrounding buildings before I turned to face Angel.

My heart stopped in my chest for a moment. He was naked from the waist up, fingers working to unclasp his belt.

"I would love a shower, but I'd rather not take one alone," he said and smiled, pulling his belt free from his jeans.

Oh.

My face wasn't the only thing on fire. I felt hot, and not because of the Louisiana humidity. Angel gave me a final lustful look, his eyes roving over me head to toe before he moved to the bathroom. I heard the shower turn on. I took a step to the left, just far enough that I could see the entire mirror of the bathroom before I remembered that he wouldn't appear in the reflection.

Ugh. My stomach twisted at the thought of what he might look like. The anticipation of watching him undress was my favorite foreplay, and I feared I'd missed it.

I kicked off my shoes and pushed my shorts to the floor, stepping out of them and starting toward the bathroom as I pulled my T-shirt over my head. I let out a squeal of surprise when I pulled the fabric away to see that Angel was just inches away. I walked right into his chest, and he held me there, tight against his bare torso. He was still wearing his jeans, though they were unbuttoned and sagged low on his hips.

He pulled my hips tight to his so I could feel how ready he was. He leaned in, keeping his lips just far enough back that they barely brushed mine. He inhaled deeply and when he exhaled, the air tickled my neck and sent delicious chills shooting up my spine. He pressed a single kiss to my throat before he stepped away, lifting his belt from the tile floor and folding it in half. He tapped his thigh with the leather once before he looked up at me.

I could hardly stand still as the images flooded my mind.

"Are you going to spank me with that?" I asked, my voice barely a whisper as I dared myself to say the words.

He chuckled and took a step forward to join me in the doorway again. Oh my. Embarrassment warmed me head to toe, my face so hot that it had to be obvious. Angel reached up and brushed my cheek with his fingers. "As much as I like to watch your skin turn pink, no, Mouse. Not tonight."

I opened my mouth to speak, but no words came out. I was still so stunned that I'd actually asked him that. It wasn't hot with embarrassment anymore though. It felt like something else might consume me, like I might melt if he didn't touch me soon. As though reading my mind, he led me farther into the bathroom, moving behind me so I could see myself in the mirror. It wasn't at all intentional, but I was glad that I managed to pick the thong that matched my black bra. He tugged on my ponytail, so I leaned back against him. I couldn't see him in the reflection, but I could feel his lips at my shoulder, trailing soft kisses up my neck before he took my earlobe between his teeth and gave a gentle tug that I felt in my core.

"I caught you peeking earlier," he whispered. "Forgot vampires don't appear in mirrors, didn't you?"

"Yes," I giggled, reaching my hand back to find the waistband of his jeans. Before I could slip my fingers beneath the fabric, he'd captured my hand, moving it to the small of my back. The cool leather of his belt slid across my behind before I realized why. He wrapped the belt around my wrist, tight enough to form a single cuff before he took my other hand and did the same, binding them together behind my back.

"I may not have a reflection, but you do, Mouse," he said, letting go of my hands. He wrapped one of his around my pony-tail and gently pushed so I was bent halfway over the counter. He nudged my feet apart, his other hand brushing over the curve of my butt. His fingers slid aside the fabric of my thong enough that they could find my center. "I want you to watch, to see how beautiful you look while I touch you."

My mouth was already parted, his fingers barely stroking me and I was nearly there, on the edge, just a few more touches from falling ...

"Angel!" My bound hands fought for something to hold onto. I tried to straighten up as the pleasure washed over me, only to be made that much more intense when he held me in place by my ponytail, forcing me to watch as I bit down on my bottom lip to contain my cry as my face reddened. God, this was hot!

Just as the last of the waves receded, I realized he wasn't holding me anymore. My hands came free and I heard the buckle of the belt hit the tile. I whirled around to face him, my lips crashing into his. He groaned as my hands moved to his waist, allowing me to push his jeans from his hips before I hooked my thumbs into the band of his underwear. Once both were in a pile on the floor, I worked on my own.

I slid my thong down my legs while he unhooked my bra, and then we were stepping under the warm spray of the shower, our naked bodies sliding against each other as we fought to find our rhythm. We finally found it when Angel lifted me into his arms, pressing my back against the tile wall before sinking deep between my legs with a groan. His body tensed against mine as he moved, his hips rolling faster and faster until he stilled, his body trembling against mine.

"I love you," I said, my insides still squirming with excitement.

He raised his eyes to mine and smiled. "I love you too," he said and kissed my nose before lowering me back to my feet. Somehow, I'd kept my hair dry and I pulled the elastic free just so I could pile my hair into a bun to ensure it stayed dry. Angel approached me with a handful of body wash and began to wash me, his hands sliding over every inch of me and taking pause only to massage my sore muscles.

"I take care of what's mine," he growled into my ear before pressing his lips to my temple. My entire body warmed in response. Yes. I was his.

CHAPTER 7

I was so hungry by the time we finished our shower. I didn't bother with my hair, leaving it in a bun, and pulled on a gray cotton dress with spaghetti straps. The entire look was so casual and comfortable that I decided last minute to wear a pair of black heels I'd packed just to make it look a little nicer for the restaurant.

Angel had put on a pair of black slacks and a white button-down, no tie. He kept the top button undone enough that I could see the chain of his necklace that held the small vial of dirt. It was the only thing that enabled him to walk under the sunlight as a vampire.

"I'm ready," I told him and grabbed my purse from the bed, turning toward the door as he approached me.

"One last thing," he said. He held up his belt for me a see with an onery smirk before he wrapped it around my middle. "I want you to wear this so you'll remember all the things I can do with it. Maybe even come up with a few of your own?"

I didn't reply as my face burned from the memory. He tugged on the belt once it was fastened around me, pulling me close enough to press a kiss to my lips.

"I already have a few things in mind," I said, reaching for the next button on his shirt before he pulled my hands away. He kissed my knuckles.

"Dinner first. Your stomach has been growling for far too long."

It was true, and the sound was loud, nagging me. I was hungry and that restaurant downstairs smelled so good. I groaned as he led the way to the door, part of me cursing my body for needing food before sex.

The lobby was empty, but the restaurant was nearly full. It was noisy and the host apologized for the fact as he led us to a table near the front window. I was glad about the noise actually. It meant that we could talk without worrying about being overheard.

"Sarah will be your server. She'll be here with bread and water shortly," the host said as he sat a pair of menus on the table between us. The restaurant was dimly lit, leaving me to keep my menu flat on the table so I could read the entrees by the candlelight.

"Red or white wine?" Angel asked and closed his menu.

"Red," I told him, still not sure what entrée to choose. There was a lot of seafood, which I was allergic to. Angel was nice and made sure to tell the hostess when he asked for a table. "Maybe I'll just get an appetizer for now ..."

I caught that chiding look on Angel's face when I glanced up from the menu. It was so subtle the way he lifted one of his brows in reproach. He didn't have to say anything for me to know what he meant.

I needed to eat. I did this when I was anxious.

The menu was a lot and the room was a lot and I really just wanted to talk with him about what tomorrow would look like. We came here for a reason, not to vacation.

"Or maybe the duck," I said, watching the humor light up those dark eyes.

"Did you tell your parents you were coming here?"

"No."

"Anne?"

I didn't respond quickly enough before that look of concern returned to his face. Before he could speak, a waitress approached us with a basket of bread and two glasses of water on a tray.

"Would you two like a cocktail, maybe a couple glasses of wine?"

"A bottle of Cabernet, please," I told her before Angel could speak. I wasn't usually the first to talk in a group, so maybe he would forget about our conversation.

"How about appetizers?" she asked.

"I think I'm ready to order, actually," I said.

"We'll take the charcuterie board," Angel interjected before sending me an apologetic smile. "I'm sorry. I didn't mean to interrupt, but the place is pretty busy, and I thought we could snack while we wait on our entrées. Go ahead and order, Lily."

I wasn't sure if I was actually annoyed with him or just hangry. I forced myself to look away from him to order the duck and then I waited quietly while he ordered a steak. Our waitress promised our appetizer would be right out and left us alone again.

"Okay. Um, the obsession with food—"

"I'd like to go back to the fact that no one knows that you're here, across the country," Angel said, his voice even despite the pointed comment.

"We literally packed and left on the same day."

"I thought you told someone where we were going."

"I'm here with you, so I don't see why it's a big deal, and also," I started, making a point to grab a slice of bread from the basket and slather more butter on it than I normally would. "I'm not starving myself. We just ordered so much food that I'd be sick if I tried to eat even half of it. So, you can ... You can relax, Batman."

"Batman?" Angel snorted.

"Yes. Batman," I said, fighting the smile pulling at the corners of my mouth. "That's what Anne calls you."

He shook his head in disbelief, thankfully seeming more

relaxed than before. "I know that's what she calls me. I just didn't think you would, too," he said.

"Oh? Was there something else you'd prefer?" I teased, my insides squirming when the corner of his lips ticked upward in that onery smirk I liked. He didn't speak. He pulled his phone from his pocket instead, tipping it upward.

"What are you doing? Did you take a picture of me?" I asked.

Angel finished typing before he turned the phone screen. I noticed the photo he'd sent of me first. My cheeks were pink, and I looked a little like a deer in headlights. Just behind my head, outside the window, was a shop that sold Venetian masks with the words *French Quarter Masks* above them in purple, green, and yellow. The message he'd typed to accompany the photo explained that we'd gone to New Orleans to enjoy a final trip before the semester started. He'd apparently surprised me with the trip, which was exciting to whomever he'd texted.

That's when I saw my father's name at the top of the screen.

"You have my dad's phone number?" I asked.

Angel smiled and tucked his phone back in his pocket. "I have your mom's, too."

My phone buzzed in my pocket, and I pulled it out to read my mom's text wishing us a safe and fun trip. I didn't get a chance to speak before our waitress returned with a wooden board covered in a variety of cheeses, meats, breads, and sauces.

"And a bottle of Cabernet," the waitress said and began to pour our glasses. Angel shot me a satisfied look across the table as the waitress worked, adjusting the items on the table to make space for the bottle.

"Don't look so smug," I teased and lifted my wine glass to my lips.

"I'm just making sure you stay safe," he said and slid the charcuterie board closer to me. I knew he meant it to be reassuring and also a reminder of where the line was. He said no one would ever hurt me, including myself. It wouldn't be the first time he scolded me for taking risks—or more than scolded me ...

I heard him scoff. I looked up from the charcuterie board to see that onery smile that told me he was thinking the same thing.

"What?" I asked, fidgeting with a piece of cheese I'd picked up.

"You know the lengths I'd go to, Mouse," he said, licking his lips.

I cleared my throat and reached for my wine glass. "I know. Lectures."

God, the way my cheeks ached from the blush. My core warmed deliciously at the memory.

"I think I give a good lecture," he said, raising his glass to me in a toast.

The way I both wanted to avoid another lecture and earn one all the same.

"Um, so, tomorrow ..." I started, lifting the glass to my lips and taking a sip.

Angel pulled his phone out again, and after a moment, he turned it so I could see the map of New Orleans. There was a little red dot marking our location. "Does anything trigger any thoughts?"

I studied the area, letting my mind go through all the vision's details again. Wherever Night Owl Apartments was, those intricate wrought-iron balconies were up and down the street. They'd been there since the first day I had the vision. I just hadn't thought anything about them until now. There were so many small indicators of this city in my vision, now that I was aware of them.

"Maybe close to the French Quarter?" I said, sitting back in my chair and letting him pocket his phone again. Our waitress returned with our meals and Angel didn't ask any more questions so I would eat.

We ate in comfortable silence, and as I finished the last of the duck, I said, "I wish I could figure out how to control the visions. What's the use of being a seer if I can't do anything with my abilities? I feel less supernatural and more ... mental case."

"Firstly, you aren't a mental case," Angel said and poured the last of the wine from the bottle into my glass. "And having you here is a good thing for several reasons. I wouldn't have brought you if there hadn't been so many things for you to gain."

"I would've come anyway," I told him after a moment of consideration. It was the truth. The visions would come regardless of whether he was around, but at least with him, they were bearable. Not only that, but I could process them enough to begin understanding what they might mean.

"And you wouldn't have been able to sit down the next day, but ..." He let out a deep sigh as a smile stretched across his lips. He raised his eyes back to me. "I would still take you out for dinner regardless." My heart skipped in my chest from the look he sent me. His eyes sparkled with such boyishness that I almost forgot he was immortal.

"You make me feel so safe, even when we are in the middle of supernatural trouble," I said, hoping it all made sense to him.

"I'm starting to think that *you're* my supernatural trouble, Mouse," Angel said with a smile. "I know that you like me to be in charge, hold you accountable, call you out when you're being unfair to yourself. But, damn, I want to take care of you. Whatever you need, I want to be that for you. I love that entrepreneurial side of you that sees creative potential in everything, the way you write the most beautiful pieces of music from nothing. I love the way you smell, the way you feel in my arms, the little sounds you make when I'm buried between those beautiful legs, and the way you taste on my tongue when you submit to me and find your release ..." Angel let out a deep breath, looking back at me with awe. "I don't know what kind of supernatural hold you have on me—"

"I think I belong with you." The words felt so heavy, and not just because it was the most truthful thing I'd ever felt. My eyes burned because I already knew what he would say. There was only so long he would stay with me if we couldn't find the cure. He wouldn't want me to spend my mortal life bound to him, grow old without him, or be left behind after I died. He wouldn't want that, which was just another reason why it was so important to me that I came with him. There had to be something I could do as a seer. If I could figure out how to use my visions rather than be controlled by them, then maybe I could find all the answers we needed to find the cure.

His expression was somber as he nodded, nearly breaking my heart.

"We should go to bed," he said and pulled a couple of bills from his wallet and sat them on the table next to his barely touched meal. "We have a witch to find in the morning."

CHAPTER 8

Angel wanted to stop for a nice, sit-down breakfast at a café, but I convinced him to grab coffee and a breakfast sandwich to go. He held my coffee as I ate the bacon, egg, and cheese sandwich and walked alongside him. I kept getting distracted by all the sights. I couldn't help myself. New Orleans was just a totally different place: the history in the architecture and the jazz music that seemed to be everywhere no matter the time of day.

Angel dropped a few bills into a guitar case as we passed a busker on the corner. The man began improvising as we passed, changing the lyrics to his song to describe my blonde hair, blue dress, and tennis shoes. I paused just long enough to toss a few more bills into the guitar case before I joined Angel on the corner to wait for the light to change.

"Have you ever performed live like that, not in concert?" Angel asked, handing me my coffee after I'd tossed the sandwich wrapper in the trashcan.

I shook my head. "Not anything non-traditional. I've done a wedding before, but never anything more casual. Why?"

Angel shrugged and took my hand as the light changed. "I just wondered. I'm sure your music would be a great fit for live events."

My stomach twisted with nerves for a moment. I didn't have the sound equipment to do a live event, not really anyway. Then, there would be everyone knowing what I looked like, possibly my real name ...

"Eventually, maybe," I said and flashed him a shy smile. He gave my hand a squeeze and we started down the next street.

"Anything seem familiar?" he asked, slowing our pace.

The street had been dark in my visions. I wondered if that meant that we would just stumble on it if we kept walking, maybe did a few things in the meantime to take our minds off of the search. When I looked up from the sidewalk, I caught the name of another mask shop not far from the next corner ahead. I held tighter to Angel's hand and led him inside.

The shop was massive, much larger than the façade outside suggested. Part of the shop was dedicated to Mardi Gras with purple, gold, and green beads, masks, and feather boas glittering near the front of the store. The farther back you went, the less costume-like the masks and décor got. They were so well crafted, the faces so humanlike that some were a little eerie to stare at for too long.

"I think I'll ask around," Angel said, stepping from my side and pulling my attention away from a display of elegant masks. "I'll see if any of the employees recognizes the building from your vision."

"Okay. I'll just, um, keep browsing," I told him.

I turned back to the long aisle of displays. I began to slowly walk past them, admiring the intricate details and the colors until I found a mask hanging on the back wall that made me stop—and not just because it was so striking. It felt like my entire body had come to a halt, like someone had directed my attention there specifically.

The mask would entirely cover the face, the material metallic and covered in beautiful vines and roses. I reached for it, feeling that pull again telling me to touch it. I took it from the wall and gasped as that pull made my heart lurch and my stomach roll.

Suddenly, I wasn't standing in that shop but sitting on a stool with my cello between my legs. I could see myself in the full-length mirror that was just in front of me. My hair cascaded over my shoulders, framing that metallic mask as it peeked around the neck of the cello. I wore a long, black dress made of sheer tulle that did nothing to cover the black bra and panties I had on beneath it. I drew my bow across the strings, swaying to the music, and when I looked up, there was a Black woman no older than I was pointing a video camera at me. She looked up from the camera for just a second before looking at the camera's screen again, giving me just enough time to realize why I recognized her.

She had the same face as the woman from Angel's photo. Angular. Long hair with the same tight curls, only she wasn't the same woman. This woman's lips were fuller, but I could sense that they were related. Maybe a granddaughter, guessing at the time that had passed since Angel took that photo.

I looked away from her and into the mirror again, the scene suddenly different. I was standing in a hallway alone. I wore a silver venetian mask and a long black dress, this one not see-through. My silver heels, the pair I'd brought on this trip, peeked from the bottom of the dress. The ruby necklace Angel had given me hung around my neck. I turned to my right when something brushed my temple. A pair of lips, Angel's lips. He smiled at me. He was dressed in a dark suit, his hair cut short, and he wore a similar mask to mine but in black. He reached past me and when I followed his gaze, I saw him pick up an old-style skeleton key from the table that had a keychain with the Night Owl Apartments logo etched into the silver.

My vision blurred, and I was back in that mask shop with the metal mask in my hands. When I looked away from it to make sure no one had witnessed the episode, my stomach dropped.

On the nearest table were busts of a man and a woman and they were wearing the very masks Angel and I had on in my vision.

I hurried to the table and pulled both masks from the busts, feeling excitement pound in my chest as I realized I was right. These were the masks. I took a deep breath and focused on the details. The masks. Our outfits. The key. There was the woman. The vision always showed me the details that mattered, revealing more as I needed it. At least, that's what it seemed like it did. The closer I got to figure them out, the more was shown to me.

I took the three masks and made my way through the store, finding Angel at the front counter with an employee. I joined him, setting the masks on the counter and sliding them across to the employee who had just noticed me.

"Did you find everything okay?" she asked as Angel looked over my haul.

"Yes," I said with enough enthusiasm to garner a surprised smile from her. "Everything." I looked at Angel for just a moment, noticing the curious look that crossed his face.

"We just need a dress and a suit," I told him as I finished paying for the masks. I took the shopping bag and started for the door.

"What do you mean?" Angel asked, catching up with me as I found my way back to the street. I wasn't sure where to head next, just that the apartment hunt had turned into a shopping trip. "You want to go dress shopping?"

"Yes."

"Why?"

"I don't know. I just— I had another vision and I'm following the details," I said and stopped at the corner to wait on the light. It felt like I'd chugged my coffee despite only having drunk a few sips so far. I held tight to the details of the vision, repeating them in the order they appeared because surely that mattered too.

"Do we need to go back for the car?" Angel asked.

"No," I said, looking down at my phone now. I waited on the light. I searched for the nearest shops and found several along Canal Street that looked promising. It wasn't far from us, just a little farther ahead. "I know where we're going."

Angel didn't question me. He actually looked a little amused when I finally caught a glance at the smile on his face when we got stuck at yet another crosswalk. He was enjoying himself despite the random detour from our original plan. We made it to Canal Place, a shopping center where I found a couple of higher-end stores that might have clothing to match whatever fancy masquerade we were apparently going to.

It wasn't until we arrived at the second men's store that I recognized pieces from the vision. Angel looked eager to choose his own outfit but allowed me to take the lead in fitting him. We made sure the fitting room was empty before he went back to try on the suit, finding his way back into the main area of the store looking just like he had in my vision.

Almost.

"Here," I said and pulled the black mask from my shopping bag. He turned around so I could tie the ribbons around the back of his head. He moved the end of his bun out of the way so it didn't get caught, making it a little easier to tie a bow.

"I've been thinking," Angel said, straightening up to his full height and turning to face me again. I smoothed the front of his shirt so his black tie would lie flat over the white button-up. "It's about time I get a trim." He brushed the ends of his bun with his fingers.

I almost suggested that he cut his long hair short, but I was so confident in my vision that I didn't think I needed to.

"You get a haircut while we're here. I saw a place on the first floor," I told him. "Get this suit and we can meet up."

"Okay. Just text me the name of the store you're in and I'll come find you," he said and pressed a kiss to my forehead.

"No," I said and patted his chest. "Let it be a surprise. I'll meet you near the entrance once I'm done."

He looked a little nervous, like leaving me alone for so long might justify as another one of those safety risks he talked so often about. He nodded and the corners of his lips turned upward slightly. "Okay. At the entrance."

"You can see my location, Angel. I'll tell you where I am if you ask, but don't expect to see the dress," I teased, pointing a finger at him. He grabbed my finger and pulled me closer to kiss my lips before he went back to the dressing room.

I walked the hall for a while to window shop, the crowd growing as I did. It must have been getting closer to dinner because my stomach growled and I noticed the restaurant down the hallway had a wait. We hadn't stopped for lunch. We had spent most of the day here at the shops and Angel never once stopped to point it out. I was glad he'd let his guard down, worried about me less. Part of me was excited to be the one to suggest a meal once we met up again.

I finally chose a shop that had several elegant dresses in the window. I kept my eye trained on anything black, finding several before I felt drawn to one. The dress I picked looked relatively plain, black satin that draped at the neckline to create just a little cleavage. The spaghetti straps were thinner than I usually liked, but the back was worth the risk. It was completely open, stretching all the way to my lower back, where the fabric gathered in a similar style to the bust. It was beautiful, and I knew then that it was the right dress.

I picked my size and tried it on to be sure before leaving the store with the dark garment bag. Angel was looking down at his phone when I saw him standing near the entrance, no doubt checking my location. His hair was cut short, just like in my vision. It suited him, made him look even more like a businessman in his golf pants and dark T-shirt. He looked up and smiled, taking the bags from me before I could say a word.

"I can't wait to see you in this dress at whatever ball we're headed to," he said and kissed my temple. His lips lingered near my ear just long enough to whisper, "And get it off you after."

I felt the crimson burn across my face as I pulled away, lacing my fingers in his and leading the way back into Louisiana humidity. "Your hair turned out nice. You look handsome," I said.

"I needed to up my game if I'm going to be standing next to you," he said, making my insides melt. I looked away from him and at the street, realizing for the first time all day that I had no idea where we were going.

"Um, so ..." I stopped on the curb. I hadn't really seen anything else in my vision. I couldn't believe it. Fate or whatever supernatural power guided my visions had come through in the spookiest way because, at that moment, a city bus approached a covered bus stop and when it stopped, I saw the woman from my vision sitting inside wearing a Tulane T-shirt.

CHAPTER 9

The doors of the bus opened with a mechanical whoosh to let an old lady on with her shopping bags. I ran.

"Lily!"

I hurried up the steps after the woman, apologizing to the scowling man behind the wheel when he noticed me. Angel let out a grunt from behind, his back foot getting caught in the doors before the driver opened them again with a grumble.

Angel spoke to the driver as I looked over the bus for seats. The woman from my vision was seated halfway down the bus, on a bench seat that stretched the whole side of the bus. The bus wasn't entirely full, but I couldn't spot any seats for two. A man with all but two teeth missing from the front of his mouth scooted over to make space for me, shooting me a lascivious smile before I felt Angel's hand slide around my left hip.

"Grab one of the handles there," Angel told me, guiding me farther down the bus to grab on to the metal bar that stretched overhead. His arm only tightened around my middle as the bus lurched forward. "We're being watched."

Chills shot up my spine as I thought about that man with the missing teeth sitting in the front of the bus. I sucked in a deep breath, part of me regretting the decision to get on the bus until I thought about the woman. I decided to take a quick glance her way and realized she was the one watching us.

"Is this another part of the plan?" Angel whispered in my ear. "Because a little warning would've been nice, Mouse."

"Sorry," I said and held on to the hand around my waist, deciding not to tell him that I ran on a whim. I was glad for his steadying arm as the bus ebbed and flowed, moving so quick that you'd have thought we were late for the next stop. I kept my eye on the woman as we approached each stop. She didn't move until the third stop just past our hotel.

She stood up quickly and strode to the front of the bus with purpose, waiting a moment after the doors had opened to get off. I left Angel to hurry after her, hearing him groan behind me as he rushed for the doors. The driver yelled at him as we reached the street. I kept my eyes on the woman as she walked ahead, going the opposite direction from our hotel and taking a right.

"We have to follow her," I told Angel before I jogged ahead this time.

"The one in the green shirt?" he asked, following me.

"Yes," I told him as we ran. "I think she's the witch, or a relative anyway."

He didn't question me as we ran around the corner. We were the only people on the entire block. No. There was no way I'd lost her that quickly. Had she done some kind of magic? Was there another turn or a door? I looked around us only to see a lot of the same wrought-iron fencing.

Black wrought-iron fencing.

That tingle slowly built across my skin, that feeling that came before a vision. I started walking again, Angel keeping close to my side as I followed the fencing until I saw the owl and moon symbol on the gate.

"This is it, isn't it?" he asked.

I nodded and pushed open the gate to reveal the courtyard and the red doors ahead. "Take out the code for the door, the one written on that paper."

I walked ahead, reaching the red door only for Angel to cut me off and type in the code. It swung inward to reveal a dark hallway with sconces that gave off warm light. To the left was a wall of gilded mailboxes and hanging just above them was that large bell from my vision with the engraving that told us to ring it for service. Standing beside the mailboxes was the woman in the Tulane T-shirt.

I let out a scream when she charged at me. She tugged me behind her, shielding me from Angel's view.

"He's with me!" I reached out to tug on the woman's shoulder, but she turned around just long enough to point a hand at me. I was propelled backward into the wall and was pinned there by an unseen force. She'd turned her attention just long enough that Angel had her pressed to the red door in seconds, freeing me from the magic so I could rub at the sore spot at the back of my head.

Angel clapped a hand over her mouth before she could call for help. "Yes, I'm a vampire. No, she's not. I think you already sensed that, though," he said, voice low. "She's with me. We aren't going to hurt you. I need your help. I'm looking for a witch who I think lives here."

I could see the bewilderment on the woman's face before Angel even lowered his hand from her mouth. She let out a laugh in disbelief, looking at me before looking back at Angel again. "Why would any witch help *you*?"

"Because the one I'm looking for did once and promised to again," Angel said and released her. "Years ago, I found a witch who knew a spell to reverse vampirism. She said she could make me mortal again. I found what she needed. Now, I just need to find her and I think she lives here."

"How could you know that? This place is shielded from vampires and tracking witches isn't as easy as tracking humans," she said, looking back at him in disgust now.

"M-Me," I finally said, nervously, taking a step away from the wall to join them. She looked over me, studying me like she was having trouble figuring out what exactly I was.

"You have something magical about you. Witch-like," the woman said before finally raising her eyes to me. "Almost."

"I'm a seer, and I had a vision. You were in my vision. We weren't here. I don't know that we were even in New Orleans, but you were there, and you look like—" I stopped talking as all the details flooded my memory, making it difficult to organize them into coherent sentences.

Something I said must have made sense to her though because her eyes widened, and she looked back at Angel. "How many years ago was that?"

"1968."

Oh my. It felt like we were in that photo right now, frozen in time, the woman and I both staring in shock at Angel's serious expression. He'd been looking for this woman since he got the guardian blood over a year ago. He'd been searching for a guardian willing to hand over their blood since 1968. For all we knew, the witch he was looking for was dead.

"Okay. Um, well ..." the woman started, finally letting out a deep breath. "You said she looks like me?"

"Yes," Angel and I both said in unison.

She nodded, staring at a spot across the room as though working out what to do next. A pit had formed in my gut. Angel only looked back at her more intensely, like he was on the verge of heartbreak if she couldn't help.

"Bebe Laveau," Angel said as he pulled the envelope from his pocket.

"Y-You sure it was Bebe?" the woman stammered.

"Yes," Angel said and finally handed over the photo. "She went by Bebe."

The woman let out a shaky breath, her eyes glazing over as she looked at the photo. "Oh God."

"Oh God? What do you mean?" I asked, pulling her attention from the photo.

She glanced down the hallway for a moment before she motioned for us to follow her. She led us down an adjacent hallway, through a door labeled for employees, and locked it behind us. The room was large, with four leather couches facing each other on top of a red rug, the only color in the otherwise dark room. She sank onto one of the couches with a groan, rubbing her temples. It made me wonder for a moment what Bebe Laveau must've done to be such a headache.

"You're looking for my grandmother. No one but me called her Bebe. Give me a moment. That kind of shook me a little," the woman said and continued to rub her temples before moving to a spot on her brow. "I'm Nova Laveau, by the way."

"My name is Lily Thompson. This is my boyfriend Angel," I said, rounding the edge of the couch opposite her and taking a seat. "We just need help with the spell. We need to know what's next."

"Yeah? Well, my Bebe doesn't know much of anything right now," Nova said under her breath. "This is what my mom said would happen."

"Could we talk with her? Does she know something, maybe how to contact Bebe?" Angel asked, joining us around the coffee table but not taking a seat.

Nova lowered her hands and looked up at him. "My mom passed away from cancer a few years back. It's just me and Bebe. I'm her caregiver."

Oh no.

"She'll remember me, I swear. Will you take us to her?" Angel asked.

The woman shrugged. "She doesn't always remember me. My grandma has dementia."

I closed my eyes against the burn, fighting the tears that threatened to spill over.

"Maybe she will remember me," Angel continued. "Will you take me to her, let me try?"

The woman shook her head. "You don't understand. She doesn't always remember things, but she always remembers her magic."

"Exactly why I need her."

"And that's the best way to get you killed!" Nova stood up

and walked toward the bookshelf that covered the wall behind her. "You're a vampire, a vampire with a supernatural snack." She directed a look at me.

"I don't feed from her," Angel shot back with enough force that the room rang with silence after. "I love her. I've wanted to be human since the day I turned, but I ache for it now because I have her. I don't feed from her."

"Okay, but you clearly aren't desecrating either," Nova said with a snort. "And most witches won't accept a vampire among them, especially not in their coven home." She gestured around them, confirming what we had suspected. These were apartments, but they were reserved for the members of the coven. For Angel, this was the most dangerous place for him to be and yet here we were among his natural enemies.

"He's not a monster," I said.

"Lily—"

"He's trapped as he is, and he does his best not to hurt anyone. He only feeds on the worst people in society, people who do horrible things, and not just once," I said, tasting the salt on my lips. "Can you help?"

The conflict on her face told me everything I needed to know. What Angel had said about Bebe being different ... That applied to her granddaughter too.

"I don't know," she said and started toward the door. I followed her as she led the way back to the main entrance and to a large counter to the right. She opened a door and appeared behind the counter a moment later. There were numbered compartments along the wall behind her, almost like the mailboxes in the entryway. She pulled a piece of paper from beneath the counter and turned it so we could read it.

"This is a lease agreement. The rent is listed. You both need to sign your full names at the bottom to get keys," she said.

Angel groaned. "We don't need an apartment. We need to speak to Bebe."

"Renting an apartment is the only way I can protect you from the coven."

"How can you protect us?" Angel asked.

She looked a little annoyed as she leaned on the counter and lowered her voice. "My family owns these apartments in a kind of magical sense. We own them because my grandmother, Beatrice Laveau, is the High Priestess of our coven. She's the strongest in the coven, even with her condition. If I welcome you to stay, the magic says you can't be removed unless another Laveau rescinds the lease. It protects you from magical attacks. Our coven bylaws are also written so that it means no one here will harm you. You are my guests. They have to accept you. It's literally illegal for them not to."

The muscles in my shoulders relaxed, and I saw Angel's lower with his sigh.

"Thank you," he said. "Thank you, Nova."

"It's what Bebe would do," Nova said with a shrug. "And my Bebe is always right."

She pushed a pen across the counter and I took it first, signing my name at the bottom. Angel did the same before handing the lease over to her. Nova signed her name at the top and turned to the numbered compartments, nudging a stool along the floor that she then used to better reach one of the top compartments.

"This one is next to mine," she said and opened the door to compartment 7G. She sat the folded lease inside the compartment before closing the door. There was a metallic clank and the end of a key protruded from the keyhole. There was a small flash and a keychain dangled from the end. Nova removed the key from the lock and turned back to us, setting it on the counter.

It was the same one from my vision, the owl and moon engraved on the little silver keychain. Angel lifted it from the counter, turning it over so I could see our names engraved on the opposite side of the keychain.

"Welcome to your new home, Angel and Lily," Nova said with a small smile.

CHAPTER 10

Our new apartment was large, at least as big as my apartment back in New York City. The biggest difference was the décor. It came with dark leather furniture, black walls with elegant trim, and lots of wall sconces and lamps with that same warm light from the building entryway. There was a wall of books and a bar fully stocked with whiskey and wines next to the bookshelves.

"What's in the bags?" Nova asked as she carried two glasses of red wine from the bar to the living room. I sat on the L-shaped leather couch in front of the mahogany coffee table. She handed me a glass before she sat down in the leather armchair.

"In my last vision, the one where I saw you," I started, turning the glass between my hands, "I saw Angel and me standing in front of a mirror wearing black-tie attire and masks for a masquerade."

"In front of a mirror? Vampires don't have a reflection, do they?"

"They don't. It was just my reflection in the mirror, but he was beside me. He took a key to this apartment from a table," I said and looked around the room, finding the spot near the door. "Right there."

Nova's eyes followed my point to the spot where the full-length mirror was just steps away from the front door. "This is wild. I've never met a seer before."

"I've never met a witch," I countered.

She smiled, pushing her curls behind her ears. "Well, since you came prepared and all," she said and lifted her wine to her lips, "there is a masquerade tomorrow night. We have them every season."

My skin chilled from the accuracy.

"Something wrong?" Nova asked.

I shook my head and then shrugged. "I can't control the visions. I don't know how they work. They only happen at night, and I know that sometimes I can trigger them if I'm near a place or an object that's important, but there's not really any pattern to them."

"I don't know a lot about seers, but maybe someone in the coven does," she said and adjusted in her seat so she could fold her legs beneath her.

I took a sip of my wine. "That's what Angel was hoping."

He'd gone by himself to retrieve our luggage and check out of the hotel. All it took was a few minutes for Nova to settle into our apartment and for me to understand how I could possibly end up comfortable enough letting her film me in lingerie while I played the cello. After I told her about the parts of my vision she was in, I had to show her my channel.

Nova loved it. She was going to college at Tulane for a fine art degree. As soon as she told me, she was quick to tell me how she was taking business classes too and how she thought about staying longer to get a bachelor's degree in business, too. I knew what she was compensating for. It was the same response I often got when I told people I was studying music.

How will you earn a living?

Not many people get in the big orchestras.

Maybe you can teach at a high school or something.

What if you got a business degree instead and taught cello on the side?

Thankfully for me, my family had never had any doubts with my music, but sometimes I wonder if that was because I was consistently a top student. I was never great in school, but I was a great musician and that made my future a little more promising than it did for others pursuing artistic fields.

"What's your favorite part of art?" I asked, hoping the change in subject would ease the tension that always came whenever my abilities came up.

Nova sucked on her bottom lip for a moment before she spoke. "I like design and creating a vision," she said with a sigh, as though there was so much to unpack that it would be difficult to explain it all. "I love all kinds of art, but really, I like the planning that goes into creating a single shot of photography or video. I've been doing some photography and videography and uploading them on freelancing sites for people to use. It's sort of hard to explain, but those clips on cooking shows that are only maybe a couple of seconds, and it's a small clip where someone is mixing cookies or an aesthetic shot of that moment a perfect apple pie comes out of the oven ... The moment lasts a second, but it changes the entire video because it's there. Does that make sense?"

It felt like everything inside me sped up, like a jolt of electricity shot down my arms and legs because I did understand. That was how I felt about layering different sounds together. It was that one chord in one of my first songs I ever wrote that made people on my YouTube channel describe the entire piece as sad. Without it, the whole song would be different.

"It makes sense to me. I feel the same way about music and audio elements," I said, mirroring her and pulling my legs beneath me on the couch and nearly spilling my wine in the process.

"Maybe we can work on something together? I don't mean to intrude on your business, you know?" Nova said, waving her hands immediately as though it was a terrible idea we should both forget right away. "It would be too much. You're a musician."

"No. Not at all," I told her, hesitating before I divulged my more recent ideas, how I envisioned the way I could include myself in my videos for YouTube without giving away my identity. I ran to the kitchen where I'd left our shopping bags to retrieve the masks I bought that morning, showing them to her as I explained how I might style my clothes and create a story.

In just minutes, Nova was every bit as excited as I was about the idea, and we'd begun to craft a story around a piece I'd just started working on. Angel came in during the middle of our brainstorming with our luggage in tow, making carrying it all to our new bedroom with much more ease than should be humanly possible.

I noticed how Nova's demeanor changed when Angel joined us in the living room. She smiled, but it didn't touch her eyes the same way as it had as we talked. Angel noticed too and gave her an understanding nod, placing his hands on his hips with a sigh.

"I hope my being here doesn't make things—"

"Oh! That! No, don't worry," she said and waved a hand in dismissal. "It wouldn't really be any different than normal, trust me."

I exchanged curious glances with Angel at the comment. I had an idea what she meant from the blush on her cheeks, but I couldn't bring myself to ask.

"Um, Nova said there's a masquerade ball tomorrow night," I said, reaching for the pair of masks I'd chosen for us, which were sitting on the coffee table on top of the plastic bag from the shop.

Angel smiled and joined me on the couch. "Your visions seem to be getting clearer."

"Maybe," I said and sat the masks back down, lifting my wine from the table and resting it in my lap between both hands. "I still don't know how they work or how to trigger them. It seems like I'm getting more information when I have them though."

The room was quiet for a moment before Nova sat forward in her seat.

"I don't know that I can help with that part, but you said something earlier about them coming at night," she said.

Angel's hand rested on my knee, and it wasn't until I felt his gentle touch that I realized how I'd tensed at her words. The visions did come most consistently at night. It was the only time they were consistent, actually. I wasn't sure why, but it made sleeping difficult. Having Angel with me had chased them away and made getting a full night of rest easier. Still, I woke up sore and still had small flashes of images throughout the night that I recognized as visions and not just dreams.

"Yeah," I finally spoke, looking up from my glass at her. "I have them every night, but less so when Angel is around."

Nova considered the words for a moment before nodding. "I can't tell you what that means or how to control them, but I think I can do something to help you sleep."

Something released deep within me, easing the tightness in my chest and making my entire body relax. Being able to sleep without a vision waking me or finding myself twisted in the sheets in the morning would make such a difference. I heard Angel let out a deep breath next to me.

"Can you do a spell?" he asked.

She smiled. "Yeah. I think I can. It wouldn't be a forever kind of thing. I'd have to do it every night, but it should give you the time you need to sleep without the visions."

"Thank you. That would be great." The words tumbled from my mouth. It was almost embarrassing how eager I sounded, like a child relieved to hear that their parent would check beneath the bed for monsters before tucking them in for the night.

"It's kind of late now," Nova said and finished the last of her wine. "I can do it and leave you two alone to settle in. I live just next door, so you can come and knock, if you need anything. You can always text me too." She blushed as she pointed to my phone lying on the coffee table.

"Thank you. Text me if you need anything, too, Nova. I mean it," I said. The way her skin turned a deeper pink told me I might have been right. She was different and didn't fit in with her coven the way you'd think the High Priestess's granddaughter would. It's what she meant when she said that no one would be surprised that she invited us here.

I stood up, Angel rising beside me, and Nova stopped directly in front of me. She took a deep breath and raised her hands to my head, resting the fingers of both of her hands on my temples. She whispered a few words to herself before lowering them again.

"Thank you," I told her again, grasping her hand for a moment. "We'll talk in the morning."

"Yeah. Sure," she said and smiled before turning for the door. Angel followed her, standing in the doorway as she moved into the hallway.

"Thank you, Nova," he said, his tone holding enough emotion that it made Nova pause in the hall. "I mean that, and not just for helping Lily with her visions. I know what it means to allow me to stay here. I don't take your blessing lightly."

Nova shifted from one foot to the other, glancing past him and at me for a moment before focusing on him again. "I know what it feels like to be misunderstood. I'd want someone to take a chance on me."

She gave us both a final smile before going next door to her apartment. Angel waited until her door shut again to close and lock ours, crossing the room to join me on the couch again.

"You saw her in your vision," he said, pushing a piece of my hair away from my face. "What did you see?"

I sat my wine glass on the table and scooted closer to him. "Enough." I was so used to his long hair that it was a little strange to run my fingers through his short hair. He was just as handsome. "I think we're going to be best friends. She's important."

He smiled and gave me a nod before leaning in, brushing his nose against mine.

"That's enough for me."

CHAPTER 11

I used my new friendship with Nova to my advantage the next evening to make the most of Angel's and my date to the coven ball. He dressed in our apartment, and I dressed in Nova's next door. Her dress was similar, though rather than revealing her back the way my dress did, her black gown had a neckline that plunged nearly to her navel. She filled out the silhouette better than I would have. After smoothing her curls and pinning them perfectly away from her face with silver clips, she helped me get into my dress.

She didn't have Anne's high-fashion touch, but the way she did my makeup was closer to what I would've chosen for myself and she managed to curl my blonde hair in a more loose and bouncy way than Anne normally did, making it look a little more natural and less styled. Once I felt as put together as I knew how, we left the apartment for the hallway where Angel was waiting.

He leaned against the far wall with his phone in his hands, looking up from it as soon as I pulled the door shut behind me. My stomach twisted tightly as his eyes roved over me. He straightened up, pocketing his phone and sending me an onery smile that made me want to dart into our apartment before I could melt right there in the hallway.

"No one should bother you," Nova told us as she turned from her door. "I have to go help Bebe get ready, so I'll meet you guys down there. Just keep your key with you."

"Thank you, Nova," Angel said, waiting for her to pass between us before he closed the distance. He stopped in front of me, not touching me for a moment as he looked over me again. Instead of brushing my face like I was used to or leaning in for a kiss, he reached past me. I heard the key click into the lock of our apartment and I moved to the opposite side of the hallway to wait as he finished, admiring the way his suit clung to his muscular shoulders and tapered just slightly along his legs.

I waited in the hallway for Angel to lock the apartment door, smoothing my black dress over my hips and wondering as I stood there in my silver heels and diamond necklace if I had dressed up too much for this coven soirée. He turned from the door with a smile and pocketed the key, lacing his fingers with mine as he led the way toward the elevator.

I pressed the button and watched as the digital screen at the top counted up until it reached floor seven and the doors slid apart. I got a full-body view of myself and for sure thought I was overdressed. As always, Angel didn't appear next to me in the mirror despite giving my hand a reassuring squeeze and inviting me to go ahead of him. I let out a deep breath of nerves as he pushed the button for the main lobby. Before the doors had even completely shut, his hands slid along my hips from behind and I felt a tickle of his breath at my ear.

"Put your hands on the rail," he said.

My heart fluttered in my chest and my face warmed. He held my hips firmly against him, pulling me against the pressure at the front of his slacks. I leaned over until my hands reached the rail and he guided my heels aside to make space for him. The elevator dinged, reminding me that we were alone for just a few moments. My heart sped up and the knot in my stomach tightened with desire, aching for him to step into the space between my heels.

"You'll keep them there, yes?" Angel asked, sliding the silk of my dress up my knees and thighs until I stood in just my thong and heels from the waist down. "Hmm, Mouse?" he prompted.

"Yes," I breathed.

I looked up at the mirrored wall, forgetting that vampires didn't appear in mirrors, and found my flushed expression instead. I chewed on my bottom lip, resisting the urge to let go of the rail to reach back and touch him.

"Good girl," he said and moved from the space between my legs. I realized what he was about to do a moment later when he lightly pressed against the small of my back so I'd arch my back and press my ass into his waiting hand. He ran his palm from one cheek to the other before it was gone, landing again with a loud slap. I barely stifled my squeak before the next came and then the next, four in total that left me with tears in my eyes. I reminded myself to keep my hands on the rail as my shock faded and I felt the sting fully set in. This was worse than that time in my apartment and while it hurt, it filled some kind of need I didn't know I had, made me more eager to feel him, made me crave the gentleness of his fingers after the roughness

...

"Keep them there," he reminded me as he slipped his thumbs into the elastic band at my hip and dragged my underwear down, his fingers softly following them all the way to my ankles where he helped me step out of them. I let out a moan as I realized he had to be crouched behind me. He was inches from the most sensitive part of me and as the realization came to me, his lips were on me. I gasped, biting hard on my lower lip to keep quiet as he teased me with his tongue. I could feel my muscles tightening, a wave rising and nearly at its peak.

Then, he was gone and as the wave receded and I was left trembling with need, he stood beside me. He took my hand and guided me into a standing position before him, the silk of my dress confirming that I would be better off on the dance floor all night than sitting in any chair. He reached out and brushed a stray tear from under my eye. He lifted the other hand, showing me my black thong, eyebrows raised as though making a point. I felt a little like prey as I stood inches from him.

"I will keep these, and you will keep your cute nose out of any vampire cure business tonight or later, you will find it in a corner somewhere and you won't be able to sit down all week," he said, a mischievous smile tugging at the corner of his mouth. His dark eyes were piercing and even though I felt a little like I wouldn't sit down all week right now, I knew those beautiful eyes held a promise. A part of me wanted to see just how much of a promise it was.

I was speechless, still reeling from desire and a little frustrated that he'd stopped just as I was at the precipice.

"I don't like your games," I whispered, unable to hide my smile and feeling my face flame immediately. He smiled fully now and pocketed my underwear.

"Then be a good girl," he laughed and cupped the side of my face, pressing a gentle kiss to my lips. "And you'll be rewarded later instead."

Ugh! The way my stomach twisted into knots! I stamped my right heel against the elevator floor and he laughed again.

"I do enjoy punishing you too. So, it's really your choice how this night ends, Mouse," he said.

The elevator gave a final ding. He laced his fingers in mine, and we stepped into the lobby before I could contain my embarrassment.

The crowd in the lobby was thin, men and women dressed in black gowns who didn't pay us any attention as we joined them. I wondered how it was that they could sense Angel and if maybe his mask or the fact that we looked like any other guests kept us concealed.

"Do you have the key?" I asked. It was a stupid question. I'd watched him lock the door, but I was still a little lightheaded from the elevator ride. I squeezed my thighs together at the memory, unable to keep the heat from rising to my face as I thought about my underwear sitting in his pocket now.

Angel chuckled just behind me, pulling me to his chest by my hips and letting a hand linger at my waist as he moved to my side.

"I want you to enjoy the party, Mouse. Let me take care of the details."

"Okay," I said, my face only heating more when I caught his sly smile.

"Ready?" he asked and laced his fingers with mine.

I gave his hand a squeeze and turned toward the open doors of the banquet hall. "Ready."

The dark academic vibe of the rest of the building was evident in the hall. Four stone columns lined the room, rising to the glass dome in the middle of the ceiling. The moonlight filled the space below bright enough that the sconces along the walls and large chandelier at the front of the room provided all the light the space needed. Surrounding the glass dome were images I'd expect to see in a cathedral; winged angels and lovers holding hands staring down from the ceiling among the vines and trees. It was a woodland scene, almost *A Midsummer Night's Dream* inspired.

Anxiety tugged hard enough at my gut that I steered us toward the bar set up just inside the room. I noticed a buffet not far away once we'd fallen in line before an elderly couple. Angel was already looking over the spread, no doubt making plans to fill a plate for me and find a place to sit. About half of the witches and warlocks were seated, talking with the others in a way that told me most of them knew each other. It wouldn't take long for them to notice us, and realize we didn't belong.

"What can I get you?" the bartender asked, pulling my attention from the room.

"Champagne," I said as I noticed the bartender next to him opening a bottle.

"I'll have the same," Angel said before the man could ask.

He nodded and pulled two glasses from beneath the bar. "May I see your key?"

Angel withdrew the skeleton key, and the man glanced at the number, hesitating for a moment before turning to fill our glasses. My nerves must have been obvious because Angel squeezed my hand before the man returned with two glasses.

"I'll find us a table. You go grab a plate," Angel told me and took my champagne flute. I wasn't that hungry, but the line for the buffet was growing longer. I joined the line behind a couple close in age to me and waited until I was close enough to the long table to pick up a plate at the end.

"You are new here," a woman said to my left. I adjusted the plate in my hands and glanced at her. She was maybe fifty, slender with enough curves to her exposed arms to tell me she spent time in the gym. She looked dressed for business, almost like a politician in her black knee-length dress with her dark hair slicked back into a bun at the nape of her neck.

"Um, yes. Just got here today, actually," I said and moved forward in the line when she motioned for me to.

"Yes, I know," she said sweetly, masking that tell-tale lilt I recognized. I grew up around some of the richest families in upstate New York. I knew that sickeningly sweet tone, the subtle way a woman's voice would rise just enough to indicate their superiority. I knew it so well that it was irritating to hear it here too.

"Oh?" I asked, my heart doing a leap in my chest as I braced for confrontation. "I'm sorry. I don't remember you. Have we met?"

The woman laughed. "Of course not," she said and motioned for me to move forward in line again. "And you're not a witch, much less a member of our coven."

My cheeks heated, but I tried to hide my embarrassment with a smile. "How could you tell?"

"Well, a witch would notice the sign of the CC," she said and tapped her index finger to a silver brooch on the lapel of her blazer. It took me a moment to put together what she meant, why she had the symbol of the Night Owl Apartments pinned to her. She was important, but not just to the apartments. She was important to the coven somehow.

"Sorry. I don't quite ... What's the CC?"

The woman took a plate from the end of the table. "It stands for Coven Council. I am a coven elder, and I have more knowledge of coven business than most on the council. It's, in part, my business to know everything about our tenants."

That's why she knew about me.

"Um," I started and cleared my throat, plopping a scoop of potatoes onto my plate even though I didn't like mashed potatoes. "You are right. I'm not a witch, which is why I know what it means that I was invited here. I'm grateful, believe me. So thankful for the coven's hospitality."

The woman allowed me to ramble until she'd filled her plate with potatoes and green beans, finally looking up when I was too embarrassed by my word vomit to continue. She flashed a smile and stood a little straighter before she spoke.

"You're quite welcome to visit, honey," she said with a chuckle. "I can't deny that I'm intrigued by you. I've only met one other seer in all my life, so I know how rare your kind is and how wise beyond your years you often are."

I wasn't hungry anymore. I placed a roll on my plate next to my helping of mashed potatoes. The woman placed a scoop of green beans on my plate like she was an aunt at a family reunion.

"Thank you," I said. I wasn't sure what to say, but I could tell that she had more to discuss and it had me on edge.

"Your companion, however, will not be well-received," she said, finally getting straight to the reason I was sure she approached me at all. "The CC is very careful about our secrecy and protection. Forgive me for being so bold, but it is obvious that you are young in your abilities and have not had the appropriate training to see this world for what it is. You are not in good company, no matter what you think you are to him."

"My boyfriend and I are in New Orleans on business and not the type you may assume. I promise you that he is not what you think he is," I told her and decided to skip filling the rest of my plate. I was prepared to leave, but what she said next had me frozen in place.

"I see that he's scented you."

I hesitated long enough that a gap formed between myself and the couple in line in front of me. "Scented?"

The woman smirked and nodded. She reached out to take the small ruby around my neck between her fingers. "Yes," she said before dropping it so that it hung on my chest. "He marked you as his as his kind does. They are very territorial, enough so that most wouldn't dare encroach on what belongs to another. That goes for most supernatural beings as well, which is why he gave you that necklace. It's not a ruby, by the way, though humans would assume so. You're naive enough in your skills that it's not a surprise that you didn't know, honey."

It's not a ruby. Angel told me that he'd had it made. If he'd marked me as his then it made sense that the ruby was something of his. Blood.

"You don't know what I've been through," I said defensively, and looked down at my half-full plate. "The necklace helps to protect me. He gave it to me because we are surrounded by the supernatural here. Look, I appreciate the coven's kindness, but I haven't met many supernatural beings who are what they claim to be."

"I see," the woman said and used the tongs on the table to add salad to her plate. "I'm happy to see that your lack of experience hasn't made you too trusting. You are correct in saying that not everyone is what they claim to be. Not everyone has pure intentions, so forgive me for questioning yours." She looked up at me with a waiting expression, leaning in as though she expected me to whisper some secret.

"It's not your business why we are here," I told her. It made my stomach twist to say the words, but I'd learned that I tend to put up with things too long.

The woman's smile returned, that fake-sweet look. "Your intentions here are entirely my business, Miss Thompson. It's my duty to the CC."

"Well, we are guests of the Laveaus," I said, watching that smile melt off her face. It was the most honest expression I'd seen from her yet, almost horrified like a villain caught before they could enact their scheme. "And my boyfriend has had a long-standing business arrangement with Mrs. Bebe Laveau herself. Excuse me."

I skirted around the couple in front of me and scanned the room. I found Angel sitting at a table near the front of the room next to Nova. She looked concerned as I approached, waving me over as though I was moving at snail's pace rather than nearly jogging to meet them.

"Have you eaten any of that?" she asked with concern and pointed to my plate.

"No," I said and pulled out the chair next to Angel who was equally as confused. I sat down, letting out a little gasp when the soreness reminded me of our agreement in the elevator. Nova didn't notice, but Angel had and slid a hand up my thigh. I grabbed it before the heat in my core could spread further. "Why?"

"Don't," Nova said sternly and took my plate. She tapped the table between us twice and my plate rose into the air and levitated away. I would've watched to see where it went except she leaned across the table, drawing my attention back to her serious expression. "That was Poppy Nolan. Her family has held a seat on the council forever. My family's sure they've done it with magic, but no one can prove it. Don't keep anything she gives you."

"Okay. Well, she's not happy about us being here," I said and glanced at Angel. He wasn't looking at us. I followed his gaze toward the main table just ahead where Poppy took a seat alone, sitting in the second largest chair. The one to her left looked like a throne and remained empty. I imagined that was where Nova's grandmother would sit later.

"I doubt many witches would be happy to see a vampire among the coven," Angel said with a sigh.

"True, but she knows that you're only here because you have my family's blessing and she doesn't like my family," Nova said.

Angel looked away from the table, conflicted. My stomach twisted as I looked back at the annoyance in Nova's expression. She offered a kind smile when she noticed me staring and it only made me feel worse. I opened my mouth to offer to leave, tell her we could meet somewhere else and Angel and I could stay at the hotel. Angel spoke before I could.

"Thank you again, Nova. It means a lot. It really does."

"It's not a secret that our families don't get along and besides," she said and looked to the entrance on the right-side of the room. "What my Bebe says matters a lot more to the coven than what Poppy says. She's not well-liked."

I knew that she meant it to be reassuring, but something tugged at my gut telling me there was more to worry about. Angel sat a hand in my lap, giving my thigh a gentle squeeze. I turned just as he leaned in to kiss me and stopped.

A whoosh swept through the room, making the sconces on the wall flicker and ruffling the napkins and dark tablecloths around the room. The air above us seemed to sparkle as though magic itself was dancing through the room the way we would later. The room went silent aside from the occasional gasp in awe and amused chuckle.

"What's that?" I asked, turning to look at Nova's smiling face. "My Bebe."

She kept her eyes trained on the entrance to the right. A pair of large double doors swung open and more of that sparkling air took flight ahead of a woman with graying curls. The room filled with applause as Bebe Laveau entered the room and began waving to the witches and warlocks, greeting the nearest guests personally with handshakes and hugs before she noticed Nova across the room. She blew her a kiss that Nova returned.

All twelve members of the Coven Council rose from their seats as she approached her throne. Bebe waved for them to sit before turning to the room of people with the most matronly smile. With the flourish of a hand across her throat, her voice was amplified so her sweet hum of a laugh filled the space. She let out a deep sigh and spoke.

"What a magical night it is to be here with all of you, family," she said and glanced toward our table, her eyes sparkling with recognition as they found Angel beside me. "Old friends."

My body relaxed with relief.

CHAPTER 12

There wasn't so much as the scrape of a fork on a plate as Beatrice Laveau stood at the head table. She moved her gaze from us and back to the room of witches and warlocks.

"It's such a privilege to be the High Priestess of this coven. I have served as your leader for many years, longer than some of you have been alive. I've taught many of you personally, heard your troubles, and celebrated your triumphs. There is truly nothing better to witness than seeing the members of this coven thrive and grow into such wonderful people and I hope that when my life comes to an end that is what I am remembered for; rejoicing in your success and providing support in your struggles," she said, arms open wide as though trying to embrace the entire room. Then her expression changed, her smile faltering just a little, and a strange coolness settled in the grand hall.

"My magic may be untouched by time and strong as ever, but none of us can escape the passage of time and I am no different. My body ages and my mind does not remember the way the magic in my veins does. So, as the High Priestess of this coven, I have decided that it is time to step down from leadership rather than risk my condition becoming a problem for the council and our coven."

The hall filled with gasps and murmurs. Nova was stiff to my left, eyes wide and mouth parted in shock. Poppy sat a little taller on Bebe's right, trying and failing to hide her smile behind her wine glass.

"As the rules of this council dictate, I have a right to choose the next High Priestess so long as that person is within my bloodline. From this night, the next High Priestess of our coven will be Nova Laveau," Bebe announced, lifting her champagne glass from the table as excited gasps and whispers filled the room. Suddenly glasses all around us were lifted and all eyes were turned on Nova who sat in shock, the color fading from her face. "To High Priestess, Nova Laveau!"

The room echoed Bebe's cheer and applause erupted. The noise faded when Poppy rose from her seat and began tapping her fork against her wine glass, the lines around her mouth deepening with her frown. She launched into the agenda, and I leaned toward Nova.

"Congratulations."

"She's right that she can pass leadership to a blood relative, but that's only if they've been allowed access to council business," Nova said, the words falling from her lips in a rush. "She trained my mom for the priesthood, not me. I've never wanted that role and she knows that. Mom always called me Little Bebe because I never planned on staying here. I wanted to leave like Bebe did and find my own way without the coven. I never ..."

"Maybe she sees something in you. Bebe left once too. Maybe she sees that strength and leadership in you too," Angel said, scooting his chair closer to me to keep from drawing the attention of the nearest table.

Nova shook her head. "No. She's confusing me with my mom."

"Well, you shouldn't have to carry the weight of that if you don't want it. What would happen if you refused the position?" I asked as she took a sip of her champagne.

She groaned as the room filled with applause, taking another long drink from her glass.

"Thank you all for your patience. That's all for the agenda for the quarter. Enjoy the evening!" Poppy flashed that politician smile at the crowd before motioning toward the band in the corner. A trumpet blared and then the rest of the group joined in with an upbeat jazz song that immediately drew a crowd to the dance floor.

"If I don't take the priesthood, then Poppy would swoop in," Nova said and downed the last of her drink. "I don't want to think about it. Not right now. I'm going to get a shot from the bar."

She rose from the table and I followed, glancing back at Angel for his encouragement before I hurried after Nova. She reached the bar ahead of me, asking the bartender for a shot of tequila.

"Make it two," I blurted as I joined her at the counter. Nova looked at me. After a moment, she let out a long sigh and turned to fully face me.

"I'm sorry to derail your night with all this drama," she said as the bartender placed two shot glasses between us with salt and lime wedges. "You should be enjoying the party with your boyfriend."

"You didn't derail anything and I am enjoying the party. We both are," I told her and looked back at our table. Angel wasn't there anymore, but I wasn't too worried about where he might have gone. He asked me to enjoy the night. He didn't want me to worry about the cure or my visions or any other supernatural problems. Maybe Nova needed that boundary too.

I lifted my shot glass from the counter. "You said you didn't want to think about it. I don't want to think about our drama, either. So, let's not."

She smiled, let out a deep sigh, and lifted her glass. We pressed them together with a clink before downing the shots. I was quick to bite the lime, but it was so tart that I accidentally spat it on the floor. Nova laughed, a squeaky sound I hadn't expected from her that had me laughing too as I picked up my lime and set it in my empty glass.

"I don't do tequila shots," I told her in defense.

"Then we'll do something else instead," she said, still recovering from her fit of laughter as she turned to the bartender. "We'll take two lemon drops."

I almost told her that I'd never had a lemon drop but decided not to ruin the moment. There was a first time for everything, and I was already starting to feel myself relax. I would enjoy the night; Angel would handle the rest. He always did. There was nothing to worry about, and as I ran through all the reasons this night was perfect from Nova to Angel, there wasn't a worry keeping me from reaching for the next shot glass.

"To new friends," I told her and raised my glass.

She smiled. "Besties."

The lemon drop wasn't as bad as the tequila shot. I'd left my champagne on the table, so I ordered another, and Nova got a margarita before we started for the dance floor. It was thick with witches and warlocks dancing to jazz music. I held Nova's hand as we joined the crowd, holding our drinks aloft to keep from spilling. I drank half my champagne once we found a spot to dance so I wouldn't spill it.

The band moved into a new song and I couldn't help but let out a cheer when Nova did. The music still had all the markings of a good jazz song, but I recognized the lyrics the man sang from a pop song. It was my kind of mashup, a similar style to Wilted Rose Strings that made it easy to fall into the rhythm and dance. I felt my heart rate climb as we moved, swayed, and I let myself relax enough that I found myself dancing in ways I never did in public. Not even when I was out with Anne did I dare get this bold, but here I felt safe. Nova cheered me on, making me laugh and fully embrace this side of myself that felt so light and full.

The song ended only for another pop song to begin, the blend of jazz and slower pace blending together seamlessly to form a sensual song. Nova shook her glass, rattling the ice at the bottom before leaning close to tell me she was going to get another. I swayed to the sexy song as I watched her disappear into the crowd. No sooner had she left did a pair of hands slide along my hips.

A jolt went through me until I turned just enough to see Angel's smile over my shoulder. I continued my dance, rolling my hips against him and leaning against his chest. No one around us paid any attention. They were too busy dancing with their partners or just enough drinks into the night not to care. Angel must have noticed too because his hands only wandered more, sliding over the silk at my hips, fingers finding the slit along my leg and slipping beneath the fabric just far enough to send warmth flooding my core in anticipation.

He let out a low groan in my ear and kissed the spot just below. "I don't know how much longer I can resist you."

I had stopped swaying, forgetting where I was as his finger traced circles on the inside of my thigh. His hands were gone and when I turned to face him, he took my right hand and raised it to his lips. He kissed my knuckles and sent me a sly look that only made my stomach twist tighter with need. I practically skipped after him as he led me by the hand toward the double doors at the side of the room.

"This isn't the way to the apartment," I giggled as he led me down the hallway. He took the next right, leading us down an empty hall lit only by those dim scones along the wall. The only other door was a fire exit at the end of the hallway, not a well-traveled route in the slightest. I gasped when he twisted me so my back was against the wall and then I giggled when I saw that smile spread wider.

"At least let me finish my drink," I laughed.

That look returned, that sensual half-smile that always made my heart stop and speed up all the same. It made me feel small in the best way, like I really was a mouse cornered by a wolf. Angel took my glass from me and with the other hand, he pushed me flush against the wall by my chest. His hand slid up the length of my neck, cupping my face. His thumb went to my chin as he raised the glass to his lips and drank the last of the champagne. Only, he didn't swallow. Instead, he used his thumb to part my lips before he drew close. He pressed his lips to mine, spilling the champagne into my mouth. The coolness of it was such a contrast to the heat threatening to consume me from the inside out, only making me want him more.

A small amount of champagne dripped from the corner of my lips, sliding down my chin and neck and leaving a cool path between my breasts. Angel licked what was left of it at the corner of my lip before he sucked the final trace of the sweet liquid from my bottom lip. He followed that trail down my neck, cleaning the sticky mess with his tongue as he went.

I tipped my head back, arching against the wall and giving him full access to my breasts as he continued his kisses, dipping as far as the fabric at the front of my dress would allow. His hand returned to my cheek, again pressing his thumb to my chin so that I would meet his dark gaze. I'd only seen that look a few times before, the moments when he let down his guard, wasn't afraid of who he was. I could feel every nerve sing at that look, already so sensitive to the rough touches I knew would follow because they always did after that look.

God, I loved this side of him, this side that was so raw and honest. Mine.

"If I were to move my hand lower ..." His voice was soft as he gently dragged his hand down my neck, over my breast, and all the way to the slit in my dress again. I whimpered at his touch. "If I move my fingers just a little farther," he said and moved his fingers closer to that aching spot, making me gasp. "Would I find that you are dripping for me, Mouse?"

"Please," I begged, grabbing on to the front of his shirt and nearly pulling it free from his slacks.

Angel smiled. "So close for me already, Mouse?" He looked like he wanted to say more, but his smile faded, and I nearly groaned when he took a step back until I understood why.

There was a loud laugh at the end of the hall and a pair of men appeared a moment later, one pressed tight to the other's side before they noticed us. Both looked from me to Angel who was adjusting his shirt and blazer so that it laid flat. My face was burning from the embarrassment.

"There's enough hallway for four," one of the men said, eyeing Angel.

Angel let out a laugh and reached for my hand. "I appreciate the invitation, gentlemen, but I don't play well with others, and I most definitely don't share."

Oh.

I couldn't look at the men as Angel led me toward the end of the hallway. I heard the men whispering as soon as we rounded the corner. I held tight to Angel's hand, ignoring that hum of a laugh behind me as we walked back toward the hall where the jazz band played a ballad. I felt him tug on my hand as I reached for the double doors. When I turned to look at him, he pulled me closer. He handed me the empty champagne flute and then reached into his pocket. For a moment, I thought he might pull out my thong right there in the hallway, but he pulled out my phone instead.

"Keep it with you. Go have fun with Nova. I'll catch up with you," he said and placed my phone into my hand.

I was a little surprised. "Where are you going?"

"I won't be gone long. I want to feed. It will make it easier to keep on my best behavior around all these witches," he said and leaned in to kiss my cheek, an onery smirk spreading on his face when he pulled away. "And make it safer for you if you want me at my worst."

I playfully slapped his chest, barely able to contain my excitement at his eagerness. Finally, he was letting me in deeper, letting me have that primal side of him I loved so much. "I like when you misbehave."

Maybe Anne was right about him bringing out a more assertive side of me.

"Okay, Mouse," he said with a laugh. "But I don't like it when you *do*, so keep your phone with you just in case. I don't mean it to be—"

"I know," I said, cutting him off and holding up my phone for him to see. "Safety first."

"Always," he said and hesitated as though the words were for a goodbye. He stepped closer instead, kissing me in a way that lasted just long enough to make my heart flutter in my chest. He flashed a final smile my way before he started down the long hallway that I suspected emptied into the lobby. I waited until he disappeared around the corner to rejoin the party.

CHAPTER 13

Something fell onto my face, waking me. I was curled up on the end of a couch in someone's living room. My heart raced until I noticed Nova lying on her side at the other end. This was her apartment, which brought all my memories back. Nova was drunk by the time I found her in the hall. We stayed for one more drink before I could tell that all the margaritas she'd had throughout the night were finally catching up with her.

It wasn't hard to convince her to go back upstairs, and since Angel had the key to our apartment, I sat with her and listened to her talk about how much she didn't want to be the High Priestess until we had both fallen asleep.

I realized as I sat up that I was still wearing my black gown, except someone had laid a blanket over me. No, a coat.

Angel's blazer fell away from my chest and onto my lap. A glass of water sat on the coffee table near Nova along with a bottle of painkiller and a protein bar. Leaning against the hallway with his white shirt untucked was Angel. I set his blazer on the coffee table and began looking around me for my phone.

"It was just here," I said, finding it just behind me a moment later.

"It's okay, Mouse."

"It died. Shoot, I forgot that it died," I said, remembering that detail from the elevator on the way up to the apartment. I'd realized the battery died when we reached the elevator, but Nova was drunk enough that she accidentally knocked it from my hands, and I got distracted with making sure she was okay. "How did you find me?"

Angel smiled. "I'll always find you." He said it so simply, like it should've been obvious, and it reminded me of the ruby necklace I wore and what Poppy had said earlier that night. I held the pendant between my thumb and forefinger, trying to decide how to bring it up when Angel moved away from the wall and extended a hand for me. "Will she be all right here on her own?"

"Yeah. She's okay," I said and rose to my feet, not bothering to put on my heels again. Angel took them from me along with his blazer and we left her apartment for ours next door.

The clock on the oven said it was just past three in the morning, meaning I hadn't been asleep very long at all, and he hadn't been gone long either. Just like usual, there was no sign at all that he'd fed, no evidence to point to him, not even a single drop of blood on his shoes as he kicked them off by the door.

"Did you have fun with Nova?" he asked, following me into the bedroom. I stopped in front of the vanity mirror, only my reflection there despite feeling Angel's hands behind me working to unzip my dress.

"The girl time was nice," I said as he slid the straps from my shoulders and let the satin pool on the floor, leaving me completely naked in the mirror. "How was yours? I saw you making rounds in the hall. Did you talk to anyone who can help us?"

He groaned in my ear, patting my butt before giving it a tight squeeze. "What did I say about vampire business?" he teased.

My stomach twisted and I chewed on my lower lip at the memory from the elevator. "Well, I didn't get involved or anything."

He laughed again and nuzzled my cheek, scooping me into his

arms and, a moment later, plopping me onto the bed. I watched as he undid the buttons on his shirt.

"I mostly watched and got familiar with the other witches and warlocks who live in the building. I figured out who our neighbors are and who's on the council. I thought it best to know who might be around just in case," he said as he shrugged out of his shirt and moved to the button of his pants.

He thought it was best to know who might be around for safety. That's why.

He removed his pants and slid into bed next to me in just his boxers, pulling the comforter over us both before pulling me to his side. I moved my hand to his waistband, where he captured it and raised it to his lips, kissing it before replacing it on his bare chest.

"You should rest. You're tired," he said with a laugh.

I almost argued as I thought about the elevator and that hallway, but I couldn't deny how sore my legs felt from all the dancing and how comfortable I was resting my head on his chest now. The way he traced soothing patterns at the small of my back only made it easier to relax against him.

It was light when I woke up. I was still lying against Angel's chest and he smiled when I raised my head to look at him.

"It can't be comfortable to lie like that all night," I told him, sitting up and reaching for the closest article of clothing. Angel's shirt hung loose on my shoulders, long enough that it covered my butt as I pulled it around myself like a robe and went to the bathroom to wash my face. He was still lying in the bed when I returned, motioning for me to join him.

He pulled me close, guiding my left leg across his lap so I was straddling him. He smiled and sat up until those dark eyes were even with mine. He kissed me softly, hands wandering past his dress shirt to cup my breasts. In a single move, he pushed the sleeves down to my elbows, baring me again. My body warmed beneath his gaze, and I tried pressing my thighs together, but they were held apart by his.

"You are beautiful, Mouse," he said, resting his arms on my thighs and clasping his hands at my lower back.

"So are you." I placed my hands on his chest, feeling the curve of him as I slid them over his collarbone and draped my arms over his shoulders. I leaned in to kiss him again, feeling the ruby brush against my chest. I remembered what Poppy had said last night, and my hand went to the ruby pendant in response.

"What's wrong?" Angel sat back against the headboard as I turned the pendant between my index and thumb.

"This necklace," I started, looking down at the ruby as it sparkled in the sunlight that peeked through the curtains. "It's not a ruby, is it?"

When I looked up, I could tell from the way the corners of his lips twitched that I was right. Poppy was right. I wasn't sure how I felt about it. I didn't think he meant it in a bad way. But still, it bothered me that he hadn't told me the truth about what the necklace was from the moment he clasped it around my neck.

"What did Nova tell you?"

"It was Poppy," I corrected, my stomach twisting nervously when he exhaled. "She said you scented me."

Angel nodded slowly, sitting up again. "I did."

"Okay. So, um, what does that mean exactly? It sounds like something ..." I was going to say that it sounded like something an animal would do. I didn't want to make him feel bad. He already felt like a monster. He didn't need to feel like an animal, too.

"It's exactly what you think. Maybe I shouldn't have—" He let out a deep sigh, his hand instinctively going to the crown of his head where he used to tie his hair before he cut it. He lowered his hands between us, looking at them as he spoke. "Vampire blood is different, and it leaves a trace on whatever it touches, a scent that only certain supernatural beings can pick up on. Witches can feel it, like a magical sensation. That's why Poppy knew what it was."

"The ruby is actually your blood?" I asked and twisted it between my fingers again.

"You should've heard it from me," Angel said and finally looked up at me with such intensity that it made me drop the pendant. He brushed my hair behind my ear, fingers lingering along my jaw. "It was primal of me. I wanted to protect you. I can rip apart anyone who tries to harm you, but marking you as mine …"

Oh. This was the part of him I ached to see more. He acted like it was all vampire, but the sounds he made when he let things get rough told me he loved it just as much as I did. I liked this primal side, how protective he got of me, and how he talked about my music like I was on my way to the top of the charts. I even loved when I was on the receiving end of that harsh edge of him because it made me better, less anxious, grounded in what was real and less in the what-ifs that so often sent me spiraling.

"So, leave your mark," I said, feeling my heart pick up pace when I saw the way his eyes lit up. He licked his lips and shook his head in disbelief.

"You do wear it well," he laughed and gave my ass a light slap before lifting me off him. "Get dressed. Wear comfortable shoes. There's somewhere I want to take you."

"Where?" I asked as I went to my suitcase still packed in the corner of the room.

He shook his head and flashed an onery look my way. "You'll see."

***

I felt groggy as we walked the steamy New Orleans streets, but not for too long. Angel led me to a little shop with a green and white awning. I could smell the coffee and hot pastries from Café du Monde.

"It's a New Orleans staple," Angel said as he led me inside.

"Coffee and beignets sound perfect."

We placed an order, and I immediately sipped from the Styrofoam coffee cup, thankful for the caffeine. Angel held a container of beignets just moments later. It was busy enough inside the small shop that we moved back outside to sit under the awning with the rest of the tourists. After a late night of drinking, the fried pastry was the perfect breakfast. They were so good, and I devoured two before I thought about how to keep the powdered sugar from getting all over my dark blouse.

"Here," Angel said with a laugh and handed me a napkin. I used it to wipe off my hands, but promptly sent a cascade of powder over my lap when I lifted the next beignet. Angel smirked and shook his head.

"Don't laugh," I told him through a mouthful of pastry. "You're the one who chose such a messy breakfast date."

"Maybe you're the messy one in this equation."

"Funny," I said and blew the remaining powder on my fingers at him. He waved away the cloud before reaching across the small table to brush away some powdered sugar that clung to the corner of my mouth. "So, what is the plan for today?" I asked.

Angel lowered his arm to the table. "I thought you might like more time with Nova. You said that your vision made you think you two will be best friends. You might as well get to know her," he said and nudged my phone closer to me from where it sat on the table.

I wasn't against a little more girl time. I'd had a fun night with Nova, and maybe we could talk more about my music and her art. We'd already brainstormed and had a few ideas that I would have loved to talk about more.

"I'll text her," I said and cleaned my hands on my napkin before I picked up my phone. I was almost finished with the message when he spoke again.

"I do have one favor."

My thumb hovered over the send button as I looked up. "Okay. What's that?"

He let out a sigh like he was still debating if he wanted to ask or not. "See where she stands on helping us. I need to talk person-ally with Bebe to see if she remembers enough. In the end, it doesn't have to be her, just someone who can do the spell. But I need Bebe to remember what spell that is."

I nodded slowly for a moment before I hit send on the text message and sat my phone down. "We'll figure this out," I told him and placed my hand on top of his. "There's a cure. We'll figure out how to use it."

He smiled a little, both of his hands sliding into mine on the table.

"This is what I love most about you. You see nothing but potential in even the darkest of things, life's most challenging moments. You're a little bit of light and it's what brought me out of the shadows."

"A little bit of light is all you need," I told him and let go of his hand to take the final beignet from the plate. "You don't need to see the entire path to know it's a way forward."

I popped the last bite into my mouth and before I could brush the sugar from my fingers, he'd grabbed my wrist. His expression had me frozen, the sadness behind his eyes not matching the smile.

"I have more reason now than ever to be mortal," he said and pulled my fingers to his lips. He sucked on the end of my index finger and then my thumb, licking the last of the powder from my skin. "Almost as sweet as you are, Mouse."

I felt my cheeks heat as he lowered my hand back to the table just as my phone buzzed. In a single message, Nova said she was dressed and ready to meet.

"Ready for company?" I asked and showed him the message.

He stood from the table, taking our trash to the nearest bin while I slipped my purse over my shoulder.

"Our new friend is waiting," he said and took my hand. I felt light, warmth spreading in my chest and not just from his touch. *Our new friend.* He was right. Nova and I would be the best of friends and I didn't need the vision to tell me. I just knew.

CHAPTER 14

Nova met us down the street from Café du Monde. She wore a cute tennis skirt and a band T-shirt. She paired the entire look with a pair of biker boots with bright pink laces. She wore her curls loose around her face, smiling when she joined us.

"I promise I'm better than any of those tour guides you'd pay for," she said and pulled out her phone. I could see as she looked down at it that she'd already created a list. "You're getting the *real* New Orleans today."

"You two have fun," Angel said, pulling me to his side so he could kiss my temple.

"Wait? You aren't coming?" Nova asked, finally looking up from her phone.

"He thought I might like some girl time," I said, noticing the way she glanced back down at her list. It made me wonder just how far ahead she'd planned the day. "If that's okay with you?"

"Oh. It's fine. I just assumed," she said with a shrug. "I'm totally down for girl time. I thought we'd need a table for three, but I can call ahead and get one for just us."

"Where?" I asked, holding on to Angel's hand before he could pull away from my side.

"There's a place not too far that I love going to for brunch. I'm feeling mimosas," Nova said.

Angel chuckled. "I'd think after last night you'd rather have a strong cup of coffee."

"They have that too," she smiled and tucked her phone into her pocket. "Sure you can't join?"

"Another time," Angel said and stepped away from my side, giving my hand a squeeze before he let go. "How's your phone?"

"Fully charged and I'll keep you updated," I told him, surprised at the butterflies that filled my chest. There was something so reassuring about how seriously he took my safety considering everything we'd been through. It was like having a guard dog.

Angel nodded and sent me a final smile before he promised to join us once he was done with whatever he planned to do to buy Nova and me some alone time. I watched him walk for just a moment before I looked back at Nova. Her eyes were locked on Angel's back and a frown spread across her face.

"Everything all right?" I asked.

Nova let out a deep sigh and turned her attention to me. "Do you forget your phone a lot or ..."

"No. I'm not forgetful or anything," I said. Then it hit me what she meant and why she was glancing down the street where Angel had gone. My skin cooled as I thought about the last few months, being locked in the wine cellar with Angel, the way I'd barely sleep in that bedroom ... I focused on Nova instead, studying the smaller details about her as I tried chasing away those memories. "He's not controlling like that. At least, not in any way we haven't both agreed to."

Her eyebrows rose, and a coy smile spread on her face. "Oh."

"I just mean that safety is kind of a touchy subject for us. We went through something recently that really rocked us and I haven't always felt safe. God, I don't always help that either with some of the things I've done." The words came tumbling out, and my face warmed more and more as the blush on her cheeks grew. "Why are you looking at me like that?"

"Sorry," she laughed. "I thought it was a Christian Grey kind of thing."

The embarrassment hit hard, making me regret everything I'd said all of that before. I should've just brushed her off. But then she'd think Angel was some controlling boyfriend. Still, the answer was simple. All I had to say was that he just wanted to keep me safe.

"Well, it's not." What was it anyway? "I mean, it is kind of a rule. After everything, it makes him nervous if he can't find me easily. Sure, he's a vampire and could track me down, but it's still easier to open his phone. It's a direct line to me if he needs it. It goes both ways. I use it to keep track of him too."

"I didn't mean to judge. I just wanted to make sure he wasn't being toxic," Nova said, her tone even and reassuring despite the deep blush on her cheeks. "Still, if it's a rule ... Christian Grey wouldn't tolerate rule-breaking."

She laughed again when I groaned, hiding my embarrassment behind my hands for a moment before I remembered we were walking on the sidewalk. She wasn't wrong though, and that only made my insides squirm more for a variety of reasons. It had become a rule to keep our phones with us at all times, not to do anything risky without the other being involved, and I knew broken rules came with consequences, consequences that made my heart race and my skin ache for his touch.

"God! Christian Grey. Batman. He's got a strange list of nicknames."

"Batman?"

I relaxed a little. "My roommate calls him Batman."

"Ah," Nova said and moved close so we could walk around an older couple on the sidewalk. "That makes sense. What do you call him?"

"Angel," I answered. "What else am I supposed to call him?"

Her face turned red again and I realized what she meant. She burst into laughter when I reached out and shoved her shoulder playfully.

"I think he's great, and you two together seem natural," she said, pulling out her phone and checking the GPS before steering us down a new street.

"It feels natural," I told her as a heaviness settled in my chest. "That's why it was so important for us to come here."

Silence landed between us for a moment. There were less people along this street, but I could see a crowd of people going through the doors of a restaurant ahead.

"The cure," Nova said with a sigh.

"I don't want it to make things weird between us, because I really do think we can be friends—"

"Lily, you've already seen that we are," she snorted. "I've been thinking about it a lot, actually."

"Really?"

"Yeah. Really." She paused for a moment as a jogger ran past us. We slowed our pace as we approached the restaurant, finally stopping on the corner across the street. "I don't want my Bebe to respond badly to Angel and accidentally hurt him or you. I've thought about us all meeting somewhere public, but I don't want to risk her using her magic in front of non-magical people either. Maybe we can figure something out over brunch."

It felt like all of my muscles relaxed at once. It was almost overwhelming to hear her say that, knowing that there wasn't just hope but a chance at action, too.

"Thank you. Yes. Let's talk," I said. Nova smiled and then we started for the doors of the restaurant.

I had one more mimosa than I'd planned to, but only because Nova and I couldn't stop talking. In the end, we decided that it would be best to talk with her grandmother somewhere that would be comfortable but also help remind her of Angel and how they met. The apartments had another courtyard behind the building with a pool and tables with umbrellas similar to the one Bebe was sitting at in the photo Angel took. Bebe liked coffee after lunch, and Nova or one of her friends would join her most days.

Comfortable and familiar. Hopefully, familiar enough to trigger a memory.

After it was all planned out, we moved on to the rest of our New Orleans tour. Nova and I went to a jazz museum and we visited an art museum before we decided to stop for an early dinner after I'd told her I'd never had a Sazerac, much less knew what it was. We waited a long time for a table but it was worth it. The Sazerac, which I learned was a cocktail, was good enough that I had two before we finished our meals and walked the French Quarter some more to check out the street musicians.

There were lots of jazz musicians, a few playing pop songs with a bit of swing to them. We'd been at dinner long enough that it was dark out and a decent crowd was gathering along the street to bar-hop before the nightclubs were in full swing. It was busy enough that I shouldn't have felt anxious, but I did. I slowed our pace, glancing around at the laughing faces in the crowd and the groups of people on their way to their next stop. I nearly walked into a woman in a bikini top carrying a tray of Jell-O shots, declining when she offered me one and invited me into the bar she worked at for a drink.

"You okay?" Nova asked, pausing in the street so I could catch up with her.

I opened my mouth to tell her I was, but that feeling I had … I recognized it now. That strange tingle that started at the base of my neck and slowly moved to the back of my head, that unnerving feeling before I had a vision, or before something happened anyway.

"Lily?"

I quickened my pace to close the distance between us. "We're being followed."

"How do you know?" she asked, keeping her voice low.

I didn't know how to answer that, but I didn't get a chance to before the vision clouded my eyesight, transporting me into an alley. A hooded figure shoved Nova against a wall, holding her several feet off the ground. She drew a knife from her hip, but fumbled enough that the figure was able to snatch it with lightning speed and had it lodged in her stomach a second later. He let go of her, and Nova fell to the ground. The figure turned to face me. It raised a hand that had only three fingers: the thumb, index, and middle fingers.

"Where's your mate?" she asked.

"Lily!" Nova snapped. I was back in the streets, Nova standing directly in front of me and looking horrified. "What did you see?"

Her eyes shifted from me to something behind me and her mouth parted. She grabbed my wrist and began shoving me forward. No one around us seemed at all concerned that we were practically jogging through the street.

"This way," she said, pulling me around a corner only for dread to settle in my bones and panic shoot through my veins.

"No!" I shouted, but it was too late. I could sense the figure behind us and we had no choice but to run for the end of the alleyway. I kept right behind Nova, hoping that the figure couldn't attack if I kept close. Instead, it appeared a second later directly in front of us and Nova slammed into its chest. I bounced off Nova's back and onto the ground.

As the figure grabbed Nova's shirt, I lunged for Nova's hip and felt a rush of relief as my hand met the handle of that knife. I pulled it free as the figure raised Nova from the ground and smashed her against the wall.

"Run!" Nova yelled, her voice cut off with a choke.

I didn't. I lunged instead, plunging the knife into the woman's back. She let out a shriek of pain and dropped Nova. She staggered backward, fighting to pull the knife free from where it was stuck in the middle of her back. Nova let out a yell and pointed both of her palms toward the woman, sending her flying into the opposite alley wall with a bang that shook the building.

The woman slumped to the ground, her hood falling away

from her face to reveal dark hair, a face so beautiful that it would make most women jealous, and a pair of scarlet eyes. She lifted her three-fingered hand to replace the hood as she stood in just seconds. She sprinted for the opposite end of the alley, making it halfway before wings sprouted from her back that nearly brushed both alley walls as she rose into the air.

"Get Angel here," Nova said as she turned to face me. "Now!"

I'd already dialed his number. He answered on the first ring.

CHAPTER 15

Angel swooped into the alley just minutes after I'd called him. His wings remained as he approached us.

"I stabbed her," I said, not realizing I was shaking until he grasped my hands and I felt the vibrations up my arms.

"Are you okay? Are you hurt?" he asked, looking over me before drawing closer to take my face between his hands.

"No. I'm fine. I stabbed her!" I said again, glad when he pulled me to his chest. His wings obscured us from view, only starting to retract after he exhaled into my neck.

"Shit," he said under his breath. He was back to his human form now, and he glanced at Nova, who leaned against the wall, still recovering. "Are you okay?"

"Yeah. Fine," she breathed, straightening up a second later and moving closer to join us. "How did you know I had a knife?"

I was still in shock about what happened, so it took me a moment to think. "I had a vision of the attack. It happened pretty much exactly the same way, except—"

I was glad I didn't have to finish for them to understand. Nova's eyes widened and she glanced down the alley where the woman had vanished. Angel pulled my attention back to him, brushing my hair from my face.

"Who was it?"

"A vampire," Nova said. "She had wings like yours."

"Like mine?"

"Three fingers," I started, taking a deep breath and closing my eyes to keep everything from overwhelming me. I didn't want to remember, but my vision had led me to saving Nova and getting more details about the woman. "She had dark hair, long. She was beautiful. Her eyes were red like yours get when you haven't fed. She only had three fingers on her right hand." I held my right hand up and showed him my thumb, pointer, and middle fingers.

His expression was more shocked than I anticipated. I figured he'd would be surprised that a vampire old enough to have wings had found us. That was rare from what he'd told me, but the look he wore now said that wasn't the worst of the details.

"Why did she attack? Did she say anything?" he asked, looking at Nova when she shook her head.

"She did in my vision," I told him, my stomach twisting to the point of nausea. "She asked me where my mate was. She was asking where you were."

Angel raised his hands to his head and groaned, glancing down the alleyway before moving closer to me again.

"You know her, don't you?" Nova asked.

"Come on," he said, taking my hand and motioning for Nova to follow him.

"What do you know?" she asked, jogging to catch up with us.

Angel didn't answer, leading us back into the crowded street. He reached back to grab Nova's hand too, holding tight to us both as he led the way down the street. I realized as we went that he was keeping to the busy routes as we made our way back to the apartment building. He kept his eyes moving when we reached the empty street Night Owl Apartments sat on, making sure we weren't being followed as we passed the iron gate and went to the door.

"Who is she?" I asked once he'd shut the front door behind us and I heard the lock click in place. He shook his head in disbelief.

"Magdalena," Angel said with a sigh. "It's a long story."

My stomach plummeted. I exchanged nervous glances with Nova before she led us back into the large study to the left of the entryway. My hands were still shaking, and I felt worse now as every possibility ran through my head. Was Magdalena a former lover? How did he know her?

"Okay ..." Nova said slowly, locking the door before she joined us around the coffee table. Angel sat on the couch opposite from me, still in shock. He would suck in a deep breath and then blow it out, adjusting in his seat until I couldn't stand the anticipation.

"Tell me," I said.

He looked up at me, compassion overtaking his shock. He shook his head and scooted to the front of the couch. "She's not anyone I knew in that way. It's the opposite, actually."

"What does that mean?" Nova asked, sinking onto the couch next to me.

Angel adjusted again as though preparing for a long story.

"I've told you about my life before I was turned," he said, keeping his eyes on me. "I need to tell you about how I became a vampire and the family that is responsible."

The air was heavy between us. For so long, he swore never to tell me how a vampire was created. He'd told me very little about those early days aside from how he'd nearly withered away in a tomb, determined to never feed on a human being.

I nodded, not able to reply for a moment. "Okay. Tell me."

"I came from a noble family. My parents were swept up in the panic of the Spanish Inquisition and were killed. I was sent to live with my grandfather. He took on their wealth along with his own. When he died, I had been working as an apprentice at a bakery in a small town and I inherited his wealth and estate. I wasn't sure what to do with the money, so I let it sit and went about my life, learning a trade. I stayed on at the bakery," he said.

"I don't think I'd know what to do either after all of that," I said.

Angel smiled, but that smile didn't last for long. A pit formed in my stomach.

"I saw a woman on my walk to the bakery one morning. She was clean. She had long brown hair and scared eyes that told me she didn't belong there. She looked terrified, but spoke up without a tremor in her voice. She asked for money. I told her to come with me and I took her to the back entrance of the bakery. I came back out with all the old bread and pastries I could carry. I could tell she was disappointed, but she thanked me and took the food. I watched her distribute it to the beggars along the street until it was all gone," Angel said with a laugh of disbelief. "The next day, she was there again. She looked the same, though I could tell that the clothes she wore beneath her cloak were different. She tried to hide them, but I just knew she wasn't really a beggar. I smiled at her and she smiled back. She didn't ask me for anything this time, but after I passed, I heard her offer herself to a man behind me. He accepted. I turned around and chased him off, telling her I would pay thrice what she normally accepted."

"She was a prostitute?" Nova asked.

Angel shook his head. He almost looked offended. "No. Not at all. It was the first time she'd tried selling her body. She tried providing her services, but I told her I didn't want them. She told me she was a virgin, and the truth came out. Her family was wealthy and influential. Her father and her brother were abusive to her. They planned on giving her to a more influential family to create an alliance—a much older man with no relatives to inherit his wealth. She had been begging on the streets of my town to save enough money to run away. I didn't have much with me, but I gave her the money I had. I told her to come back tomorrow and not to ever try to sell herself that way again."

Angel cleared his throat and continued.

"She came back every day, and every day I gave her money until she asked me where it all came from. I told her about my family and more about myself. We became good friends. One day, she wasn't in the streets, and I got worried. I knew where she lived, so I went to look for her and I found her at her home alone. She had been beaten. She wanted me to leave, saying her father found all of the money and taken it, and that she was going to be taken to her fiancé's home later that week. I stayed with her. I wanted them to find me there. I didn't want to leave her alone with them anymore. When her father and brother got home, they accused her of sleeping with me and I told them they were monsters for hitting a pregnant woman."

"Pregnant?" Nova gasped.

"She wasn't, though, right?" I asked, feeling my stomach plummet further as I remembered how the story ended. Angel shook his head, which eased my nerves a fraction.

"She wasn't pregnant. We had never been together. We were nothing more than friends, but that was all it took to shatter their plans for her. Her father was livid. He beat me. They wanted to know how I thought I could dare touch a noble woman like Maria, so I told them the truth. Few knew of me, but many knew my grandfather, and they all knew he'd inherited my parents' money to add to his fortune. Her father was still angry, but it was impossible not to see that part of him was happy with the turn of events. Honestly, the only difference between the old man she was betrothed to and me was our ages. I had many years of potential left to bring her family more notoriety and fortune. That, or as the sole heir, I could be killed, and my family's fortune would go to them."

Nova let out a hum of understanding. "You married her."

"I did," he said, speaking the words toward the ground before looking up at me. I wasn't sure what I felt. He'd told me that he'd never felt as deeply about anyone as he did me. I believed him. I still did, but he had lived hundreds of lives before me. Of course there had been others, regardless of how he felt about me. He'd told me I wasn't his first. I knew that and it didn't bother me, except that he'd married Maria so easily. He tied his life to hers, but told me he wouldn't let me tie mine to his as long as he was immortal.

"We were wed, but still never anything more than friends. We were never intimate past our kiss at the altar. Maria told her father she must've been mistaken about being pregnant. We lived simply. I continued working at the bakery, saving away my family's fortune in case we needed it. Her family accepted me. More than just that, her father was quick to tell the town of me, and her brother was enamored with my wealth even more than his own. Together, our union made our families more desirable, which is how Maria's brother Alonzo met his wife, Magdalena. It wasn't but maybe a year later before things with the family changed. They made fewer appearances. One day, Maria went to visit them and she was frightened when she returned. She thought something terrible had happened to them because they were all more ruthless than before. People around the city had started to go missing, and she knew them well enough to fear that her family was behind it. She said the three of them even *looked* different and she was afraid that maybe something demonic had taken root in her family home."

He didn't need to say it for us to know. Even Nova's frown deepened, and she sat back with a nod.

"How were they turned?" I asked.

"I went to the home to see it for myself. Once I saw what they were, I planned to go to the church to tell the priest, but Alonzo got to me first. I tried to kill him. He hadn't been a vampire for long, so he wasn't yet skilled, just strong. I lost the fight. He'd intended to kill me, so he was angry when I turned, but he knew it meant I wouldn't tell anyone what they were. I tried to end my life that same night. When you first turn, the hunger is excruciating. I resisted, even when they offered me one of their maids. When it was clear that I would not tolerate my existence, they agreed to help me end it."

I'd heard this part of the story before, but I knew more about vampires now than I did then. If they had wanted to kill him, they would've put a stake through his heart or burned him. They didn't, though.

"They didn't want you dead," I said in nearly a whisper.

"The vampire who had turned Francisco taught him everything he knew about vampires. Francisco turned Alonzo who then turned Magdalena. The three of them killed the other vampire, burned his remains. They knew how to kill a vampire. Instead, Alonzo told me I could desecrate until I turned to ash. I believed him. I allowed him to lock me in the family mausoleum. I planned on dying there and it felt like I was in the days that followed. I was a skeleton of my former self when that stone door opened again. One of them had given Maria the key when she came looking for me. They probably told her I had died and was laid to rest there." He paused, his breath shaking. "I was so out of my mind with hunger that I drained her of life in seconds. She was gone before I knew what had happened," he said, voice cracking and dark eyes glazed.

"It wasn't your fault," I told him, half-extending my hand to him before realizing he was just out of reach. He noticed the effort, though, and sent me a small smile.

"That's when I realized what the plan had been all along. They had money, but it was nowhere near what I had left untouched from my grandfather and parents. I had no living family except for them and they knew that. They knew that I wanted to die for being a vampire. Killing Maria, making me kill her ... it was just a twisted way of getting rid of her and gaining my wealth."

"All of that for money when you have eternity?" Nova gasped. "Why?"

"If they wanted to get back at you, why didn't Magdalena kill me? She didn't even attack me. In my vision, all she did was ask me where you were. She called you my mate. She knows we are together," I said, ignoring the way Angel flinched when I mentioned my own death.

"I took something that belonged to them," Angel said. "They want to take everything from me."

Silence hung in the air for a moment. I wished we weren't separated by that coffee table as I saw him look down, hiding the single tear that fell from his face and onto the floor before he looked back up at me with that stoic expression I was so used to.

"I'm with Lily. I still don't understand," Nova said slowly as though still thinking through the details. "From the way you've described it, you're nomadic. You don't have many possessions or even a home. If they wanted to take everything from you, wouldn't Lily be everything?"

Angel let out a deep breath, and a smile pulled at the corners of his lips. "After I killed Maria in the mausoleum, I'm sure the plan was to kill me in response. I knew they'd sent her. There was no other way for her to have found me there. She was my best friend and not the kind of person to give up. She would make the best of shitty circumstances and if she couldn't have what she deserved then she would provide it for others, which is what she did for many of the people in need in our town. She taught me that fighting fire with fire only left behind a pile of ash." Angel laughed and shook his head. "So, I left behind a note for her family. I told them they could endure eternity knowing that I had escaped them as the better man, my fortune earned through the honest work of my family rather than through the bloody history of theirs, and that while their reputation was already tarnished due to the whispers in town about their missing workers and their dismissal of those poorer than them, my name and Maria's name would always be gold."

"And the money?" Nova asked.

Angel smiled. "I left it at my grandfather's estate. I never quite knew what to do with it, so I kept it hidden there and only took what I needed or chose to give away. It's still there as far as I know."

I was frozen in place, suspended between shock and panic. Magdalena really wasn't after just me, maybe not even after Angel. They wanted the money, they wanted everything Angel had. This grudge had lasted for centuries.

"Eternity is a long time, even longer if instead of allowing time to heal old wounds, you allow them to fester," Angel said. The room was quiet. I could tell that Nova was still digesting the information. She looked invested, ready to ask more questions even.

"That's enough for tonight," I said, standing up. I paused for a moment, wanting to say something, but no words felt like enough. I was angry, or hurt, I wasn't yet sure. I just knew that I didn't want to sit in this room anymore. So, I turned and went back to the lobby instead and straight for the elevator, the silver doors sliding closed just as Angel appeared on the other side.

CHAPTER 16

It wasn't until I was standing outside of our apartment that I remembered that we only had one key, a key that was in Angel's possession. I tried twisting the doorknob several times, shaking the door in the frame, panic rising in my chest and choking my efforts to take deep breaths.

He gently brushed my hands aside and unlocked the door, letting me rush inside ahead of him. The tears threatened to rain down my face, but I kept them at bay, held on to the anger that I still didn't understand. I allowed it to build, letting all of my frustrations bubble to the surface. I was tired of being so scared all the time, panicking at the normal things in life like being successful or putting myself out in the world. I was mad at myself. Why was I like this? Why did facing Magdalena in the alley feel easy in comparison to revealing my true identity on YouTube or accepting that I didn't want the easy success that my upbringing offered me? Why had my heart raced faster when I told my parents about my YouTube channel than when I stabbed Magdalena in that alley? Why couldn't I just have this, Angel, the two of us however we were, for as long as time would allow?

"My marriage to Maria was not loveless, but it wasn't

romantic either," Angel said as he closed the door behind us. I kept my back to him, folding my hands on top of my head and then placing them on my hips before folding them across my chest. "She didn't deserve the treatment she got or would get. She was kind and we were friends. I married her just to give her what she deserved from life."

I let out a deep breath, still deciding if I wanted to say the words before I turned around and they came flying out of my mouth anyway.

"So, you tied your life to her and didn't love her. You love me, and you say you can't tie yourself to me because I deserve better."

"No," Angel said and stepped toward me, stopping when I held a hand up. "I love you. I can't ask you to—"

"That's the thing, though. I am so tired of being afraid of going after what I want, worrying about the things I shouldn't be afraid of, like what people might think about me, or looking stupid, abandoning my future with a prestigious orchestra so I can make stupid songs on YouTube."

"It's not stupid and you definitely don't look stupid, Mouse," he said. His voice was gentle, but I could sense a subtle edge to it. It made my heart skip, but I ignored that anxious voice in my head telling me to back off. It wanted me to soften my tone, telling me that this wasn't that big of a deal, that he'd already told me he loved me more than anyone before despite what had happened in his past. But, I was getting bitter from my lack of action and if I didn't say what I thought and express what I wanted I was afraid I would never have a shot at achieving it all.

"I'm mad at myself all the time for not speaking up. I don't want to sit behind a music stand in my black dress with the New York Phil. I don't want to play the classics or even instrumental music. I want to create something new, something all mine. I don't know what the hell I'm doing, but I know what it looks like in my head and I know that you're always there by my side. And maybe I'm a little mad at you too for ..." I couldn't finish. I wasn't even sure where I was going with the phrase, how to express the pit in my stomach when I thought about my future with him.

"You can tell me, Mouse," Angel said, more insistent than before.

"I have," I said. It was like the dam finally broke, my entire body relaxing as the truth came out. "You say you've never loved anyone the way you love me, but you don't want me to spend my entire life with you if it means you're immortal. You told me you'd leave me if we can't find a cure because you think it's what I deserve. Somehow, though, married Maria on a whim because she deserved better than her abusive family."

"Things were different back then. I was still young, and I didn't know what I wanted from my own life yet."

"You're constantly torturing yourself because you think you're damned for being a vampire, but it doesn't seem like you cared about yourself then, either."

He scoffed, uncrossing his arms and letting them hang by his side. "I was doing what I enjoyed by working in that bakery. I didn't care about the money or my family's good name. I wanted to make something of myself by myself, and I did. Marrying Maria was me just going along with the times. I had no interest in anyone in my town, and I wasn't about to uproot my life and start over during a time when communities were tight-knit. So, I married a woman I considered a friend."

"Okay. Fine," I said, shaking my head. "That doesn't change the fact that you're so concerned about me that you make yourself miserable for simply existing."

His jaw tightened and I saw his shoulders rise as he inhaled. He looked at the floor as he let out a groan before raising those deep eyes to mine, his expression firm the way I remembered after he'd flown me onto my apartment balcony and then chided me for leaving the sliding door unlocked.

"I'm mad at you too, Lily," Angel said, pushing his sleeves roughly to his elbows. "I want nothing more than to protect you, emotionally and physically. I would tear this world apart to keep you out of harm's way, but the way that you put yourself there anyway ... You know exactly what you want and you know that. Hell, you just told me the whole plan, yet you self-destruct when things go well. You know you do. That's why you're stuck, and you know it. You make a change and things go well, because you're so damn talented, and then you run away rather than ask for help. Not only that, but you make bad choices along the way, like not taking care of yourself, skipping meals to work, not sleeping, working harder than you should—"

"I'm not working at all right now, not that it even matters—"

"Stop!"

The room echoed with the silence, his tone so sharp that I barely remembered what I was saying. He was angry, his entire body tight. He pushed his right sleeve up to his elbow from where it had fallen to his wrist, his fingers rough with the fabric. He took a sobering breath before looking up at me again, his expression almost apologetic.

"Lily," he started, letting out another groan as though he was struggling to find the right words. My chest ached.

"Say it," I whispered.

He froze, looking at me with surprise before he scoffed and looked down at the floor. When he looked up again, his eyes didn't meet mine. He shook his head in disbelief before he spoke again. "You say you like the vampire side of me. You like it when I'm rough; when I'm dominant."

"I love it because it's real. It's you," I told him, closing the distance between us. I was still mad, but not nearly enough to push him away. The opposite, actually. I wanted to have him closer physically and emotionally.

Angel nodded, his shoulders relaxing when I rested my hands against his chest. He still looked mad as his forehead met mine, his jaw tight despite the gentle way he cupped my face with one hand and wrapped the other around my lower back.

"I want to punish you," he said so firmly that it sent a jolt through my body. "I want to fuck you so that you'll feel it in the morning and remember how you promised to take care of yourself and keep yourself safe. I want to leave reminders on your skin when you self-sabotage. I want to put you across my knee, kiss away your tears when I'm done, and hold you in my arms because you are mine."

"And you think I need to be punished?" I asked. It felt like a wave was rising in my chest, higher and higher and I was just waiting for the break.

"I think you want to be," he said, sending that wave crashing and a tear of relief rolling down my cheek. "I think you want the release, someone to hold you accountable when you're doing yourself a disservice, someone safe you can let go with, be that person you know you are inside until you feel confident enough to share it with the world."

"Yes," I said, breathless, standing perfectly still in his arms.

"You want rules, Mouse?" he asked. All I could do was nod. I tried to kiss him, but he kept just out of reach, pulling my lower lip free from between my teeth. God, I was melting, full-on pouting as he looked intently back at me, determined to make a point that I was sure would only make me squirm more than I already was.

"Please," I said and not just because I wanted him to touch me. I did want his rules. It was comforting knowing what to expect with him, knowing he was nothing but supportive and also quick to shut down all the destructive things I did when I got caught up in my emotions. He was my safe place to let go, someone I trusted enough to hand all control.

"You sure you want this?" Angel asked, his hands already stroking my skin through my clothes, tracing the top of my shorts until they found the clasp between us. "I take care of what's mine. I can give rewards and punishments. God, Mouse. The way I want to punish you for the hold you have on me, for making it impossible for me to walk away when I should. I can't. Not anymore. Cure or no cure, you are mine."

"Yes," I said and tugged on the front of his shirt, "And you are mine."

He lifted me by my ass so I could wrap my legs around him. He kissed me with more intensity than he ever had, claiming my lips. Once he sat me on the counter of the kitchen, I pulled his shirt up his abdomen. He broke our kiss just long enough for me to pull the fabric over his head. Instead of finding my way back to his lips, I kissed the hollow of his throat instead, tugging on his short hair so he would expose more of his neck to me.

I left a trail of kisses down his neck as he unbuttoned my shorts. When I reached his left shoulder, I sucked on his skin, leave my own mark there. He let out a hum of satisfaction and then a groan when I bit his shoulder, the sound of him sending a flood of heat to my core. I gasped when he gripped the front of my shirt, ripping the fabric in a single tug so that only the sleeves remained on my arms. He slipped a finger under the band of my bra, tugging it down and then releasing so the cups pressed my breasts up and exposed most of them to him. He pulled back just far enough to look at them, tracing the curve of them lightly with his fingers before he looked up at me again.

"Mine," he said and stepped closer. I lifted my hands, barely touching his chest when he gripped them both in his right hand.

"I want to touch you," I said, aching to get back to rough touches. I wanted to feel his tight muscles against my skin. Part of me wanted to bite him again to see what else he might do. I felt a smile tug at my lips as I admired my work from moments before.

"Eyes on me, Mouse," Angel said and placed my hands by my sides, the dark granite beneath me cool to the touch. "Let's see how good a listener you are."

I arched my back, just enough to lift my breasts free from my bra, catching his attention. I couldn't contain my smile, and it only spread when his did. Those dark eyes met mine and told me that he knew exactly what I was doing.

"Good listeners get rewards," he said, placing his hands on top of mine. He pressed them to the granite, a clear message to keep them there before he gripped the top of my shorts. He slipped them off and let them fall to the ground beneath us. "You will do as you're told, Mouse. Understood?"

God, I could barely sit still. I tried to press my thighs together, but he was standing between my knees. He gently slid his hands up my thighs and then back down, giving my left leg a sharp slap that pulled me from my trance.

"Understood?" he asked again.

"Yes," I gasped, heart pounding with anticipation.

Angel didn't move, still standing between my knees. He was just far enough away that he could look over my body, and I could practically feel his gaze on my bare skin. He lifted his eyes to mine, his tongue flicking out to lick his bottom lip.

"Touch yourself."

My stomach clenched with desire, part of me protesting that it wasn't his fingers that slipped beneath my underwear now. I kept my eyes on him, spreading my legs wider, determined to drive him wild enough that he would have to touch me. My mouth parted when I reached my slick center, my heart picking up pace when he smirked.

"Please, touch me," I breathed.

"No."

"Please."

"Show me what a good girl you are, Mouse," he said and took a step closer, holding my legs a fraction wider. "I want to watch you come undone."

I did, my muscles tightening before I melted right there on the counter. I let out a loud moan, my hand gripping his shoulder while the other ushered the last of the wave to shore. I groaned, a shaky mess, when he held both of my hands in one of his.

"I told you to listen, Mouse," he said and began to wrap a piece of fabric around my wrists. My shredded top. He was tying me with my shirt, tightening the fabric so I couldn't slip free before he released my hands.

I groaned again as he lowered my back to the counter. He lifted my arms so they were above me, stretched to the other side so my bound wrists hung off the edge. "Good girls listen and do what they're told," Angel said, sliding his hands down between my breasts, over my stomach, and between my thighs.

I was nearly sent over the edge again when his fingers moved against me, coaxing me closer. Just when I thought I would explode, he slowed his touch enough to dull the ache. He continued his torture, each time sending me deeper and deeper into that floaty headspace, reducing me to a mess of pleasure until I was begging him for release.

My hands were still tied, but together they grazed his chest. The air whooshed around me and now my chest was against the cool granite, Angel's hand against my back to keep me there. He slapped my ass hard and then he was there, filling me, thrusting deep. He had me pinned so effectively that there was nothing to do but take it. Realizing it sent me over the edge immediately, shattering into so many pieces that I wasn't sure I'd ever recover. That wave continued, relentless, leaving my legs shaking and slick with desire.

The cool granite was replaced with the warmth of his skin. I was still coming down from that otherworldly space when I felt the sheets around us. I was sitting in Angel's lap on the bed as he worked to undo the fabric around my wrists. He rubbed them both once he'd freed me, kissing away the marks on my forearms from where I'd bumped them against the granite.

"Wow," I said in an exhale, making him laugh.

"So, about those rules—"

"I'll follow whatever rules you want," I said with a giggle.

Angel smirked, pulling me closer to his chest as he leaned against the headboard. "Let's not move too fast. I can think of one rule that I'd like to set if you agree. It's a hard limit for me."

I already knew the rule. We'd set it months ago, though informally so. I raised my head from his chest to look at him, the importance of the subject in his expression.

"I know," I told him, brushing his cheek. "Safety."

"It's more than just that," Angel said with a sigh, the concern in his voice making my stomach twist with guilt. "Keep your phone with you at all times just in case anything happens. You can call for help, and I can find you faster. Don't take unnecessary risks. Eat three meals a day. Get enough sleep. I don't like it when you're in danger, and I especially don't like it when you've done it to yourself."

"I know, and you're right," I said, my face heating. "It's what I do when I'm anxious."

"We're going to find you a better coping skill," Angel said and kissed my brow.

"Yes. Better," I said with a sigh.

"I mean it. It's a hard limit for me, Mouse. There's nothing more important to me."

"It's fair," I told him and kissed his nose. "I accept the rule."

He let out a sigh, a smile spreading on his face as I said the words. "Just don't make me enforce it." He playfully slapped my ass, and I snuggled closer to his side. We sat like that for a long time, long enough that I noticed how sore my muscles were from our games.

"I meant it," Angel said.

I lifted my head from his chest, sitting up when he adjusted. He turned on the bed to face me, our knees pressed together and our hands entwining.

"You are mine, regardless of the cure. I can't keep doing this, living like this without you. It may be selfish of me to ask you to spend your mortal life with me if we can't find the cure. But I can't keep existing knowing you're somewhere else, with someone else ... You are mine, and while my marriage to Maria wasn't, I know that ours will be the kind of bond to make my existence mean something."

Everything stopped for a moment. It was like the air was sucked from the room. The meaning of the words finally settled around me, sending a jolt through my chest.

"Is this—are you asking to marry me?"

Angel smiled and kissed my ring finger. "Not just yet." He lowered my hand to his lap, running his thumb over the spot where an engagement ring would sit. "I know there is very little between us that is traditional, but I would like to commit myself to you in all the ways I can. I want your family's blessing. I want to ask them for your hand, then put a big ring on yours. I want the engagement, the wedding, and to peel you out of a white dress after."

I laughed and he brushed a tear from my face, and when I looked back at him, I saw that there were tears in his eyes too.

"A spring wedding sounds nice," I said.

He smiled. "Be patient with me, Mouse." He kissed my forehead. "I want to be mortal when I stand at the altar if I can, but I will stand there as I am if I must."

I nodded. For that, I could wait. "I love you."

"I love you," he said and lowered his lips to mine. In a matter of seconds, I was beneath him again, and the world around us faded into the background.

CHAPTER 17

Angel was tense as we took the elevator down to the lobby.

"It'll be okay. It's going to go fine," I told him, squeezing his hand tight. He forced a smile my way before looking ahead when the doors slid apart.

"I hope so," he said as we started through the lobby.

Nova told us to meet her at the back patio. She wanted to talk with her grandmother first and make sure she had a heads-up about us coming before we showed up for her afternoon tea and disrupted her routine. When I got the text to go ahead with the plan, Angel and I made a beeline for the elevator.

"She recognized you from across the room. That counts for something." I let go of his hand so we could walk opposite ways around a pillar, rejoining on the other side. The door to the back patio was just ahead, a warning posted on the glass telling us that the door would lock behind us.

"It's going to be fine," I said again before he opened the door.

The patio was large, bigger than I had imagined. To the right was an expanse of grass large enough for dozens of children to run freely. To the left was a rectangular pool that I was sure felt perfect on a hot day like today. Around the pool were lounge chairs and metal tables beneath black umbrellas. Nova and Bebe sat at one of those tables.

Bebe Laveau wore a flowy black dress and a pair of pink sandals to match the large sunhat on her head. Her hair hung in tight curls around her face just like Nova's, and she smiled at us as we made our way toward them. Nova stood up, moving to her grandmother's side and pointing to Angel.

"Bebe, this is—"

"Angel," Bebe said with a smile. "It took you an awfully long time to find that first ingredient."

I heard Angel sigh in relief beside me. He let go of my hand and surged forward to take Bebe's hand. He kissed the back of her hand and dropped to one knee before Bebe pulled away and shook her head.

"Sit in a chair like a grown man," she said and patted the seat next to him. "My daughter tells me this is your girlfriend."

I saw Nova open her mouth to correct her, tell her that she was her granddaughter, but she rolled her eyes instead and introduced me. "This is Angel's girlfriend, Bebe. Her name is Lily Thompson and she's a seer."

"A seer?" Bebe asked, looking at me curiously. She gave a harumph and looked to Angel who stood next to her. "Did she see you coming?"

"She did," Angel said and smiled at me.

I could feel the blush spreading. "I didn't know I had. I didn't know I was a seer until he told me, and I didn't know what that was."

"Really? Are there not others in your family?" Bebe asked.

I shook my head. "Just me."

"Has anyone taught you how to use your abilities?"

"No. That was part of the reason we came here. The other part ..." I hesitated and glanced at Angel in case I was giving away too much too early in the conversation.

"I know why he's here," Bebe answered and then motioned toward the empty chairs around the table. "You all have got to sit down. You're making me nervous with all these looks you're giving each other and the shifting ... You'd think you were all in trouble, and I'm the one to give you what for. Sit."

Nova shook her head in annoyance, but there was no denying the humor in her face as she sank into her seat again. Angel pulled a chair out for me before sitting in the seat next to Bebe.

"It's funny you think you'd tell us off," Angel said and withdrew the envelope from his pocket that held the photo of Bebe. "I remember buying the girl in this photo a drink. Tell me, how old were you here?"

"Bebe!" Nova gasped as Angel slid the photo across the table. The old woman looked down at the photo and then sat back with red-tinged cheeks.

"Now what was an old man doing trying to give a twenty-year-old girl a drink anyway?" Bebe teased. "How old were you *really* when you took that photograph, Angel?"

"Well, you're just as stubborn as the day I met you," Angel laughed.

Bebe patted him on the knee. "You're every bit as handsome as I remember, so it's no surprise to me that you came with such a pretty girl on your arm. I have to say that I am surprised you didn't come sooner."

The humor faded from Angel's face. "Finding a guardian who wouldn't kill me on sight was hard enough, not to mention one willing to give me their blood."

"You have the blood then?"

"Yes."

Bebe clapped her hands together and then extended a hand to Angel, palm up. "Let's have it then."

Angel paused for a moment before he withdrew the vial from his pocket. He sat it in her palm and Bebe raised the glass vial in front of her face to look at it, tipping it from one side to the other to watch the blood as it slid along the glass inside.

"So, what do you have to do with it?" Nova asked, peering over her grandmother's shoulder to look at the vial. "They told me you knew a spell."

"A spell for what?" Bebe asked, looking at Nova. My

stomach fell, but just as Angel groaned next to me Bebe let out a gasp and looked back at us. "Ah! The cure for vampirism. That's right."

Nova, Angel, and I all exchanged relieved glances while Bebe gently sat the vial on the table. Angel stowed it away in his pocket before anything could happen to it.

"So, you know the spell to cure vampirism?" I asked, scooting to the edge of my chair.

"It's a kind of binding spell similar to a blood bond," Bebe said as though it was last week's news and not a spell powerful enough to undo a centuries-long curse. "It's in one of my personal spellbooks."

"You wrote it down?" Nova asked.

Bebe turned to look at her in annoyance. "How do you think I'd remember it? Do I look like I cure vampires every day?"

"Where's the spellbook?" Angel asked, pulling her attention back by placing a hand over hers on the table. Bebe stared at him for a long moment, and I worried that she was drifting, forgetting our entire conversation. She adjusted in her seat.

"Well, only a blood relative can open those books. They have my greatest hits in them, my best recipes. You see, the trick is to use the best apples. The ones out back behind the barn are the perfect apples. The secret is to sprinkle a little cinnamon on it when you roll out the dough."

"What is she talking about? Is that the spell?" I asked, looking to Nova.

She shook her head. "No. That's great-grandma's apple pie recipe." Nova let out a deep sigh and got up from her chair, placing a hand on Bebe's shoulder that was enough to keep her from telling us how long to bake the pie in the oven. "Bebe, I have your recipe book in my apartment. They want to know about your spellbook."

"Oh. That's right," Bebe said with a laugh. "I wrote the cure for vampirism down in one of my spellbooks. I don't remember which one, but I do know that because that spell is a binding spell. You have to do all the steps in order for it to work. One at a time. I made sure to write it all down so that the book will tell it to you exactly the way you need to do it."

"You don't remember which book it's in?" Nova asked. Her tone was sweet, but her expression told a different story. Judging by the frustrated look on Nova's face, Bebe must have had dozens of spellbooks from, and I doubted there was an easier way to figure out which one we needed than to go through every single one page by page.

Bebe shrugged. "No idea, but your mother would know. I told her that a vampire would come back looking for it someday, so I told her how it worked. It's important because that spell could change everything for vampires. That's why I explained to her how it worked. I even gave her the dagger."

"The dagger. You—" Angel scoffed and then sat forward in his seat, resting his elbows on his knees. "I gave you my dagger, my father's dagger. It was the only thing I had left of him. I thought it was payment for helping me with the cure."

Bebe laughed. "Not payment. You have to bind to something, and weapons make the best objects, especially in this case. I took your dagger because that's what I planned to bind all the steps of the spell to. Do the binding spell with your dagger. You use the dagger to kill the vampire. Once you kill the vampire, his heart restarts, and his body becomes mortal. That's the cure."

It was quiet for a moment, so much so that we could hear people talking in the distance.

"It's like a reverse death," Angel said slowly. My heart skipped in my chest.

"Wouldn't that kill the vampire once he's mortal?" I asked, trying to keep my panic from seeping into my voice. Angel placed his hand on my knee and began stroking back and forth with his thumb. I followed his lead, matching my breathing to the pattern.

"I know it sounds kind of paradoxical, but that's how the spell works." Bebe shrugged. She looked around the table before turning toward Nova. "Where's my tea?"

"So, where is the dagger now?" Angel asked, looking from Bebe to Nova.

"I gave it to my daughter. You'd have to ask her where she put it," Bebe said, still looking around the table. "Where's my tea?"

"I'll go get the tea, Bebe," Nova said and rose from her seat. She sent me a sad smile before Bebe reached for her. She looked nervous and then confused.

"You aren't Jackie," Bebe said. Nova hesitated before she placed a hand on Bebe's back.

"No. I'm Nova," she said. She rubbed her back for a moment. "I'll go get the tea."

"No. I think I want to go to my apartment. I think I need ..." Bebe didn't finish. My chest tightened, and I wished there was something I could say. Nova held Bebe's hand as she stood up. They walked just a few feet before Bebe turned to face us again, pointing her finger at Angel. "Just find the spellbook. It will tell you what to do next."

She started walking toward the door with Nova, who didn't look as optimistic as she had before.

Angel had been quieter than usual despite the reassuring smiles he sent me across the table as we ate dinner. The restaurant was close enough to Night Owl Apartments that we walked, holding hands. He didn't say a word during the entire walk. I could see the contemplation on his face whenever I glanced his way, wondering if he needed reassurance more than I did or if he just wanted a moment to think.

"Are you okay?" I finally asked, setting my fork down to keep from further scooting the last ravioli around my plate.

Angel let out a deep breath and nodded. "I just have a lot on my mind."

"Do you want to talk about it?"

He smiled back at me and then reached across the table to ease the fork from between my fingers. I hadn't realized I'd been turning it over and over on the table until he set it aside.

"I think a part of me had been focused for so long on getting the guardian blood and then finding Bebe again that I forgot there are more things needed for the spell." The corners of his mouth twitched, but he kept the good-humored façade for me. The tightness of his jaw told the truth. It made me wonder if he would've said what he had about getting married regardless of his immortality. Had he thought he was close to breaking the curse then? How much more did we need to gather to complete the spell? How much longer would Bebe's memory last to perform the spell?

"Do you have any idea what's left?" I asked, hoping there had been more to their conversation so many years ago.

Angel looked away from me, licking his bottom lip as he thought. His expression changed; his eyes focused on something behind me. I didn't even turn fully in my seat before Nova slipped into the chair next to me, dressed in a pair of sweatpants and a crop top that made me wonder how she made it past the hostess station.

"Nova, what's wrong?" Angel asked.

"How did you find us?" I asked.

She held up her phone. "You shared your location with me."

"I did?"

"I know. I was just as surprised as you are. I bet we did that at some point during the soirée and were just drunk enough not to remember the next day."

"Why are you here?" Angel asked, speaking loud enough to pull her from our discussion.

She smiled wider and sat up straighter, looking at both of us in turn before she spoke. "Bebe named me as her successor, using the blood rule to pass her position to me as High Priestess. I already had some magical privileges because I'm her blood relative, but formally naming me before the coven gives me the right to all aspects of coven business, even if she hasn't fully stepped down yet. She gave me full rights."

"What does that mean?" I asked as Angel pulled several bills from his wallet and set them on the table.

"It means that I have access to the coven archive and artifacts room. Bebe wouldn't keep anything that important lying around her apartment, even if she does have a protective spell on them. Her spellbooks are in that room, and I can get us in there to find them," Nova said.

Angel was already on his feet. Nova and I followed him, hurrying onto the sidewalk to catch up with him.

"We'll need a plan," he said once we joined him.

"Already got one," Nova chimed in. "So, want me to explain it at your apartment or mine?"

"Ours," I told her before Angel could speak up. I had a feeling that Angel might need a drink to relax, especially because this plan would include me. I wasn't going to sit on the sidelines anymore. I had supernatural abilities too, and it was about time I learned to make use of them.

CHAPTER 18

"N o."

"Angel," I groaned.

It was a good plan, and it wasn't like it was dangerous. Nova and I would go into the archives together to find Bebe's spellbooks and hopefully Angel's dagger too. He would make sure no one interrupted, which should be easy because there were so few people with access to the archives anyway. Poppy was the only person Nova worried about finding us, so Angel would keep tabs on her whereabouts. As late as it was, that meant making sure she didn't wake up extra early for work and catch us.

"You don't know what's down there," Angel told me, his hand gentle as it laced with mine in his lap despite his firm tone. "The coven's most important records and artifacts are there. Things won't be sitting there unattended. There could be spells or traps."

"What would the coven think if they caught you down there instead of me?" I asked, looking at Nova for support. She nodded, waiting for Angel to answer. "The coven accepts me because I'm a seer. Catching me with Nova, who has a right to be in the archives anyway, would be more forgivable than finding you there."

"Lily," Angel said softly. He knew I was right. I could see it in his face. He hesitated before sighing. "Be careful."

A mixture of relief and excitement flooded my body. A smile spread on Nova's face when I looked up at her.

"We'll have more time if we go now," she said and stood up. Angel and I followed her back into the hallway, finalizing the last of our plan as we waited for the elevator to take us to the lobby. Angel would stay in the lobby and call me if anyone approached the back room. It was easy enough and not even Angel looked that concerned as we rode the elevator.

The elevator doors parted to reveal the empty lobby. It was quiet and I hoped that it would stay that way as Nova started toward the employee lounge on the other side of the room. I don't remember there being a door in that room, but Nova said the entrance to the archives was there. Angel caught my hand before I could follow her.

His expression softened, but the concern was still there. "Be careful and call me if you need me."

"It'll be fine," I said, moving closer to him so I could rise on my toes to kiss his cheek. He let out a deep breath and nodded, letting go of my hand so I could hurry after Nova.

She'd already unlocked the back room, waiting for me to enter before she closed it and locked it again. I looked around the room, studying the walls for any sign of a hidden door along the wall. Maybe one of the many books on one of the shelves worked as a lever like in spy movies.

"Stand by the wall for a second," Nova told me, waving for me to move away from the coffee table. I did, joining her by the door again. She held her arms in front of her. The couches rumbled as they scooted apart. The coffee table rose into the air and moved to the wall beside me. The red rug rolled up to reveal a wooden door along the floor with a metal ring set into the wood where a handle would be.

Not a ring.

There was a loud hiss that sent ice through my veins and that ring uncoiled, the black head of a snake rising from the wood to face us. Nova eased me behind her with one arm and extended her other arm to the snake. She barely flinched when it struck, sinking long fangs into her hand with a hiss. It lowered back to the wooden door and coiled into a circle until it had stopped moving and looked like a simple piece of décor against the wood.

"Magic has to be so theatrical," Nova scoffed and reached for the snake that now served as a handle. She groaned as she lifted the door, and once I realized it was safe, I helped her open the door the rest of the way to reveal a set of stone stairs that went down into the dark.

"Are you okay?" I asked, looking at the hand she had cradled against her middle. She brushed her fingers against the snake bite, and it vanished.

"I'm fine. It's just annoying how dramatic witches are," she said and led the way down the stairs. Sconces lit the path ahead of us, guiding our descent into the room. The stairs were long, going down so deep that the air chilled my bare arms and legs. Only the sound of our footsteps on the stones greeted us as we went, the only noise for several minutes before the sconces lit ahead of us to reveal a landing.

"Finally," Nova said, her voice echoing off the enclosed stair-well. "I was worrying how much longer we'd have to go."

"You didn't know?" I asked. She reached for the sconce on the left. It had three metal feet, clearly intended to be used to carry throughout the room beyond.

Nova glanced sheepishly back at me with the torch in hand. "I've never been down here."

"That's okay. It's a records room. There's got to be a system," I said as she started into the room. We only made it a few feet into the space before she raised the torch above her so the light fell over the first of many shelves. None of them were labeled and I could see that those tall shelves held everything from files to boxes to strange glassware I assumed was used for potions.

"Oh," I gasped. It was too dark to see how far back the shelves went or how high they stretched. "We have our work cut out for us."

"Hang on. I think I can speed things up," Nova said and held the torch to me. After passing it, she turned to the room and cupped her hands under her chin. A little flame burst into existence, and she began to twist her hands together until she'd molded the flame into an orb of light. It got so bright that I had to look away before she sent it floating high into the air. It lit the space around us for several yards, revealing just how massive the shelves were and how large the room was.

"I'll go left," I told her.

She held a hand in front of me to keep me from moving. "I'm not done yet."

I waited while she closed her eyes and mumbled to herself. She let out a groan and started again, and then again before she sighed in relief and pointed toward the right. There was a purple glow barely visible through the shelves, maybe four or five rows away from where we stood.

"Bebe's spellbooks," she said and clapped her hands. "Let's go. We'll try that again to find the dagger after we figure out which book we need."

I followed her down the rows until we found the right shelf, jogging halfway down where a row of books were. There were four books in total, all several inches thick and bound in dark leather with Nova's surname etched into the spines. It was impossible to tell which glowing book was the right one. I reached for the first one only for my fingers to meet something firm. It was like there was a wall in place between me and the spine.

"Here," Nova said, easily taking the book from the shelf and setting it in my arms. "I bet only a Laveau can touch them."

The books were so heavy that I could only comfortably carry two. Nova took the rest of the books and we carried them back to the stairwell. The slap of the books on the bottom stair echoed off the walls, reminding me that someone might hear us. I glanced up the stairs as though expecting to see Poppy herself storming down to catch us.

"Let's try this again," Nova said, pulling my attention back to her. Eyes closed, she began murmuring to herself, casting that same location spell. Only, this time nothing happened. We moved away from the stairwell, looking down the aisles in case the purple light was just hidden behind something. Her expression when we reconvened at the bottom stair told me all I needed to know.

"Guess that means the dagger isn't here," I said.

She nodded. She let out a deep sigh and turned for the stairs, lifting two of the books into her arms. "Well, there's no reason to hang around."

"Didn't Bebe say she gave the dagger to your mom?" I asked before lifting the heavy books into my arms. Dread filled my gut at the journey ahead. I wasn't sure I could carry the books all the way up without a break.

Nova adjusted the books, so they rested on her right shoulder instead. "My apartment used to be my mom's apartment. I was living in a dorm on campus. I moved in to her apartment after she passed away. I never found a dagger when I went through her things."

"Maybe it's hidden in the apartment," I said, following her lead to rest the books on my shoulder. It did make it a little easier to carry them.

Nova groaned. "I'm worried that Bebe remembered wrong."

"Then maybe it's hidden in her apartment."

"Maybe. I don't know," Nova adjusted the books on her shoulder again, pausing a few steps ahead of me for a moment before she continued. My back had started to hurt and from what I remember of the trip to the archives, we were only halfway up.

"Could we try—" I had to pause to catch my breath. Nova didn't interrupt, too busy trying to pace herself. I moved the books back into my arms, trying my best to stretch my back before I started climbing the stairs again. "Could we try the spell on both apartments?"

"Yes," Nova said. The books wobbled on her shoulder, and she paused to adjust them, but not quickly enough. One of the books slipped over her shoulder and slapped loudly against the step between us. It was so loud that it hurt my ears and made me jump. I let out a scream when my own books fell on my feet. I was sure my big toe would be bruised, but I was more concerned with how loud we'd been.

Nova turned on the stairs with her eyes wide in surprise, one book held in her right hand as she watched me massage my right foot.

"Everyone okay?" Angel asked.

I looked up to see him standing just behind Nova. He skirted around her when he saw me, holding my right bicep so I didn't fall as I rubbed my foot.

"Fine. We just dropped the books," I said and lowered my foot to the floor. Angel bent down and took the three books into his arms before turning and taking the one in Nova's arms too.

"You're supposed to keep watch," Nova told him as he balanced all four books on one hand.

Angel nodded up the stairs. "I did until I heard you two. I wanted to make sure everything was okay. Now that I know, we should get out of here."

"Say less. Let's go!" Nova turned and hurried up the stairs, moving at a quicker pace now that she didn't have the books weighing her down. My foot ached as I followed, focusing on each step and the light ahead rather than how much farther there was to go.

The stairwell started to brighten, the sunlight from the back room spilling into the final stretch of stairs ahead. My aching muscles felt a fraction lighter as we approached the door. Nova climbed into the room and looked back at me, taking a step away from the entrance to make space. I sighed in relief as I stepped into that room again, turning in time to see Angel duck as though something had bumped him on the top of the head. He lifted a hand, muscles tensed like he was pushing against an invisible door above him.

No. There was no way.

"Maybe it's the books," Nova said and brushed past me to step back into the stairwell. "Here."

Nova took the books from Angel one at a time and handed them to me. I set them on the couch to the left in a neat stack until all four were on the cushions. I stepped aside so Nova could step into the room again, both of us looking back at Angel who was using both hands to push against that invisible barrier. His expression fell, his jaw tight as he shook his head.

"I'm stuck down here," Angel said with a groan. "Just a witchy booby-trap." He slapped the invisible wall above him once before leaning against the wall to the right.

It felt like I was still stuck down there with him, the walls tight on either side, the air thin, my chest heavy ...

"Do you know a spell?" I asked Nova. It felt like it took all of my breath to ask that single question. "Maybe in the books?"

I turned for the stack of Bebe's spellbooks only to watch them rise from the couch and shoot behind me. I whirled around to watch them settle in a neat stack on the floor next to Poppy Nolan. She wore her signature pantsuit with her dark hair smoothed over her shoulders. She crossed her arms as she pinned us with those judgmental eyes, a slight smirk pulling at her lips.

"Those aren't yours," Nova said, pointing a finger at Poppy's chest.

Poppy's smile only grew wider. "They aren't yours either." She looked down at the pile like she'd just won the first-place trophy in a race, only when she bent down and extended a hand to brush the cover of the top book, her fingers didn't reach the cover. She tried again only for her fingers to meet an invisible barrier. Her smile faltered for a moment before she looked back at us with that feigned smugness.

"Those aren't yours," Nova said again, this time surging forward and snatching the book from the top of the stack. Poppy was appalled and she acted like she might try pulling it away from Nova before she hesitated, likely remembering how she was unable to touch the spellbooks before.

Nova gathered the books in a stack on the floor between herself and me, and Poppy watched with annoyance as she did.

"Your kind may be welcome here among the coven, but his is not," she said, keeping her eyes locked on me.

"You have me locked down here. Leave them alone," Angel said.

Poppy let out a laugh. "They are as guilty as you, which is why I've already called a meeting of the coven elders."

"That doesn't matter, Poppy. They're here as my guests and have the blessing of the High Priestess," Nova said, and pointed toward the door.

She only smiled wider. "Well," she said and smoothed her blazer along her hips. "They are gathering now in the great hall. High Priestess or not, any member of the council has a right to call a meeting, a right that you do not possess."

"Bebe named her as the High Priestess," I said. It was hard to forget the look on Nova's face when her grandmother had announced that at the soirée.

I heard Nova sigh next to me as though already anticipating what Poppy said next.

"The next High Priestess has not been formally accepted, and I can promise you that the elders are looking into the legitimacy of appointing Nova Laveau in the first place."

"Legitimacy?" I asked, glancing at Nova who looked surprisingly defeated. "We were all at the soirée. We heard the announcement,"

"She means they're questioning if my Bebe was in the right state of mind to make the decision," Nova said under her breath, just loud enough that I could hear.

So, the only card we held was that Beatrice Laveau was the current High Priestess. Our only hope was that she remembered Angel and their history together.

"Bebe still gave us her blessing to be here," Angel said. He kept his voice calm. "I swear that I'm not here to harm anyone and I haven't. Lily is here to learn what she can about her abilities as a seer. I'm here for Bebe's help. We're old friends."

Poppy laughed again. "That doesn't matter. The council will decide if you can stay and you will stay right there until they do." She didn't allow any more time for conversation, casting Nova and me a smug smile before she turned and started back to the lobby.

I glanced at Angel before looking at Nova. "What do we do?"

"We get the books to my apartment first," she said and lifted two of the large spellbooks into her arms. "Then we haul ass to the ballroom to make our case."

I looked at Angel again, worried about what might happen if I wasn't with him.

"I'll be fine," he promised, motioning for me to go.

I took the remaining two books and Nova and I hurried for the lobby. The elevator thankfully opened right away and we were able to take it to our floor. Once inside, we dropped the books on the kitchen counter and began to scour the apartment for Angel's dagger. I looked over the shelves in the living room as she darted for her bedroom.

"This is all I have left of her," Nova called out. A moment later, she walked backward out of her bedroom, towing a medium-sized trunk with her. She stopped when she reached the kitchen and I knelt beside her. She twisted the key on the front and pulled the top open on its hinge.

"I expected there to be more with how heavy it is," Nova said with a sigh.

The trunk wasn't even half full. The bottom was littered with papers and notebooks. Nova's and her mother's birth certificates were inside, passports, a little organizer that held hair from Nova's first haircut and all her baby teeth. We sifted through all of it until everything sat on the floor around us and we could see the cloth lining at the bottom.

"I don't know where else to look," Nova groaned. "I like to keep things organized, so I know every inch of this apartment and this trunk is the only things I haven't opened since ..."

I could see the disappointment on her face, but the way her eyes glazed over told a different story. This was the first time she'd opened the trunk since her mother died. It might have been the first time she'd looked at any of her mother's things since she died. The gratitude was overwhelming and my chest hurt for her as I thought about how important this was. I opened my mouth to try expressing how sorry I was for making her go through her mom's things, but her expression changed. She tilted her head to the left, a look of curiosity crossing her face as she reached into the bottom of the trunk.

"What is it?" I asked.

"I don't know," she said slowly, running her hand along a tear where the blue lining connected with the wall of the truck. She pressed her hands to the bottom of the trunk in several places. "No way."

"Is it ..." I didn't finish the thought. Nova slipped her fingers inside the tear and ripped the fabric away from the trunk, pulling back the lining out to reveal a piece of plywood. It was obvious that it was a false bottom, the wood sitting on top of something I couldn't make out until Nova lifted the plywood out of the trunk. We both gasped as we took in the sight.

Stacks of money lined the bottom of the trunk, thousands of dollars bound together in neat stacks. Nova began sorting through the stacks, revealing at least three layers of cash until she found the real bottom of the trunk and along with it ...

"The dagger," she said, holding up a silver dagger in a black sheath. There was an elegant R burned into the black leather sheath. I took it from her so she could go back to staring in awe at the money in the trunk. I wasn't sure what to do with the weapon. Angel had the key to our apartment, and somehow, leaving it here felt strange. I tucked it into the waistband of my shorts and draped my shirt over it before I stood up.

"We should go find the council," I told her, pulling her from her trance.

Nova nodded, closing the lid on the money and rising to her feet. "Yeah. Um, you're right. I'll just, um—" She motioned to the trunk as though it might finish the thought for her before she snatched her apartment key from the counter to her right and led the way toward the door.

CHAPTER 19

The elders were leaving the ballroom when we reached it. Relief washed over me when I saw Angel standing with Bebe outside the main doors, offering me a smile when he saw us coming. I threw my arms around him and his tightened around my middle.

"How did you get out?" I asked.

He chuckled. "The witchy cavalry came and whisked me away, had me in magic handcuffs and everything until Bebe got here."

"We found the dagger," I said in his ear. I pulled back far enough to kiss him on the lips. He relaxed, letting go of me and taking my hand.

"I put my foot down," Bebe said, stomping her foot against the hardwood for emphasis. "I know my mind isn't what it used to be, but they still trust my judgement over Poppy Nolan's."

"You look nervous, Bebe," Nova said, pulling my attention away from Angel. Bebe did look nervous, she cast a look at Angel as though preparing to tell him bad news. It made my stomach knot.

"There's more. What's the catch?" I asked, looking at Angel.

His expression had fallen too. He kept his eyes on Bebe a moment longer before he looked back at me.

"They don't fully trust me. They believed me when I told them how I feed and what my intentions are here. They took my word for it only because Bebe did," Angel said and then let out a deep breath. "They are more concerned with what my impact may be on the community. The coven has started to gossip about me being here and there are concerns. They want me out of the city by the end of the month, then we head back to New York."

We only had a few weeks. We just found the spellbooks, the dagger, and we had a few weeks to figure out which book contained the spell and how to use it on the dagger. It didn't seem like that large a task except Bebe was in no shape to leave Night Owl Apartments to perform the spell. After the end of the month, we wouldn't be allowed back here for her to continue binding the items we needed to the dagger.

"I explained the spell to Jackie. She'll know how to do it for you. She can leave to meet you whenever you're ready for the next item," Bebe said, her words only making my stomach sink further.

Nova patted Bebe on the shoulder and started to lead her toward the elevator. I turned to face Angel again, taking his free hand in mine.

"Maybe Nova can tell us the spell and we can find another witch," I said.

Angel kept his eyes on Nova and Bebe as they waited for the elevator, not looking at me until the doors slide apart. "Bebe said she enchanted the spellbook so the spell reveals itself one item at a time. There's a specific order. We need the spellbook."

I remembered how I was unable to touch the spellbooks on the shelf in the archives. Even if we stole the books, we wouldn't be able to use them. Chances were that we wouldn't be able to get them out of the building without a Laveau's permission.

I looked away from Angel when Nova joined us again, a cautious look on her face. She shifted from one foot to the other.

"I don't want to impose or anything. I don't want to be a third wheel, but I'm going to need a place to stay," she said, her arms wrapping around her middle. "I can pay, obviously." She let out an awkward laugh as she pointed toward the ceiling where the trunk of cash sat several floors above us.

"What do you mean?" I asked.

She looked surprised. "I'm coming with you. You'll need someone to do the spell and only a Laveau can use the spellbook. We'll have to figure out which book we need first, but ..." Nova shrugged, still looking anxious at us as if we might reject her.

"Oh my God," I gasped and let go of Angel to pull her into a hug. "Of course, you can stay with us!"

"I can help pay for rent or whatever," she said when we pulled apart.

Angel laughed. "You're doing me a huge favor, Nova. You can have whatever you want."

She relaxed, a smile spreading on her face. "Okay then. Let's go back to my apartment. We have a spell to find."

———

It was going to take more than an evening to find the spell. It turned out that even with Nova's permission, only a Laveau could open the spellbook. The most Angel and I could do was pass the heavy books to her so she could flip through the pages. We finally called it a night when I nearly fell asleep on her couch.

"We'll come over in the morning to keep you company," I told her as Angel and I started for the door.

Nova waved her hands in dismissal. "Don't worry about it. There's no reason for you guys to spend the last of your trip here watching me read. Go do something fun tomorrow. I'll call you when I find the spell."

"Are you sure?" Angel asked, holding the door open. "I don't want to leave you with all the work. It's only fair that I do something."

Nova and I exchanged looks as though daring the other to point out the obvious. Nova was stuck with the work either way.

"You got the blood. You'll have to get the rest of the items for the spell later. We'll call it even," she said and leaned against the doorframe. "You might as well enjoy New Orleans while you're still here. I promise, I'm fine on my own."

"I'll show you my favorite places in New York when we get there to make up for it," I told her, mouthing a *thank you* before she shut the door. I turned to Angel in the hallway as he stood in front of our door, turning the key between his fingers. "Aren't I supposed to be the anxious one in this relationship?"

He smiled, pulling me toward him as he unlocked our apartment door. He slapped my butt as I passed him in the doorway, turning to face him as he shut and locked the door behind us. He lifted me by my hips and sat me on the kitchen counter, moving into the space between my knees so we were just inches apart.

"Who's anxious?" he asked, brushing my hair away from my face.

I placed my hands against his chest before he could lean in for a kiss. "You are."

He hesitated for a moment. I knew he was going to deny it but the truth must've been obvious to him too because his shoulders rose with his deep breath, and he lowered his hands from my face to my thighs.

"Centuries I've waited for a chance to be mortal again," he finally spoke, watching his fingers trace circles against my thighs. "And not only do I have that, but I have you. There's a whole life ahead of us. It's all a little overwhelming, in a good way." He looked up at me when I draped my arms on his shoulders.

"You sure you're ready to give up life in the shadows for the suburbs?" I teased.

He smiled. "Who said anything about the suburbs?"

"Just a figure of speech," I said and pulled him closer. "I hope mortal Angel is strong enough still to give his famous lectures. Wouldn't want to lose your edge."

"Ouch. Wow," Angel laughed, stepping closer. "When did my good girl become such a brat?"

I could hardly sit still, my heart racing as I thought about how far I dared to take things. How much teasing would it take before I found myself on my back beneath him?

"I think our fight woke up something in me. I feel more confident."

"Ah, the mouse has a little pair of boxing gloves, does she?" Angel smirked, tugging on a piece of my hair behind my back. "You're right, though. Something's different since our argument."

"Maybe brat suits me," I said, unable to contain my giggle at how absurd that sounded. I was the girl who almost never skipped a college lecture and felt guilty the one time I did, even though the professor never took attendance and didn't even know I had been absent.

"Any excuse to teach you a lesson," he said, pulling my bottom lip free from my teeth with his thumb.

"Which brings us back to my point," I said and poked his chest. "Better hope you don't lose your edge if you're going to keep up."

There it was: that dark look in his eyes that sent a delicious jolt through my body. I felt light, a floaty feeling that sent every creative taunt from my mind and had me focused on him and that look. The corner of his lip twitched upward in that ornery smile.

"You better watch what you say, or I'll put that bratty mouth to good use."

I wrapped my legs around him. His hands wrapped around my wrists, holding them at my sides. All it took was a single look, and I was completely within his control, and gladly so.

"No fair," I said, tugging against his grip.

"You going to behave?"

Ugh. The way I wanted to say "no" just to see what he'd do …

"Only if you kiss me," I said and tightened my legs around his hips, trying to pull him closer. He smiled wider and leaned his forehead against mine.

"As if I could resist you," he said and pressed his lips to mine. It was too brief, but he held my wrists firm and pulled back far enough that there was no way to deepen our kiss. He only smiled wider when I moaned. "Brats don't get rewards. So, are you my brat or my good girl, Mouse?"

I was a puddle.

"I'm your good girl," I said as the heat burned me from the inside out.

"My," Angel said and lifted me off the counter, gripping the back of my shorts. "Good girl."

I kissed him, my heart speeding up as the kiss deepened. Once we reached our bedroom, he sat me down so he could pull off his shirt. I took mine off as his hands went to my shorts, unbuttoning them and sending them falling to the floor before I'd freed my hair from the neck of my shirt. He tugged my underwear down my legs, and I kicked them the rest of the way off.

He didn't reach for me right away like I expected. I undid his belt and pulled it free from the loops in one swift move that sent chills of pleasure over my skin. He kept his eyes on me, alight with that coy look, as his pants pooled at his feet. He kicked them aside and hooked his fingers into the elastic band of his underwear, sliding them down his legs until he stood there naked with the full length of him on display.

He smirked and sat on the bed, leaning back against the headboard, and then motioned for me to join him with a single finger. "Come here, Mouse."

I crossed the room, very aware that I was wearing just my red bra as his eyes roved over me. Once I was close enough, he took my hand and guided me onto the bed. I leaned in to kiss him as his hands moved to my back to remove my bra. I sat up so it could slide the rest of the way off my arms and his hands cupped my breasts, his palms warm against my skin.

"I want you to use me," Angel said and moved his hands to my hips. "I want to watch as I sink into you, be at the mercy of your pace."

My heart skipped in my chest. This was new. I was a little disappointed that he hadn't just put me there himself, slammed into me with that roughness I loved. I straddled him and positioned myself over him until I could slowly sink onto him. He let out a moan, lips parting, his eyes locking with mine, and a shiver of pleasure ran over my skin. The way he looked at me ... God, this was why he wanted this. I felt powerful as I rolled my hips, drawing out the movement just to watch the satisfaction settle over his face.

"That's it, Mouse," he said, sliding his hands along my thighs. "Take me."

I slid my legs farther apart, my heart speeding up when his mouth parted as I took him deeper. I picked up the pace as his breathing increased, growing heavier with each thrust. I could feel my own desire grow hot in my core, rising, rising, and—

I squealed in surprise when he rolled, so I was lying beneath him. I was just on the edge, that delicious wave beginning to recede as he hovered above me.

"I'm a gentleman," he said and flashed me a playful smirk. "Ladies first."

His fingers found my center and within seconds my hands were in fists on the pillows behind my head. He stifled my cry with his lips, slamming into me and picking up where I'd left off. I was still recovering from the aftershocks when he let out a moan and stilled against me. He raised his head and rested his forehead against mine, our bodies still entwined. He pressed his lips gently against mine once before leaning in again for a deeper kiss that sent another wave of warmth through me.

He rolled onto his back next to me and I snuggled close to his side, letting him pull the sheets around us. My body was sore, exhausted from the sex and the long day. I pushed away my thoughts about the spellbooks and the Coven Council. Whatever happened with the cure or the council, I still had a lifetime ahead with Angel and that was enough.

CHAPTER 20

Angel and I started the day with coffee to go and a couple of croissants in hand, deciding to walk the French Quarter and take in the sights. It was nice to take things slow. Angel had been so stressed with trying to find the cure, and I knew he was anxiously waiting for Nova to call and let us know that she'd found the spell. Despite the wait, he was relaxed as he walked beside me. I told him what my therapist had told me over and over for years, and even though I knew it was easier said than done, I told him the same thing she told me. There was no reason to stress about what would come, especially when we could spend the present enjoying ourselves.

He smiled at me when I'd said the words, the look on his face more of pride than one of comfort and I wondered if he was thinking the same thing I was. Things really did feel different since our argument. Maybe I just needed to get my fears out in the open. Maybe I just needed to release some anxious energy. Whatever the change was, I felt a little more myself than before and different all the same.

We visited a few tourist shops along the walk. I bought a keychain for Anne and a New Orleans golf ball for my dad's collection. It was something he started when I was a kid. I had been too young to realize the display in the den was a "do not touch" item in the house. I took a few golf balls he'd brought back from a trip across Europe when he and my mom were first married and immediately lost them in the vineyard when I was practicing my swing for the daddy/daughter tournament at the club later that week.

"He'd never yelled at me like that before. Well ..." I didn't have to finish the sentence for Angel to know what I meant. He'd seen my dad's temper when I stood up to my parents after I brought him home to meet them months ago.

Angel took my bag of souvenirs from the shopkeeper and offered me a sweet smile.

"Your father is a reasonable man and there's nothing he loves more than you," Angel said and took my hand as we exited the shop for the street again. "I'm sure he understood."

"Yeah. He did," I said, noticing how he only smiled wider when my stomach grumbled. "Now, I make sure to buy him a golf ball whenever I go somewhere new."

"I think it's a nice tradition," Angel said. Something behind me caught his eye and his smile faltered a little. I followed his gaze across the street to a restaurant that must've just opened for the day. The host led a couple to a booth in the large window to the right of the entrance. A waiter was setting the booth for the day in the left-hand window, with more waitstaff dressed in white and black tending to the tables behind. The Spanish flag hanging from the pole mounted just outside the entrance was probably what caught Angel's attention.

"I've only eaten a croissant today ..." I tugged on his arm, leading him into the street after a car passed. I could see as we drew closer that the couple were the only other patrons in the restaurant. We approached the hostess at the podium and my stomach growled loudly again at the smell of fresh bread and spices. I heard Angel laugh.

Before I could say a word, the hostess and I made eye contact and sent my retort flying from my brain. She looked at Angel next, her posture relaxing. She began speaking in rapid Spanish as she gathered a pair of menus from the podium. The remaining embarrassment from my noisy stomach was chased away when Angel responded to her. I didn't understand what he was saying, but the words spilled from his lips like silk, each syllable flowing into beautiful phrases. The hostess led us into the restaurant and seated us in the left window, giving us a view of the street and providing us some privacy from the main area of the restaurant where a pair of waiters were still setting tables for lunch.

"I've never heard you speak in Spanish before," I said as I slid into the booth opposite Angel.

He smiled as he adjusted the menu on the table in front of him. "The opportunity to speak has never come up when we're together."

He was right. I'd never asked him before. He was over five hundred years old, and he grew up in Spain. I knew he spoke Spanish, but it was a reminder that he'd lived several lifetimes before me. I was overwhelmed with questions. I couldn't focus on a single one to ask.

"Does it bother you that you've never heard me speak in Spanish?" Angel asked, reaching across the table to take my hands. He eased my fingers from the menu I was fidgeting with, keeping me from peeling the plastic more than it already was.

"No. I knew that you spoke Spanish. Of course, you do," I told him, looking back down at the menu when I saw the way he looked at me, as if analyzing my expression. A moment of silence passed between us and my fingers itched to pick up the menu again, to peel at that plastic edge and focus on something other than the strange feeling burrowing in my stomach.

"Your father has golf balls. My grandfather had his horses," Angel said.

I looked up at him and I could see that his smile didn't quite touch his eyes the same way it normally did. He gave my hands a reassuring squeeze before he continued.

"He loved riding. He said it cleared his head. When I was young, he had a horse he loved more than the rest, a stallion he broke himself. I'd watched him break the horse and train it. He used to get so frustrated, but he poured hours into that horse. I didn't understand why at the time, not until I was much older and I realized how stressful his work was and how hard he fought to protect our family from people who tried to besmirch our name. It was his outlet and earning that horse's trust and loyalty must have been a kind of comfort to him," Angel said, smiling at the memory. "You took your father's golf balls for practice. I stole my grandfather's horse."

I gasped as I imagined Angel atop a wild stallion, racing through the trees. "What do you mean you stole it?"

He chuckled. "I was maybe fifteen or so. I was angry. I don't really remember why. I was difficult in my youth, but my grandfather was always gentle. He rarely raised a hand to me, the opposite actually. He was calm and addressed me with so much compassion, no matter what trouble I'd gotten into. He never yelled and something about the way he never seemed angry with me would make me so mad. It made me feel worse and something just snapped that day. It was a big argument, and I said some things that finally put a chip in his armor. He didn't yell, but he'd never been so firm with me. I wasn't finished, though. I walked out on him mid-argument. I could've left on any horse, but I picked the stallion because I knew it would just piss him off more. He didn't let anyone ride that horse, and it wasn't until I was well within the forest that I realized that was because the horse was still wild at heart. My grandfather had his trust, not me. He must have realized I wasn't my grandfather after a while because he stopped responding to me and bucked me off."

I pulled my hands free to cover my mouth. I only relaxed when I saw the humor in Angel's expression.

"Don't worry. I was fine. Well, physically. My ego took a hit, and I was still pretty pissed off until I realized I had no idea where the horse was. I knew I was already in for it. Losing the horse was a step further than I dared go, so I started to search for it. The weather wasn't great, and it started to rain. I found the horse, but it wasn't happy to see me and wouldn't let me approach it. I nearly took a kick to the chest, and that happened to be the moment my grandfather found me."

"I'm sure he was mad," I said.

"Not for stealing his prized horse," Angel said, pausing as the waiter approached with two glasses of water. He thanked him in Spanish and waited until the man had gone back to the kitchen before he continued.

"He was mad that I'd ridden the horse. He finally lost it. You'd have thought it was a summer day from how red in the face he was from yelling at me. He told me off for riding a wild horse, told me how the horse was big enough to crush me, and he threatened me with every punishment under the sun. Then, he told me to come to him."

A pit had formed in my stomach. I could imagine a younger version of Angel standing in the rain. It was hard to envision a version of him that was so obstinate, though. The way he described his grandfather was the way I saw Angel. He was soft, caring, and he noticed the smallest details. There was no hiding my feelings from him because he seemed to see right through my façade anyway, not that I wanted to hide from him.

Angel let out a deep breath. "I stood in front of him. I was prepared to take the punishment. I deserved it. I felt so guilty for what I'd done and the things I'd said. It was all too much." Angel shook his head with a scoff. "He just hugged me, so tight, like he might never see me again."

I was frozen in place, my hands still on the menu. "You must've really scared him."

"I did," Angel said with a nod. "I remembered sobbing into his chest, and he just held me tighter."

"Wow," I said, barely finding my voice. I wasn't sure what to say. It was so moving, and I couldn't find words that were important enough to express the fact.

"I needed it," Angel said, easing the tension in my muscles with a small smile. "That kind of unconditional compassion, the gentle touch to melt all the anger that had been eating me up inside since my parents were executed. I hated that he never got mad at me, but I realized it was because he understood how angry I was at the world."

"He sounds like such a great man, but I'm sure he was so worried. Things could've gone much worse. You could've been seriously hurt," I said, the reality finally catching up with me. "He let you off easy, considering you could've been trampled to death."

"I didn't go unpunished, Mouse," Angel laughed, the humor back in his expression now. "I told you he *rarely* raised a hand to me, not that he never did."

He reached across the table again to take my hands, letting out a deep sigh. Something told me that he'd never told anyone that story before. I was sure it was a secret between him and his grandfather, a vulnerable moment that only bonded them more.

"Why share that story now?" I asked, worrying as soon as I'd asked that he might think I didn't think it was important. I felt the blush creep into my face. "I just mean, it seems like it was such an important moment for you. It was really emotional, more than just me losing a couple of cheap golf balls."

He chuckled and leaned his elbows on the table. "You have shared your worst fears with me, opened your family to me, loved me when I have felt so undeserving of being loved ... I want to share the same with you."

I felt like I might cry for a moment. All the questions came flooding back and I wished more than anything that there had been cameras back then so I might see what baby Angel had looked like.

"Tell me more about your family. What were their names?" I asked.

My question had to wait so we could order lunch. He spent the entire time we waited on our food telling me about his parents, his grandfather, and his time living at this grandfather's estate. La Lanza de la Montaña. His mom was very different from most women during his time. She was smart, well-read, and lively in a way that garnered admiration and admonishment. Angel's dad doted on her, and their marriage was more like one from today than from fifteenth-century Spain. Angel's excitement dimmed as he talked about their relationship, and I could tell that the difference in their relationship had played some kind of part in their arrest and execution.

"I was fourteen or fifteen when I lost them," Angel said after our waiter had left our table. The food smelled wonderful, but I was so absorbed in his stories that I didn't pick up my fork right away. "It wasn't but a few months later that I stole my grandfather's horse. I know that their deaths were still fresh."

"I'm sorry," I told him.

He shrugged. "It was a long time ago. I'm thankful for what they taught me and for my grandfather. He'd been all alone before I came to live with him. We needed each other."

The seriousness of the conversation was broken when my stomach growled. He laughed as I lifted my fork, not realizing just how hungry I was until I'd taken my first bite of the chicken. I ate most of it before either of us spoke again.

"I've been in the States for well over a century," he said in amazement.

"You've never been back home?"

He shook his head. "Not since Maria's death. I didn't take a thing with me when I left. I started over, eventually immigrated here under a different name. I've had so many through the years …"

I lowered my fork to my empty plate. "Would you take me?"

"To Spain?"

"Yeah, to La Lanza de la Montaña," I said and straightened up. I couldn't believe my stomach wasn't bursting at the seams after the large meal.

The way Angel looked at me filled my stomach with butterflies. There was warmth in his eyes as he smiled. "I would love to take you. Soon."

"I'm holding you to that." I pointed a finger at his chest and he laughed, looking up as our waiter approached our table again. We paid for lunch and went back onto the street. A boutique at the end of the block had caught my attention before I felt my phone buzz in my pocket.

"Nova," I told Angel as I answered the call. "Hey! What's up?"

"I found it!" She said the words loud enough that I had to pull the phone away from my ear. "Come back to Night Owl and meet me in my apartment. I need that guardian blood."

She hung up before I could. It felt like I'd chugged a cup of coffee. My heart launched into a race, thoughts swirling so fast that it took a moment to find the right words as I turned to face Angel.

"Nova found the cure in the spellbook."

CHAPTER 21

Nova told us she only had to flip through two of Bebe's books to find the spell. It was just like Bebe said: the book was enchanted. When we arrived at her apartment, Nova had it opened on the living room coffee table, the page blank other than the cursive words *Vampire Cure* and a single sentence beneath.

Blood of power.

"Where's the blood?" Nova asked Angel.

Angel hesitated before withdrawing the vial from his pocket and handing it over. Nova sat it on the page along with the dagger and sucked in a deep breath.

"Bebe said you have to do a binding spell," Angel said, still anxiously eyeing the vial next to the dagger..

Nova nodded slowly, staring down at the items and chewing on her bottom lip. I was starting to worry that she couldn't do the spell based on how nervous she seemed, but she picked up the vial and looked at Angel before I could say anything.

"Do you trust me to do this?" she asked.

Angel looked conflicted but nodded. "Yes. I trust you."

"Okay," Nova said with a sigh. She pulled the stopper from the vial with a soft pop and emptied the contents onto the blade of the dagger, already murmuring a spell to herself. Angel's entire body had tensed, and I was frozen with anxiety. I willed the spell to work, watched with bated breath as the blood coating the dagger shimmered beneath the living room lights. Just as Nova stopped speaking, the blood vanished. The dagger was clean.

"Did it work?" I asked as Nova lifted the dagger from the page. She turned it between her fingers to inspect it, her smile widening.

"Yes," she said with a laugh of disbelief. "It worked! I did it!"

"The book," Angel said, staring at the page where a second sentence had appeared beneath the first.

Hand of the maker.

The maker. I looked at Angel whose expression was far from excited like Nova's. He just stared at the page, his eyes far away.

"It means the hand of the vampire who turned you, doesn't it?" I asked, looking at Nova when he didn't respond. Her smiled faded as she looked from me to Angel.

"Who turned you?" she asked him.

Angel looked up from the book. "Alonzo de Palencia."

His brother-in-law, the man who allowed Maria to find him as he was desecrating in the mausoleum.

"If Magdalena is here, then Alonzo probably is too," I said, remembering the three-fingered woman from the alley. Angel didn't look comforted by this. The opposite. He looked like he was piecing everything together, his expression only growing more concerned the longer the silence stretched.

"I can help. It's us against them," Nova said and motioned to each of us with an index finger. "One vampire, a witch, and a seer. Magic makes for a strong weapon, and there's the vampire's speed and strength. Maybe Lily can trigger her visions to prepare us better for a fight."

"My visions are so inconsistent, though. I'll need someone to teach me how to target them," I said.

Nova tugged on my shoulder. "I can help you. There has to be something in one of the spellbooks or even the archives that can teach us."

"Three vampires," Angel muttered.

"What?" I asked, turning away from Nova.

He exited his trance, adjusting on the couch beside me before deciding to stand up instead. He lifted a hand to the top of his head where he used to tie up his hair before he cut it short. He let his hand fall to his side. "There are three vampires. Magdalena and Alonzo are mates, so they won't go anywhere without the other. Francisco leads the group. Whatever they do will be approved by him first."

"Okay," Nova said slowly. "Then, we will plan for three."

"We only need Alonzo's hand, not to take down the entire trio. I can handle this alone," Angel said. His brief glance my way told me all I needed to know. He wasn't wrong. We didn't have to plan a whole war, but attacking just Alonzo didn't seem like an act that would go unpunished. It didn't matter if we attacked just one or all of them, it would be like a declaration of war regardless. All he was doing was trying to prevent the inevitable. I would eventually be dragged into the fight one way or another. He couldn't protect me forever.

"We'll have to face them all anyway," I said, preparing for his retort. "How about we gather information on them for now while I learn how to target my visions. Who knows? Maybe I can get good enough and we can anticipate their moves before they make them."

"I don't like it," Angel said.

"It doesn't matter," I said, my stomach doing a flip when I saw the surprise cross his face. My entire body felt alight with pride for speaking up. I felt good about the plan and no one else had suggested anything better. "I need to get a grip on my abilities anyway. These vampires are here, and Magdalena made it clear that they want to get to you, no matter who they have to go through." I crossed my arms when I looked at him, determined to hold my ground despite the firm look he shot me.

It was a reminder. I could practically hear him talking about our one rule, my promise not to take unnecessary risks. That's where I had him though—this was very necessary and if I didn't do something, I was sure I would only be more of a liability.

Nova cleared her throat and stood up. "I'm going to put the rest of these books in the trunk and go to the bathroom. So, um, you two just talk it out. I'm good for whatever."

Heat rushed to my face when she sent me a knowing look from the doorway of her bedroom. Her arms were stuffed with the spellbooks, so she used her foot to close the door behind her. Angel didn't hesitate to voice his concerns.

"I don't want you in the middle of a fight," he said.

"Magdalena already told me I was. It doesn't matter. I promised that I wouldn't take any unnecessary risks, but I will do what I have to to protect myself and you and Nova. I can do that by learning how to control my visions and using them against our enemies," I told him, moving my hand from the couch cushion to my lap when he tried to take it. I knew what he was doing. I always melted at his touch, the way those dark eyes looked at me with longing now ...

"You're right and I agree with you. I just don't want you involved when it comes time to fight," he said, scooting closer. I should've, but I couldn't bring myself to move away. God, he made it so difficult to resist him. I could see the acknowledgment in his eyes too.

"I won't just take a knee, Angel," I said, not sounding nearly as assertive as before.

"And picking a fight with a bunch of vampires will earn you a trip across mine," he said, his tone firm despite the gentle brush of his thumb along my cheek.

"Picking fights with vampires and protecting myself from them are two different things," I said, playfully poking his chest. "So, put away that palm of yours because I'm not putting myself in any danger. I'm protecting all of us from it. Maybe I can use my vision to *prevent* a fight. How about that?"

"Sounds like you're getting caught up in semantics," he said, tugging on my lower lip with the pad of his thumb. I pulled his hand away, thwarting his attempts at distraction, and he smirked.

"Yeah, well, I pay close attention when the subjects of semantics and red handprints are brought up."

"Keep up the sassy attitude and you'll be well-educated on one of those subjects, Mouse," he laughed. I reached out to shove his chest, but he caught my hands before I could touch him. He kissed the back of my right hand and gave a deep sigh. "You're right, though. Protecting you is why I gave you that necklace; you should know how to protect yourself."

"And you," I added.

"And me," he said, squeezing my hands gently. "I think it's a good plan, but leave the fighting to Nova and me. Be our eyes. Tell us what you see. Keep us from walking into trouble."

I nodded. "Maybe I can get good enough to see where all the items are for the cure." I hoped he would be mortal soon, and we could move on from all this supernatural danger. I had leaned in to kiss him when I heard the door open. Angel and I straightened up as Nova returned from the bedroom, sending an apologetic look my way.

"So, do we like the plan or is there a new idea?" she asked.

"We like the plan," Angel answered. "Lily works on her seer abilities. I'll see what I can find out about Alonzo and how to get his hand."

"I'll be ready to do the binding spell once you do," Nova nodded. She looked excitedly at me. "I think we should talk to Bebe."

I didn't argue. Bebe said she'd met a seer before. It was clear she was the strongest and most knowledgeable witch in the entire coven. If anyone knew where to start, it was Beatrice Laveau. I only hoped she could remember.

My eyes flew open with my gasp. I was twisted in the sheets and when I rolled to my left to wrap my arms around him, I remembered that Angel had left. It was just another vision. Nothing new, but I remembered more of the details.

There was the dark figure at the end of the hallway, the flash of silver at his hip. I knew it wasn't Magdalena because I remembered the black gloves. Leather gloves. Ten fingers. Already, I was struggling to recall the vision, pushing against the protective part of my brain that was fighting to shove the images away. The dark man stood at the end of the hall. He ran at me and as I remembered him raising that silver object, I realized he was holding a cane. I thought he'd wrapped his arms around me from behind, but no. It was his cane that pulled me flush against his chest.

The vision had lasted just seconds before I fell back into the usual nightmare, and it was Paul Saxon restraining me, whispering in my ear, my skin crawling from his touch ...

"Lily."

I raised my hands in defense before I realized it was just Angel. He was still dressed in a T-shirt and jeans, hesitating before he sat down on the bed and pulled me into his lap. I took deep breaths, focusing on matching the pattern of gentle circles he traced on the back of my hand.

"Another nightmare?" he asked.

"A vision," I told him, feeling him tense beneath me. "A man with a cane."

"A cane?" he asked.

I raised my head from his chest to look at him. I recognized that look. "It was a black cane with a silver knob on top."

He nodded slowly. "That's got to be Francisco de Palencia.

He used a cane before he turned. I bet he still carries one with him."

I didn't tell him about the way he'd attacked me in the vision. It hadn't been long at all. Chances were that if I'd seen the entire event, Angel would've been there to fight him off. The hall we were in was dark. It was impossible to know where we were.

"Did you feed?" I asked, hoping it would distract him. It worked, thankfully, and he stood up and began undressing.

"Yes," he said and tossed his shirt onto the foot of the bed. "I was as quick as I could be. I know that your visions and nightmares are more likely to come when you're alone."

It was true. I hadn't had a vision since we moved into the apartment. The nightmares had gone away when he came back from his first trip. He slipped out of his jeans and threw them to the end of the bed where they landed on his shirt before sliding off the comforter and onto the floor. He didn't bother picking them up, but sat on the bed next to me. I scooted back to my side so he could slide beneath the sheets.

"I think I'll feel better after my first lesson with Bebe," I said and snuggled to his side.

"I'm sure you will," Angel said and kissed the top of my head. "I know I will."

My heart rate had finally evened out and as the panic receded, exhaustion set in like it usually did after a vision or a panic attack. I melted against Angel's bare skin, already feeling the heaviness tug on my eyelids.

"Sleep, Mouse," he said and began brushing my hand with his fingers. "I won't let anything hurt you."

I let my eyes close and slipped into a dreamless sleep.

CHAPTER 22

"Are you sure I can't help?" I asked from the floral-printed couch in the living room. The apartments were all mostly the same, though Beatrice Laveau's unit was slightly larger. The layout was the same as ours, but she had a bigger kitchen and a living room large enough to fit a small dining table that overlooked the back patio. You could see the twinkling lights from Bourbon Street and I could only imagine what firework displays looked like from that window.

"Tea is a tried-and-true method," Bebe said from the stove, her hand shaking as she poured from the tea kettle. She filled two teacups on little saucers before setting the kettle aside. I couldn't stand it anymore. I stood up from my seat when she started to carry the tea across the kitchen, the cups rattling against the saucers as her hands shook.

"Thank you," I told her and took both cups. Luckily, she didn't protest and allowed me to carry the cups to the table. "I'm not much of a tea drinker, but I've never tried ..."

"Darjeeling tea," Bebe said, motioning for me to take a seat at the table. She took the seat at the head and I sat next to her, pulling my saucer closer and looking down at the loose-leaf tea.

"I thought you said it was tasseography," I said, finally remembering the word she'd used earlier. I'd barely taken two steps into her apartment and she started telling me her plans for our afternoon. At first, we were talking about tea and basic divination, which immediately went right over my head, and then she was on a random tangent about how she always made cinnamon chicken for Thanksgiving. Her daughter was bringing home a boy one year and instead of hearing that he was allergic to cinnamon when Jackie told her about him on the phone, she thought she had said that he loved cinnamon chicken. Bebe didn't like the guy from the jump and Jackie broke up with him in the middle of Thanksgiving dinner after one of their guests punched him in the nose for being rude to her. The man who threw the punch ended up marrying Jackie and a year later Nova was born. They ate cinnamon chicken for Thanksgiving ever since.

I knew that Jackie had died from cancer. Neither Nova nor Bebe had ever mentioned a man. I almost asked what happened to him, but by that point, Bebe remembered why I was sitting in her living room and finished preparing our tea.

"Tasseography is what we are *doing* with the tea, honey," Bebe said and sat back in her chair. She lifted her cup to her lips and took a sip, her entire body relaxing afterward.

I lifted the cup to my mouth, hoping I liked it. I wasn't sure what I'd do if I didn't. I could drink it, but what if it was so bad that it made me cough or gag? Thankfully, that wasn't the case. The tea was similar to coffee, but it had a slight fruity taste. After taking a second sip, I decided that I liked it, and I made sure to file the name away so I could add it to my grocery list.

"What is tasseography?" I asked, taking another sip before lowering the cup back to the saucer.

Bebe acted like I'd pulled her out of her thoughts, adjusting in her seat and looking over me for a moment like she didn't remember exactly who I was. I almost reminded her of my name before she spoke.

"It's the practice of reading tea leaves," she said as if it was obvious.

"Oh. So, um, how do you read the leaves?" I asked, looking down at my cup and focusing on the hunks of herbs swirling in the dark liquid.

"You drink the tea," Bebe said with a laugh.

I looked up at her amused expression. "That's all? You just drink the tea and interpret the shapes left at the bottom?"

Bebe only smiled wider. "Well, you have to focus on your intentions while you drink. You can't just talk about the usual gossip with your girlfriends or read a romance novel on the couch. The point is ..." She motioned toward me to finish.

"See the future?" I asked, hoping the obvious answer was correct. Thankfully, she nodded and raised her cup to her lips again. "So, I just think about the future?"

"Well, being a seer, the leaves will come together more easily for you. Seeing is a natural ability for you. Our goal is to involve you more in the practice so you can take control of your abilities rather than allow them to butt in whenever they feel like it."

That was one way of putting it.

"I don't mean to be skeptical or question you," I said, choosing my words carefully. "I know you have a lot of experience and you're well-read, you've traveled a lot, you are very good at what you do, you're the strongest witch in the entire coven—"

"Skip to the but, honey," Bebe said and waved her hands in dismissal.

Here I was, letting my anxiety get the best of me again. I took a deep breath. "Tasseography is a whole practice. I guess, I don't totally understand how this will allow me to control my visions."

Bebe smiled. It was like she knew I'd ask that very question. "Tasseography will teach you to focus your thoughts on what you desire, what you anticipate, and to be open to the truth. It's important to envision what we want from the future, but it is equally as important to keep your mind open to interpreting what is. When we train our mind to fully picture what we manifest, when we open our mind's eye to a complete vision of the future, what we see often becomes our reality. When it takes a shape of its own however—"

"Are you saying that anticipating what I believe is the future can trigger a vision of the truth?" I asked. Bebe was silent. She was statue-like and I worried for a moment that she'd fallen into one of her episodes. After a long moment, she picked up her cup and took a drink. When she lowered it, she looked up at me.

"I've only ever met one seer before you," she said, pointing at me. "She told me once that when she felt she had brain fog she would make herself a cup of tea and it would center her."

My stomach sank. So this entire thing was a shot in the dark, something she'd heard someone say once the way my mom might call me in a panic about something she saw on Facebook. I looked down at my cup and tried not to let the cynicism sneak into the front of my mind.

Beatrice Laveau was the most highly respected witch in the coven. She was powerful, even for an old lady with dementia. Her power still dwarfed the rest of the coven's and despite confusing Nova with her daughter, she still spoke with authority that held true. I watched as the tea leaves swirled around in my cup, wondering if there was any way they could form a shape of importance and not just one of chance.

"Take a drink," Bebe said, pulling my attention back on her. "Think about the future."

I exhaled and raised the cup to my lips. I took a long drink before looking down at the small amount of liquid remaining. There was maybe a mouthful left and still the tea leaves looks like nothing but floating hunks in the dark water.

"I'm focused on what I want," I said, looking up at her when I realized how bitter I sounded. She didn't flinch. She looked almost amazed instead, like a thought had just occurred to her.

"No," she said and laughed. "What do you *need*?"

I looked down again. What did I need? God, there was so much. I needed to get a grip. I needed to find control that was outside Angel, outside his tight embrace and the comfort of his rules. It was so easy to explore that when I felt safe with him, when I knew that he wouldn't judge me or shoot down my ideas. I wanted a future with him, to be married to him, to start a life with him that included a career for myself. I liked being in charge of that. I loved that I could create what I wanted for my YouTube channel, write the music that called to me ... Yes, it was a risk, but it didn't feel like the same as the risks that I was used to. It didn't feel the same as telling my parents about my YouTube channel, or worrying about failing as a musician had felt at NYU. Somehow, those risks felt only like an opportunities. I was good at what I did, I knew that. Every teacher I'd ever had told me that I had a great future ahead of me in music. I knew what I was doing as a musician, and I ached for a life where my time outside of Angel was consumed by possibility.

"Drink," Bebe said, reaching over to slide the cup closer to me.

I lifted the cup and drank the last of the liquid, draining it like I had those shots with Nova at the coven soirée, chasing away every last fear about doing tasseography right. I sat the cup back on the saucer and let out a deep breath. I waited while Bebe finished her tea and I watched as she looked into her cup. She let out a hum of surprise and turned the cup on the saucer, taking in the tea leaves left behind.

"I've never been one to dwell on the future," she shrugged and sat back in her chair. "I like to live in the moment."

"What did you see?" I asked her. It was only fair. If she thought this whole lesson was going to benefit me, then it only made sense for her to take it seriously. Yet, here she was shrugging at her own cup the way someone might toss aside the paper fortune from a to-go order of ramen.

"Looks like a heart to me," she said and tipped the cup so I could see. Sure enough, the tea leaves had gathered at the bottom of the porcelain to form what looked like a heart. I thought about what it might look like from another angle, but still ... The closest thing I could associate to the leaves was a heart.

"And yours, honey?"

I looked down at my own cup after she spoke. The leaves looked like a scattered mess at first, but pictures began to form in my head, and I tried to keep an open mind and let them come. It was the same vision I'd had when Angel and I first walked the French Quarter. At least, part of it was. I saw Nova holding a camera in front of me, my cello positioned between my legs as I drew the bow across the strings. No. It wasn't my cello. I could sense the slight difference, and there was a mirror in the vision. This time, I could see myself in the reflection in a way I hadn't been able to the first time. I was wearing the Venetian mask I'd bought just a week ago, the silver one, and the rest of me was draped in black like the Grim Reaper.

"What do you see?" Bebe asked again, pulling me from my thoughts. I looked at the bottom of my teacup where all the tea leaves had bunched together. I turned the cup a full circle as I tried to work out what it looked like, the closest I could figure being a map.

"I don't know. It looks like something from the globe," I said as I turned the cup back to its starting position. "I don't know. France? It kind of looks like France?"

Bebe laughed, and that quickly became a cough. I stood up, not really sure what kind of help I could provide. She raised a hand for me to wait, clearing her throat for a final time before lowering her hand and turning in her chair to face me.

"Maybe I'm not ready for this," I said and collected both our cups and saucers from the table. I'd no sooner reached the kitchen than she spoke again.

"There's more meaning to the little things than you think, especially where a seer is concerned," Bebe said.

I set the cups in the sink, pausing a moment before I turned on the faucet and began to rinse the cups. I watched as the tea leaves swirled down the drain, trying not to make too much out of the shapes they formed. I turned from the sink to face her. Bebe had joined me in the kitchen, her arm resting on the countertop.

"What was that seer you met like?" I asked, the words bursting from my lips before I had fully allowed them. I'd been curious from the moment she'd told me she'd known a seer. The way everyone talked, seers were rare. It didn't seem likely that I'd happen upon one. After I'd said the words, it was hard not to think about the intention behind them. Part of me wondered if all the anxiety, the constant feeling of being on edge, was just a part of being a seer.

The humor had faded from Bebe's expression. It was the most serious I'd ever seen her. I was very aware of how close to the front door I was now, where my purse was, the coolness that seemed to settle over the room ...

"He told me that I would lose my daughter. He said I would grow close to my granddaughter only for her to leave, and I would die alone, not because I was unloved, but because I wouldn't recognize those who stood around me in the end," she said. She stared blankly at me for a moment, the room so uncomfortably silent that I could barely stand it before she gave a hum of consideration. "We all die. Whether I remember or not, I know I am surrounded by love. I know because I feel it, even when I don't fully remember the details, I feel that I'm loved, and I know that I have loved deeply. There's nothing else that matters."

I stood like I was made of stone as she gave a shrug and rounded the countertop to join me in the kitchen. She went to the fridge, opening it and pulling down a container that she handed to me before she pulled out a bag of lettuce.

"Pop that in the microwave, Jackie," she told me before going to the cabinets to pull out a plate. I watched for a moment as she covered the plate in a layer of lettuce, then looking down at the container to make sure it went with whatever salad she envisioned. After confirming the meal, I set the container in the microwave and watched as it spun around the plate inside the machine, part of me unwilling to leave even after Bebe led me to her door and wished me a good evening. I stood in the hallway a moment before I could muster the courage to go back to my apartment, glad that Angel didn't ask too many questions about how my lesson had gone.

CHAPTER 23

I met with Bebe every afternoon that week and thankfully, those lessons were more productive than that first one. I couldn't explain it, but by our third meeting, I felt more in control of myself and my visions. The lessons were strange, going from the tea leaf interpretation to meditations, but I somehow felt more confident in my abilities, and I'd already been able to see more of my visions whenever they returned, despite still not fully understanding how to trigger them.

I'd had a vision of Francisco de Palencia in a restaurant, and Angel had done enough research at that point to figure out where they were currently staying. It was close enough to Night Owl Apartments that he got nervous, and we spent the next few nights cooking our own meals in the apartment. It wasn't until I caught Nova bringing groceries to our door that I realized what he'd learned.

"You had a vision of Francisco attacking you," Angel said as he unpacked the groceries. "You haven't seen anything since, let alone seen any more of that vision. I don't mean to be ..."

He turned from the cabinet, his expression telling me he wanted to reach for me, despite waiting for my response.

"I know," I told him, raising my arms to accept his embrace. He didn't move at first, but he finally let out a deep breath and straightened up. I wrapped my arms around his middle and he kissed the top of my head. "You're worried."

"I tend to be a bit too overprotective these days," he muttered.

My mind went to the fear I saw in his eyes months ago when we were trapped in the wine cellar at the Saxon's estate. He'd been so afraid of feeding from me, and aside from telling me he never would again, it was the one thing that happened that night that I knew was still too painful for him to discuss. Having heard the story twice now, I knew how much he was afraid of the same thing happening to me that had happened to Maria.

"I understand," I said and pulled back just far enough to look up at him. My heart leaped in my chest, like a frantic bird in a cage, and I wasn't sure I wanted to open the door. Despite the hammering of my heart and the slightly sick feeling at the memory, I felt that it needed to be said. "And I agreed to your rule because I know why it's important to you. They say that time heals all wounds, but I think empathy is the only thing that can keep them from scarring. You may be a little overprotective sometimes. I know why. It's the same reason you know to take my hand, brush your knee against mine, or take control when I'm anxious. Having you set a firm structure is like building walls of stone around me when the previous ones before were made of glass. It's out of sight, out of mind for me. I understand that your rule about safety and the way you are gentler with me when you've gone a while without feeding is not just to protect me but to ease your own fears. Your trauma is just as valid as mine."

He looked more somber than before and his arms around me loosened. "Lily, I don't want you to feel—" He took a moment to think, moving his hand from around me so that they rested at my hips. "I don't want to be so careful that you never chase after your dreams or never live the life you deserve."

"You won't be. You aren't. I don't see it that way. It's the opposite to me, actually," I told him and cupped his face in my hands, waiting until his eyes were on mine. That bird was fluttering around in my chest again, making me nervous. "I told you when I was in the hospital that things with you feel like a controlled release. I still feel that way, especially now that you've let down your walls more. I want to be less anxious, and I'm working on it, but when we are alone—"

God, you'd think I wouldn't blush so much after everything we'd done together.

"You are my safe place to let go, to be a version of myself I want to be but am just not ready to be yet, and to reclaim a part of myself I felt like someone else stole. When you are that dominant, vampire version with me, it makes me feel supported in figuring out how to move on from my past. When you stand behind me, especially when you put your arms around me, I don't think about Paul attacking me in the vineyard first anymore. I think about you and how good it feels and the way you smell."

"I would never hurt you, Mouse," Angel said, taking my hands from his face. I nearly put them back when he kissed my knuckles, his subtle way of transitioning to another subject. Even when he shared his past with me and his thoughts, parts of them remained buried. He didn't want to dive deeper and for the longest time I just assumed he wasn't ready. Now, after hearing him talk about Maria and how easily it was for him to slip into that dominant role when we were alone, I wondered if maybe he felt the same in his own way.

"Submitting to you doesn't just make me feel safe. It makes me feel powerful," I said, freeing my right hand from his so I could brush his cheek. His eyes flicked to mine and I felt like I could see centuries there in their warm depths. His jaw tightened beneath my fingers, but his eyes remained soft, almost pleading, like they were asking me to let the pieces fall into place. It silenced the racing of my heart and only made me more confident in what I had assumed all along.

"I think being in charge and setting rules, gives you a sense of control over your life that you haven't felt in a very long time. I think it makes you feel safe to know that I'm yours, to know that you have my submission, to protect me the way you couldn't protect Maria and your parents, maybe even yourself. I think it's a controlled release for you the same way it is for me, like our own version of therapy. Maybe that's fucked up to say but ..." I stopped when something on his cheek caught my eye. The tear slid down his cheek and I brushed it away before it could go far. He'd managed to contain the rest by the time he pulled me closer by my hips, shaking his head.

"It's only fucked up if you don't want it, Mouse," he said softly. "Tell me what you want, and you'll have it. I want to give you everything. Just tell me."

"I want a reminder," I said, feeling everything inside speed up again.

"A reminder of what?"

"That I'm yours," I said, watching the realization set in on his face.

"Want or need, Mouse?"

I stepped away from him, looking back at him to make sure he would follow me toward the living room. He did, standing taller somehow and looking more intimidating than usual. It made my stomach clench in that delicious way. I nearly fell over the arm of the couch as I stared at him.

He grabbed my arm to steady me. "Want or need, Mouse?"

"I think you need it more than me," I said.

He smirked. "I think the opposite. I think you need a lecture, and I want to give it to you."

I sank onto the armrest before his hand could slink around my hip to cup my ass. "Not a lecture. Just a reminder." I held up my right hand to show him my index and thumb. There was a difference.

"You and your semantics," he teased, tickling my side. I couldn't help but react, allowing him to pull me closer by my arm and slap my ass.

"Ouch!" Before I could reach back to cover my butt, I was distracted. Angel pressed his lips to my throat, leaving a trail of kisses up to my ear.

"Even good girls need a little discipline," he said. "How should I punish you, Mouse?"

I leaned against his chest. He gathered my hair at the base of my head in one hand, the other sneaking under the hem of my skirt. He palmed me through my underwear, teasing me with gentle pressure.

"I could tease you, bring you close to release over and over until you're begging me for it," he said in my ear. Finally, his finger slipped past my underwear, grazing just softly enough to leave me wanting more. I realized just how much of a punishment it would be. The words were already on my lips, my plea barely whispered, when the front door burst open.

"I thought I'd help and bring in the groceries since I was coming over anyway," Nova said with a shrug. She was clueless about what was happening seconds before. My thong was barely on my hips now. I had to wait until she looked away from us to set the grocery bag down to tug on the straps through the fabric of my dress.

"I thought we got it all," Angel told her, squeezing my butt as he passed.

Nova looked up from the plastic bag as she began unpacking the fruit. "No. This was still sitting in the hallway."

"Must've missed it," Angel said, looking back at me just so he could flash an onery smile. He mouthed the word *later* before turning back to the counter to help put away the produce.

I joined them once I felt less flushed. "I'm ready to start when you are."

"Same. Is it okay if we use your apartment today?" Nova looked from me to Angel.

"Sure. You might want to take the bedroom, though. I was going to start on dinner. You can stay, if you'd like," he said as he pulled a package of chicken from the fridge and sat it on the counter. When Nova sent me a questioning look, I let go of the last of our private moment to fully transition into our lesson. We'd been working hard and I was getting much better at controlling my visions. I rarely had them overnight like before, which meant I was sleeping much better.

"Yeah. You should stay," I said and pulled on her arm as I backed toward the bedroom. "Angel may not need to eat as a vampire, but he's the best cook. You don't want to miss it."

Angel looked up from the cutting board to smile. "Centuries of practice has given me a lot of secret recipes." He winked.

"Yeah, well, just you wait," I said and pointed a playful finger at him. "If I get good enough as a seer, you won't be able to keep those secrets anymore."

His smile dimmed and that boyish light in his eyes was suddenly gone. It made my stomach drop; made me suddenly very anxious.

"I found something in one of the spellbooks that I think you should try," Nova said, pulling my arm and forcing me to look at her. When I glanced back at Angel, he was too busy prepping the meal to notice me. I joined Nova in the bedroom, shutting the door behind us as she sat on the bed with her phone in her hand.

Nova found a strategy in the spellbook that was a mix of meditation and hypnosis. I was still anxious enough from the look I'd seen on Angel's face in the kitchen that it took me a moment to get focused. It was a strange feeling once I fell into that space between the present and an unknown future. It physically felt a little like floating in a pool. Sometimes, the waves pulled me in one direction.

The lesson, as Nova explained it to me, was deciding when to go with that feeling and when to redirect. It was a learning curve for sure, but as I focused, I started to notice the subtle difference between distractions and the visions. They didn't always start as visions, rarely so. Usually, they came on just like any passing thought, but as I allowed my mind to relax, it was like another door opened in my head and allowed me inside a new scene.

"What did you see this time?" Nova asked when I opened my eyes and rubbed my temples. I was starting to get a headache from the effort, which we learned was when it was time to call it quits for the day. The more I practiced, the longer I could go before the ache would set in.

"You, Angel, and me," I told her and accepted the Advil when she handed it to me. "I think we were in an airport."

"I hope it means there's a vacation in our future. I haven't had one of those in years," she said.

I swallowed the pill along with half my glass of water. I hated how tired using my sight made me. If I wasn't so hungry, I would have curled up on the bed and taken a nap.

"Smells like he's making something spicy," Nova said, looking to the closed bedroom door.

"I think he said something about chicken and dirty rice," I said as I stood up. Nova followed me back into the living room. Sure enough, Angel was finishing piling dirty rice onto our plates on the counter. We climbed onto the bar stools across from him as he finished and turned his attention to the dirty dishes in the sink.

"Thanks for dinner," Nova said, looking at each of us in turn before taking a bite of chicken.

"You're always welcome with us," I said, Angel nodding in agreement. I could tell he was only half-listening. His eyes looked far away as he started to scrub a pot. I forced myself to take a bite of rice despite the twisting in my stomach. The spice from the meal eased my discomfort a little.

"How was the lesson?" Angel finally asked, glancing up at me for just a moment before he continued washing the dishes. I was sure it was all a distraction now. We had a small dishwasher in the apartment, so he didn't need to wash the utensils at the bottom of the sink. But there he was, scrubbing a fork with enough care that you'd have thought it was crusted over with grease.

"Um, good," I said, pausing before I took another bite of rice.

"She's getting really good," Nova corrected, already finished with the chicken on her plate. "She sees something new every time now."

"Not very much," I said, watching Angel in case that nervous look crossed his face again. It didn't. He looked relieved. "I see stuff, but I don't get any of the context."

"Maybe you will with more practice," he said.

I shrugged. "Maybe. There's no way to get all the context though. It's the future, you know? There's a number of things that could be different that I'm not seeing in my visions."

"Well, you're sleeping better and you're less anxious," Angel said with an encouraging smile. "That's better."

"Yeah. Better," I said and tried a bite of the chicken. He was right about things being better. I felt less like a ship at sea and more like a dinghy tethered to the dock. The waves still tossed me around, but I wasn't going to be taken out to sea without any direction. It was a relief that was difficult to feel at the moment; Angel's nervous expression was the only thing I could think about.

Nova ate a second helping of rice and the last of my chicken, staying just long enough to make plans with us for brunch tomorrow before she went to her apartment next door. Angel locked the front door as I started putting away all the dishes from the drying rack. He didn't speak while I worked, but the glances he cast my way told me enough. There was something on his mind and he was preparing to tell me.

The pressure in my chest grew as I continued to work. Usually, keeping my hands busy took a little bit of the edge off the anxiety so I could think more rationally. This time, it only allowed me to stew on what he had to say. So much so, that when I turned toward the drying rack to find it empty, I looked directly at him next. I opened my mouth to ask what had him so worked up, but he spoke before I got the chance.

"I'm going to feed."

I froze for a second. Angel's shoulders heaved with his sigh and he looked much more relaxed than before. He always got a little nervous when he had to leave me to feed, but there was something different in the air between us. His eyes were still a soft brown, not the usual darkness there that came the longer he went between feedings.

"It hasn't been that long since you went out," I said.

He nodded. "I know. I want to keep sharp though, and I have

one more target on my list. I don't like letting those guys go when they plan to hurt someone. If I can prevent more harm, I'd like to."

"And?" I asked. I could tell there was more. He knew that I could, smiling in response.

"And we could face the other vampires any day." He rounded the counter and leaned in to kiss me. He pulled back just far enough to flash that onery grin that made my stomach clench. "And I can do that thing you like in bed."

I slapped his chest with both hands. "You're so bad."

"I know exactly where I'm headed, so I won't be long."

He kissed me again before taking the apartment key from the counter and heading into the hall. I heard the lock click in the silence and instead of pulling out my laptop to work on things for Wilted Rose Strings, I climbed into our bed.

CHAPTER 24

Every nerve in my body was alight as I flew from bed, nearly tripping over the sheets to reach the front door of the apartment and whoever was banging against it. I threw it open before even thinking about checking the peephole. Nova was still dressed in her pajamas, a frantic look of her face.

"We have to go!"

"Nova, what's wrong?"

"Now!"

I felt sick as she pulled me into the hallway. I had enough time to close the door before she towed me toward the elevator. The doors immediately slid apart, and I was sure I'd heard her sigh in relief as we stepped inside.

"What's going on?" I asked, catching sight of my disheveled reflection in the mirrored wall.

"I don't know. I'm supposed to bring you the ballroom," she said, shifting from one foot to the other as the floors were counted down on the screen above us. "Poppy. The Coven Council is meeting."

"Right now?" I asked, remembering that I left my phone behind now that I needed it to check the time. It had to be late. I felt like I was deep asleep when Nova banged on my door. I was still struggling to understand exactly what she meant. "There's a council meeting right now?

"Yes, and I was told to come and get you. They need you specifically."

Me? My blood cooled. Angel was still gone on his hunt and Nova didn't seem at all surprised by that. She hadn't asked about him or looked for him. This meeting was about him, a follow-up to the last one. Either someone had changed their mind, or the council had new concerns.

The elevator doors slid apart, and I followed Nova into the lobby as I tried to calm my nerves. My fingers went to the blood necklace at my neck, turning the pendant between my fingers as we walked. She pushed the door open and strode straight into the room. I stopped just inside the room. It was so quiet that I could hear the door close softly behind me.

I almost threw up at the sight of them.

The twelve elders were seated behind that long table on either side of Bebe in her throne. It was like a witchy version of *The Last Supper.* The more I looked at the council members, the more I realized they too had been woken in the middle of the night. The women were all dressed for the day, but none of them wore any makeup. The woman who appeared closest in age to Bebe still wore her silk bonnet from the night. The man sitting beside her, who looked ready for an argument, was dressed in a pair of slacks and wore a blazer over what appeared to be a button-up pajama top. He only seemed to get more agitated when he noticed me staring and turned suddenly in his seat to look down the table.

"All right, Mrs. Nolan," he said and tapped the table in front of him twice before he gestured to me. "You got the lady. You got all of us here. We started the record. Please tell us why it was so important to have this meeting now and not in the morning."

Poppy turned away from him with a scoff, a dark smile growing when she looked at me. "I've been keeping track of our resident vampire, and I needed him gone to hold this meeting."

"We've already addressed this issue," Bebe said, getting murmurs of agreement from a few men and women around her.

Poppy groaned and stood from her chair. "He's been hunting more often." She rounded the end of the table and stopped in the space between the council and Nova and me. She raised her hands as though preparing to address the room, turning from the table to face us again.

"Angel only feeds on the worst kinds of people, people who routinely harm others," I said, looking past Poppy at Bebe. She looked just as annoyed to be there as the rest of the room.

Poppy shook her head. "Vampires are opportunists."

"Angel has a tracking system. He hunts strategically. He never attacks just anyone," I said.

"He's still a vampire, and he kills to survive!"

"Mrs. Nolan," the man said, his voice booming across the room. He sucked in a deep breath, pressing his fingers to the bridge of his nose. He looked calmer when he lowered them. "This is the exact argument we had the last time. If you woke us all up for another rendition of your vendetta against this young couple, then—"

"Then what, James?" Poppy asked, folding her arms.

"That's Mr. Hebert to you," he said, pointed at her.

"Can we move on? I've had enough of the two of you," a woman at the end of the table said. Mr. James Hebert sat back in his seat, but Poppy wasn't giving up.

"I think I'd like to hear the rest of your threat, Mr. Hebert."

Several elders groaned. Mr. Hebert held up his hands in resignation. It was clear from the way they all shifted in their seats, making themselves more comfortable, that this was a hole that went deep, and it would take a long time to climb back out.

"Angel left several hours ago to hunt. You knew that, Poppy. Why did you know that?" I asked.

Thankfully, she turned her focus on me. It sent a pit into my gut, but I was tired, and the anxiety of standing in front of them all like I was on trial was enough to force the words from my mouth.

"I told you that I've been paying attention," she laughed. "I saw him leave."

"You said that, but you also said he's been hunting more often. How could you know that's what he's doing when he leaves ... unless you are following him?"

The room went quiet. The elders watched us carefully now, not a disgruntled look on a single one of their tired faces. Poppy's smile grew wider, and she clapped her hands together, keeping them just beneath her chin, as though in prayer.

"Smart girl," she said with a laugh. "I mean that. I do believe you are very smart, but it's a shame that you are letting your emotions blind you to the manipulation of that vampire."

"He's not manipulating me," I said.

"Poppy, I know that you don't like me, but don't harass my friends just to get back at my family. Please," Nova said and stepped away from me so that she stood between me and Poppy. "We've already been through this. We've done the research on Lily and Angel. My grandmother and I are helping them and that's the only reason they are here, for our help."

"You're enabling and you are endangering this entire coven."

"We aren't! Lily has no one to help her control her sight. Angel is an old friend of my grandmother's and all he wants is to be mortal again. He's here because there is a cure for vampirism and we've already started the process for him. If you would just leave all of this alone—"

"It's a good thing I didn't," Poppy interjected, turning toward the table as she continued. "I've been following the vampire since we last talked about him. He has been hunting more often. It's difficult to follow vampires during those times, because they are fast. They are good at vanishing into the shadows, but the last time he left I was able to track him to a warehouse. I stayed until he left again and once he did, I entered the warehouse, and I think what I found will change your perspective."

There was a beat of silence. I was sure that my heart stopped as Poppy walked to the double doors on the right of the ballroom. She pulled one open and stepped aside so Olivia Saxon could walk in. My stomach twisted and I could taste the bile at the back of my throat as she walked toward me, flashing that wry smile that still haunted my dreams.

"This is Olivia Saxon. I think you two have history, don't you?" Poppy asked me, stopping next to Olivia.

"Yes," I said in barely more than a whisper.

"We were neighbors. I watched Lily grow up," Olivia said, glancing back at the elders, who all exchanged looks of confusion. Bebe stared straight at Poppy. I'd never seen her look so serious. My vision swam as the tears burned my eyes. This wasn't possible—the Saxons were dead. Angel said he dropped them through a gate to the Shadowlands. He said they would never hurt me again. How did Olivia get here?

"When I went into that warehouse, I found Olivia chained in the middle of a room. She was terrified. She told me that Angel Ramírez had captured her and her brother and has been holding them captive for over a month," Poppy said.

Olivia brushed away the tears that silently fell on her cheeks before she spoke. "He wanted revenge. We all had a fight months ago. My brother's jealousy got the best of him, and he did some horrible things to poor Lily," she said, pausing to take a couple of calming breaths. "Angel kept us chained, suspended in that warehouse. I watched him cut into my brother with all kinds of weapons, even his own teeth ..."

I shuddered. I remembered the way Angel had landed on Paul's shoulders in that field behind the estate. There was no forgetting the way he ripped Paul's head from his shoulders and tossed it into the grass. Paul was a guardian, so even such a violent attack wasn't fatal for him. It still shook me to my core. So even though I knew Olivia wasn't as upset as the tears suggested, I knew she was telling the truth.

I believed her when she said that Angel had tortured Paul. While part of me felt a little closure from knowing he suffered just as I had after he'd attacked me in the vineyard, the thought of Angel as torturer and executor struck me hard with such sadness. He told me since the beginning that he was a monster and I always reminded him how he wasn't. He fought against his urges and only fed on serial killers and rapists. I knew he was capable of dark things for the simple reason that it was within his vampire nature.

"He tossed you both in a gate to the Shadowlands," I said, folding my arms across my chest to stop the fidgeting. "How are you here?"

"He tossed Paul in the gate," she corrected. "He had other plans for me."

It was a slap, and she knew it. Poppy knew it. I could tell from the shocked expressions of the elders that the entire room knew I had been betrayed because I could never keep a straight face, and this hurt.

"What plans?" I asked, my voice shaking.

She shook her head in disbelief. "He's kept me chained in that warehouse. He never went on any hunts like I'm sure he told you. He's been coming to visit me instead. I've been nothing but a blood bag for him. Since I'm an immortal guardian, he can drain me and my body will heal again by morning. I told him where the gate was. He even took me with him and Paul, but when it was time he pushed Paul in and stopped me from following. I've been in that warehouse ever since."

There was no point in hiding the tears. I stood silent just feet away from her, but it felt like my body was falling apart piece by piece.

"I know how you must feel," Poppy said, her sympathetic tone not matching the smugness of her face.

"Stop," I said.

"Lily!"

Whatever force that was keeping me from crumbling entirely was ripped away at the sound of his voice. I whirled around to face Angel in the doorway. Several chairs from the long table scraped against the floor and Angel held his hands up in surrender when three of the elders approached him with their own hands raised.

"Nobody move!" Bebe was on her feet. She slowly came out

from behind the long table, walking right past Poppy and Olivia without offering so much as a glance, to stand next to me. She placed a hand at the small of my back, rubbing soothing circles.

"I came back. I was hoping to talk to you first," Angel said.

"You lied to me. You told me they were both gone," I said.

He didn't look away as he nodded, the corners of his mouth giving a twitch before he spoke. "Yes. I lied to you."

God, this was humiliating. I hated that Poppy was right. I had been manipulated. Angel let me believe he'd killed Paul and Olivia. He made me think the threats were completely gone. Olivia hadn't been the one to assault me, but she knew. She knew, and she allowed her brother to capture me again, to hold me hostage in their house, and she talked to me like I was dead weight. I wasn't sure which was worse, that Olivia was alive or that I was angry with my boyfriend for not committing a second murder for me.

"Please," Olivia said softly. I looked away from Angel to see her stare glassy-eyed at Bebe. "I need a safe place for a while to recover. I don't know what to do next. I just need a place to stay for a little while."

"Of course," Bebe said, taking her hand all the while still rubbing comforting circles against my back. She looked back at the table of elders, most of them leaning together to whisper as they stared at Angel. Bebe stood straighter and let go of Olivia and me. "Angel, you need to leave. You aren't welcome in this building anymore. You can have this last week in New Orleans, but you won't come near the apartments again without repercussions."

Angel's jaw tightened, but he nodded. "Of course. Thank you for your hospitality."

"Lily," Bebe continued, placing a hand on my shoulder. "You are welcome to stay in your apartment as long as you like."

"I'm sorry, Mouse," Angel said. I could see the plea in his eyes, the pain in his voice, making me ache to touch him. I wanted his arms around me, to hold all the pieces in place like they had so many times before, but my chest hurt knowing that Olivia stood just feet away when he made me believe I was safe from her. I had to remind myself that Olivia confirmed that Paul was behind the gate and could never reach me, because having her so close was almost like that moment in the vineyard all over again.

"I'll stay," I said, feeling just a little better when Nova wrapped an arm around my shoulders. I glanced up to see the hurt in Angel's face, sure I saw a tear hit the hardwood floor when he looked down at his feet. He raised his eyes to me and nodded.

"Okay," he said and let out a sigh. "I'll go."

He hesitated a moment before he pulled our apartment key from his pocket. Before he could take a step, the key was ripped from his fingers and shot across the ballroom to sit in Bebe's waiting hand. She handed the key to me and I turned it between my fingers, unwilling to watch as he left the room. I didn't breathe again until I heard the door close.

CHAPTER 25

I went straight to our apartment, barely making it inside before I crumpled. Nova shut the door behind her and joined me on the kitchen floor. I lay my head in her lap and sobbed until my eyes hurt. At some point, she convinced me to move to the couch where she brought me a glass of water and draped a blanket over my lap.

"He told me they were both gone," I told her, my throat raw from crying.

"I'm sorry. No one should have to go through something like that or be reminded of it like this," Nova said. I opened my mouth to ask how she knew, but I could see in her expression that Angel must have told her. She was his friend too. I wondered what he had told her about us. I wondered just how much detail he'd given her about the last few months.

I sipped the water, the coolness helping soothe my throat and ease my nerves. "I thought it was over. It felt like it was finally in the past. I don't know. I can't let him be the one to save me from everything. I can't tell him how good he is and also expect him to hurt the people who hurt me. God, it's all so violent. I just want everyone to be safe. I want to feel safe in my own space."

I held my breath against the sob building in my chest, taking a long drink of water. I was distracted when Nova's phone began buzzing on the coffee table. She glanced anxiously at me before she lifted the phone to her ear and rose from the couch.

"Hey. Um, yeah. It's all good. Don't worry," she said, taking my almost empty glass from my hands. "Of course. You know I will." She took the glass to the fridge and began to refill it. She paused with it in her hands, halfway turned toward me, before she spoke. "Um, yeah. Give me a second."

"Thanks," I said when she hurried across the room to hand me the glass. I noticed the way her eyes went to the bedroom before looking down at me nervously. I had my suspicions about who the caller was. At first, I was upset because I'd expected him to reach out to me first. He'd told me several times that I was his as long as I wanted to be. The coven may have sent him away, but I made it clear that I wasn't going with him. I needed the space, and I'm sure he knew that.

"Is it okay if I ..." Nova started, pointing toward the bedroom.

"I'll be fine. Take your time," I said.

She paused before heading for the bedroom, closing the door so I couldn't make out a word that she said. I could hear the slight edge to her voice, though, telling him off from the sound of it. Her voice got softer after a while as the conversation continued. I pulled my knees to my chest and drew the blanket to my chin. I sipped the water until the glass was empty again and I sat it on the coffee table. I lay down against one of the throw pillows. My brain was too full for sleep, even with my eyes closed I couldn't escape the way Angel looked when he admitted he'd lied or the smile on Olivia's face when she walked in.

The bedroom door opened with a creak and I looked up as Nova moved into the living room. I sat up on the couch only to lean against her shoulder when she sat down next to me.

"It was shitty of him to lie," she said after a long moment. "Worse that he didn't just throw her in the gate with Paul."

All I could muster was a hum of agreement. We sat like that for several minutes before she spoke again.

"He didn't do it to hurt you," she whispered. "He knew it would hurt you to know. That's why he didn't tell you. He planned to send her through the gate before you went back to New York. He only kept her because she's an immortal guardian and he could feed from her and never kill her. He said that he felt like he was getting back at the people who hurt you every time he went to feed from her and he didn't have to kill anyone to survive. It felt less violent to him and made him feel more human. It was selfish. That's why he did it. He kept her captive where only he knew so she couldn't hurt you, but he only kept her to make himself feel like less of a monster. He knows it's no excuse for lying to you—"

"I understand," I said. It didn't make it feel any better, but I knew how much it hurt him to do what he had to do to survive. If he didn't feed, he would eventually desecrate, but when he didn't feed, he worried he wasn't safe for me to be around. "Did he ask you to tell me that?"

"Not at all," Nova scoffed. "He told me not to. He respects your decision to stay here. He said that he knows you need time. He'll be around, because he worries too much, but he won't reach out to you unless you want him to."

"Why are you telling me then?"

"Because you're my best friend," Nova said with a shrug. "And because you love him."

I do love him.

I leaned against her, and she settled back against the couch. She promised me that things would work out and somehow, I knew they would. I wanted them to work out. Part of me wished I had left with Angel, and it was his arms around me for comfort, not Nova's. The longer we lay there the easier it was to unravel all the emotions weighing me down. I wasn't angry, I was scared. And no one made me feel safer than Angel.

I smelled waffles. The blanket was partially over my head, and when I lowered it, the light from the windows made my eyes burn. I sat up. On a paper plate on the coffee table sat a pair of toaster waffles. Angel only ever bought ingredients, not pre-packaged meals and snacks, so I knew these came from Nova's apartment.

"Hey! You're up," she said as she walked out of my bedroom. I paused with one of the waffles raised to my lips.

"Did you sleep here?"

Nova nodded and pointed to the opposite end of the couch where a folded blanket sat. "I stayed most of the night and then I went back to my apartment. I hope you don't mind. I moved some things over there so you wouldn't have to look at them."

My heart leaped in my chest. I knew what she'd moved. I understood why she'd been in my bedroom now. Angel didn't need much. The coven wanted him to leave immediately after the council meeting and he had, not even coming up to our apartment for his things. I bet she took his suitcase next door along with anything else of his she could find.

I lowered the waffle back to the plate and stood up. For a moment, I thought I might cry. I was not going to cry. I was done crying. Not just that, I felt angry. Just when I felt like I was moving on from everything with the Saxons, Olivia comes back into our lives. The only thing that made it easier was that she confirmed one thing. Angel may have lied about Olivia being gone, but he really had killed Paul and that dulled the pain from the memories a little. He couldn't hurt me. All the trauma he put me through, he couldn't repeat. I had gone to sleep reminding myself of it, surprised now that I hadn't had a single nightmare. I'd slept soundlessly, actually, and I felt good now despite the anger churning in my stomach.

"I'm going to shower," I said and stood up. "You can stay. I'll only be a minute."

Nova sat on the couch. "Okay. How about we go out later?"

"Yeah. Maybe," I said and backed toward the bedroom. Nova smiled encouragingly, not without a look of sympathy or sadness like a lot of people would have. She didn't nag me, saying that I needed to take my mind off things or to try forgetting what had happened like Anne used to tell me. It was a look that said she understood that I needed to just sit with my feelings for a bit to sort them all out and decide what to do next. I didn't need a distraction or to forget or pretend that Angel hadn't lied. I needed to cope and figure out what I wanted to do next.

God, what was I going to do next?

"Okay. Shower," I said again, before turning and going into the bedroom. I shut the door behind me. It was just like I thought. Angel's suitcase was gone, and the drawer to the dresser where he'd unpacked his T-shirts and underwear was ajar as if Nova had hurriedly packed everything. I took a deep breath and went to the master bathroom, turning the faucet of the shower to hot and waiting until my reflection in the mirror began to blur from the steam in the room to go back into the bedroom for a clean set of clothes.

I noticed the light across the bed and realized my phone was sitting on my nightstand charging. The screen lit up just long enough for me to see the notification. I dreaded it and found myself darting around the foot of the bed to listen to the voicemail. The first voicemail was from last night, not long after the Coven Council meeting had ended. The second voicemail was left just a moment ago. I clicked on the first message and held the phone to my ear.

"I'm sorry. I'm so sorry, Mouse," Angel said, pausing to breathe. "It was selfish of me. I realized after a while that I'd only kept them alive in that warehouse so I could take all my anger out on them. I wanted revenge for you, to hurt Paul over and over for how he hurt you. Fuck, I wanted him worse than dead, but after a while I just felt ..." He went quiet. I could hear his footsteps in the background, like he was pacing. When they stopped, he took another deep breath.

"Fuck. It didn't make me feel any better. All I wanted was to get rid of the people who hurt you. It didn't matter how many times I watched his immortal body heal just so I could kill him again, I was just reminded that it didn't matter because what was done was done. He hurt you, and not even killing him would get rid of that scar. All it did was remind me how it felt to want for blood, to give in to those instincts, and I hated myself for it. It's no excuse. It's unforgivable what I did, but I kept Olivia alive because knowing that I could feed from her and not kill her made me feel less of a monster. At least she was locked up. I wouldn't have to kill anyone. I could feed more often and be stronger for you. I planned to send her through the gate like I did Paul once we were finished in New Orleans. It was so weak of me, and I'm sorry. You deserve so much better."

The phone went so quiet that I checked to make sure the voicemail hadn't ended. It hadn't. I listened to his sighs of frustration. He mumbled something that sounded like "fucking monster" and "piece of shit" between the silence. He inhaled, the sound louder as though raising his phone back to his ear.

"I'm sorry, Lily. Do what you need. Take your time. Leave me if you want. Just please, stay safe. I love you," he said and hung up.

Steam wafted from the bathroom, but I wasn't done yet. I had to listen to both voicemails. I clicked on the one I'd missed today and lifted the phone to my ear, lying back on his side of the mattress.

"Hey! I just wanted to make sure you were okay and let you know that I'm tracking the de Palencias. Olivia Saxon is staying at Night Owl Apartments. I'm sorry. You shouldn't have to deal with this. It should be me, and I promise I'll make it right. I'm going to get what we came here for, and then we can go home. I love you."

It was a short message, but something about it chilled my skin, and I wasn't sure even the hot shower could ease the tension. He was planning to make a move on the vampires. It never took Angel long to find someone once he picked his target.

My finger hovered over the call button. He was fine. Nova had been keeping in contact with him. She wasn't worried. Before I called him, maybe I should talk to her about it? I was sure that the moment I heard his voice, I would forget about the lie and want to bury myself in his arms, let them melt away all my fears. But I couldn't do that anymore. The only real way toward healing was through this mess and I couldn't do that if I kept pushing away my feelings or let Angel soften the blow. I had to deal with them myself. Maybe being apart for just a little bit was an opportunity to sort it all out.

I couldn't not respond, though.

I opened a text message instead and let my fingers type, deleting and rewriting the message a few times before I finally decided it was good enough and hit send.

I'm okay. I'm mad at you. I love you.

It was so stupid. I felt like a petulant little girl reading the message back, but it was the truth. I was mad at him for lying to me, even if it was to protect me. My heart leaped when I saw that he was typing a response, those three dots lighting up the screen as I waited for his response.

I'm sorry. I don't deserve you. I love you.

I sat the phone down as soon as I saw the message. I knew I'd forgive him because I already had despite the pang in my chest I felt whenever I thought about the lie. I needed to be mad for a little while.

I had to turn down the temperature of the shower. It was boiling when I finally got in and the room was thick with steam. I stayed under the water until it started to cool and then I took my time drying my hair. I went back to my phone on the bed, my fingers snagging on the sheets when I tried to pick it up. No. Not the sheets. My finger was hooked in the sleeve of a dark T-shirt. Angel's T-shirt.

I lifted it to my face, the dark floral smell comforting. It was like he was there, holding me, telling me he wouldn't let anyone hurt me again ... Except he wasn't here, and instead of masking the panic rising in my chest it only grew until I felt like I was choking on it. I forced myself to take deep breaths, closing my eyes, remembering all the things Angel would tell me when I felt this anxious. Only, I heard my own voice instead of his. I replayed the words in my head until I was used to the sound of my voice.

Your past doesn't define your future. Your fears don't limit you.

I thought about the vision of myself in front of that mirror in the Venetian mask, Nova filming as I played the cello. I opened my eyes and looked toward the dresser where those masks sat, perfectly lined up as if on display. I looked at myself in the mirror above it, and the towel slipped away from my body. I still held Angel's shirt beneath my chin, the fabric just enough to hide my naked body. It reminded me of the time I danced in the apartment, the very music video that went so viral online and made enough money overnight for several months of rent. The explosion my channel had after *The Lion Inside* still made my head spin to think about, but it opened doors for a dream I didn't know was a dream until it was in front of me, a way to express emotions I buried deep for so long, giving me a way to take control of my life. Dancing in just that T-shirt made me feel powerful somehow.

It felt like I took back control.

It felt like I was claiming my body as mine again.

It felt like I was taking the power away from my abuser.

And it gave me an idea.

I hurriedly got dressed and went into the living room. Nova

jumped when I ran into the room, sitting straight up on the couch and dropping her phone into the seat next to her.

"I have an idea," I told her before she could speak. Her shock faded to confusion. "I have an idea, and I need your help. It's going to take the whole day though if that's okay."

A smile slowly spread across her face. "Great."

My body was alight with excitement. I could tell she was happy for the distraction as much as I was.

"I'm going to need a cello," I told her, only making her smile wider as she caught on.

"I'll start making some calls," Nova said and stood up from the couch.

CHAPTER 26

It turned out that there was a mansion in New Orleans that you could rent and it didn't take long to find a music store. Nova and I spent most of the morning at the mall putting together a few outfits, all of which matched at least one of the Venetian masks. I bought several cloaks at a mask shop just down the street from the apartment and after a trip to a few lingerie stores, Nova and I went to the mansion we'd rented for the day. I'd never spent so much money on my YouTube channel.

By the time we got there, the sun was setting. It was perfect since my vision consisted mostly of dim lighting anyway. The mansion had a grand staircase with a giant crystal chandelier in the foyer. I knew immediately that it needed to be a focal point, a large portion of the video, and Nova had the same idea.

"We'll do a shot of you walking all the way down the stairs in the black teddy," she said, beating me to the vision and only making it sound even better as she painted the scene. "When I edit the whole video, we'll cut back and forth to this shot. The whole video will be a kind of moody introduction to this new persona. It will be like you're reintroducing Wilted Rose Strings and you as this masked figure will be the frontwoman. It will be a big reveal.

We can use part of the staircase shot as a teaser to hype your fans up for the music video release. That will give me time to edit the video and might help draw more people in."

I was so excited I could hardly speak.

"Go get changed. We'll do this shot first before we lose the natural light from the windows," Nova said, turning toward the front doors to point at the large windows around them.

We took command of the master bedroom upstairs. It was as large as my New York apartment. The bed was big enough for us to lay out all the outfits we'd picked. There was an outfit for every one of the masks: silver, gold, and black. We decided to use only the black cloak, so the silver and gold were folded in a pile on the couch across the room. I slipped out of my dress and then my bra and underwear, tucking the undergarments beneath the dress on the bed even though there was really no reason to hide them. I was nervous though and something about the extra care made me feel a little better.

Three outfits. Several different scenes, but three different personas. The video would center around the black outfit, a lace teddy with black stockings connected to a garter belt. The pair of black heels I'd wear were the tallest I'd ever attempted to walk in and in hindsight, that might have been a poor choice considering the longest and most important scene to the entire music video was of me walking down the grand staircase in the foyer. It was probably a good thing we were starting with that shot so I had the stamina and focus still to descend the steps without injuring myself.

I slipped into the teddy. It took a little bit of stretching to get it on by myself. I'd curled my hair before we left the apartment even though I wasn't sure I wanted that much of myself in the video. I let it fall over my shoulders as I bent over to drag the stocking up my legs. Lingerie wasn't new to me, but the sexiest thing I owned was a little nightgown that barely covered my ass. Even then, it covered a whole lot more than this outfit. The teddy covered the front with bits of lace, but my entire ass was covered by just two tiny strips of elastic. I was glad that part would be concealed by the cloak.

I slipped into the black heels and did a practice walk across the room, turning around to see myself in the long mirror in the bathroom. Fuck. Holy shit. I could barely focus on the walk back as I watched myself in the mirror, the way my hips swayed and my hair flowed around my shoulders. I couldn't resist. I picked up my phone from the bed and when I reached the doorframe of the bathroom, I started snapping photos.

I didn't have any makeup on. I didn't need it since my face would be behind the masks the entire day, but even without it I felt the sexiest I ever had. Well, aside from the moments I shared with Angel. As I looked over the photos, I remembered how he'd lied and how I told myself I would take the time for myself. We had to be apart at least until the coven told him he had to leave New Orleans. I wanted to send him the photos, to tease him at least, but I locked my phone and tossed it on the bed before lifting the black cloak.

It was a dramatic look, the way the extra fabric of the sleeves billowed behind me, the satin fabric shimmering in the light of the bathroom. The hood was large, which I liked. It made it easier to conceal my hair. The Venetian mask covered my entire face and the beautiful swirls only added to the luxury around us. It felt so fitting to be in costume here, filming a proper music video, being in it myself...

I took a deep breath and went back into the hall. Reaching the banister, I looked down to the foyer to see Nova setting up her cameras. She had three: two on tripods to get different angles of the stairs and another she held in her hands. She looked up at me and her lips parted.

"You look so good! God, I have chills!"

"Is it too dramatic?"

"Hell no!" She hurried up the stairs with her camera, already rattling off her ideas. She made me walk down the hallway toward the stairs, getting several videos of me walking toward her at various angles before she was happy. There was a shot from behind as I started to walk down the stairs and several more where she filmed me from the knees down to show off my legs and shoes. It was just us in the huge mansion and it felt almost easy settling into the work. I was used to these kinds of artistic ventures and instead of trying to understand her vision for the imagery, I associated the moments with pieces from my song. I'd picked it before I even asked for her help. It was a dark and sexy piece, one I thought of a kind of descent into darkness. It was my villain era and the more I replayed the notes in my head, the more I felt a part of the moment. That was until she gave her next direction.

"When you get halfway down the stairs, push back the cloak so I get a full-body shot of the lingerie. Keep walking as you do that. When you reach the bottom, I want to get a shot of you from behind slipping the whole cloak off and walking away. I won't get your entire body. It will only be like, from the shoulders down. How does that sound?"

My stomach was in knots. I loved the idea. I did. It was a vulnerable thing to do—to be nearly naked on camera—but it also felt powerful.

"Yeah. Let's do it," I said from the top of the stairs.

Nova hesitated with her camera halfway raised. "Are you okay? If you aren't comfortable with it we can adjust."

"No. No, I love the idea. It's just a little ... Well, you know. It's just a little new. I've never done anything like this."

She smiled and gave a nod, letting me know to walk whenever I felt ready. I paused for just a moment before my nerves could grow. I had gotten much better at walking in the heels, so I could focus more on the way the cloak moved around me and less on paying attention to my feet. I walked quicker than I had before. Just like she'd instructed, when I reached the middle of the staircase, I pushed open the opening of the cloak to reveal the lace teddy and kept walking. Nova cheered as I went, setting my hands on my waist like a model taking charge of a runway, walking the rest of the way down the stairs.

We reset again for the final shot. After a little more thought, we decided it would look better if I walked from the bottom of the stairs to the drawing room just off the foyer and shut the door. It would be the final image and Nova told me to stay in the room for up to a minute so she could get extended footage to use for the credits.

I made sure the cloak hung just right so it would be easy to slip off my shoulders and then she called for me to go. I walked two steps before I let the cloak fall, the silk caressing my skin as it fell. I let my hands linger on the gilded doorknob as I pulled it shut behind me. I let out a loud exhale once the door clicked into place.

I was shaking, but not with fear like I was used to. It felt similar to one of my panic attacks, only I felt so free. Tears pricked my eyes, and I pulled off the mask just in case they fell. God, this was a rush! I felt more myself than I had in a long time, even more so than when I was safe with Angel. I could barely stand the wait in that room before Nova called for me to come out. I took off the heels and hurried out, both of us squealing with excitement.

"It's going to be so good! You look so sexy and I swear you look like the evil queen from a fairytale. I can't wait to get to editing!" Nova was practically bouncing next to me.

"We still have three more outfits," I laughed, already thinking about what to change into upstairs. "Let me change into the gold."

We continued to work our way around the mansion. The gold ensemble was meant for those smaller, in-between shots. We took advantage of the more ostentatious things around the mansion. Nova mostly took videos of me lounging on plush couches, walking through the spacious rooms, and several of me playing the cello. This lingerie set was the most comfortable of them all: a simple gold bra with a matching pair of cheeky underwear. I wore the black cloak, the fabric covering most of the outfit aside from the moments it was visible whenever I walked.

The final scene, which would be the beginning of the video, took place in the indoor pool. It was dark, with patio lights casting warm light onto the clear water. The moonlight gave the scene a kind of eerie glow, which turned out to be exactly what Nova was hoping for. Part of the glass dome above us allowed for the shadow from the wrought-iron balcony to project over part of the pool, casting dark swirls over the water that Nova decided to take advantage of.

This was where I started to lose part of the vision. I trusted Nova to tell the story we'd crafted together though, so I followed her direction even when the shots consisted of just my hand holding the silver mask. Once she got nearly an hour of simple shots, it was time for me to get in the pool.

Nova recorded footage of me walking into the pool in a silver babydoll dress, the fabric so sheer that it was almost ghostly as it flowed around me in the water. I walked in until I was submerged, Nova filming me from behind so only my hair might giveaway my identity. We moved to the deep end, where she filmed a few moments from the diving board above me as I dragged my arms and legs through the water, trying my best to make the nightgown flow around me in an artistic way. We decided last minute that the story would be easier to follow if I emerged from the pool again wearing the black cloak and silver mask, so she filmed that moment from two angles. She got a shot of me walking out of the pool from behind and then another from the front, the hood pulled low over my silver mask.

"This is going to be so good! I can't believe how good this looks before I've even edited any of it," Nova gushed near the steps, watching the footage back on her camera. "We absolutely need to get that teaser done tonight. Wow."

"Nova, put the camera down and relax. I think we've earned it," I told her, not waiting for her response before I took the camera from her and sat it on the nearest lounge chair.

"I need to relax? I think you need to relax," she teased.

"I feel so relaxed. I feel great!" I said and took both her hands. "And you should, too. We did something crazy tonight!"

I pulled her toward the pool, both of us screaming as we plunged into the water. Nova gasped when she rose out of the water, shock painting her face as she looked back at me. I laughed and she joined in after splashing me for pulling her in, telling me how lucky it was that she was wearing a pair of sandals and not her nice tennis shoes. We swam around the pool for a while longer, floating on our backs and looking at the stars through the glass dome above us before we went back to the master bedroom and changed.

We put the wet clothes into a dryer on the first floor. Nova sat at the kitchen table with the gold robe cinched around her, while I sat across from her in my blue dress. She looked like a boxer ready to enter the ring, and she laughed when I told her and feigned a punch.

"You think there's wine in here?" I asked an stood up from the table.

"Um, maybe. You'd have to pay for it. We're already renting the place for the night," Nova said as I located a bottle of red wine on the counter across the kitchen. I managed to find a corkscrew in the first drawer I opened.

"Then I will pay for it," I said and popped the cork from the bottle, not thinking to look for wine glasses until then. Thankfully, Nova appeared with a pair a moment later.

"To Wilted Rose Strings," she said and lifted her glass in a toast. I pressed my glass to hers and drank, the wine reminding me of the vineyard back home. It was obviously more expensive than what my family produced and it showed in the taste. This was the kind of wine that you savored, so Nova and I sat at the table again and waited for the dryer to finish and enjoyed the bottle.

"Thank you," I told her as she poured the last of the wine into my glass.

"You know this is my kind of thing," she said and took a drink. "I love making art and film is one of my favorite mediums. I've never had an opportunity to create anything like this and I've always wanted to. I should be thanking you."

"Not for that," I said, spinning the glass between my fingers. She lowered hers, her expression fading as she realized what I'd meant. I was glad I didn't have to explain. The last twenty-four hours had been a strange mix of emotions. I went from feeling so sad and betrayed to the most in control I'd ever felt and putting together a whole music video in an expensive mansion. It seemed like a rash decision, but also exactly what I needed. It was what Wilted Rose Strings needed too and I could already see all the opportunities that this might bring.

"You're welcome," she said and tapped her glass against mine. "You're my best friend."

I felt the smile tug at my lips. "You're my best friend too."

The dryer buzzed and we cleaned up the kitchen before we gathered the last of our things and left, too tired to go anywhere else but home.

CHAPTER 27

I was exhausted the next day, but that didn't dim the buzz of excitement I felt about the night before. We slept in so late that it felt a little funny to be going for coffee and breakfast, but a latte was exactly what I needed if I was going to make it through our seer lesson later today. Nova and I had met every day so I could practice my visions. She took notes on my process and did research for different methods that might help. I got better each time and while I couldn't plan for what I'd see, the visions had gotten so clear that it was almost overwhelming the amount of detail I got from just the small moments.

"I am so tired," I said as the elevator doors opened to the lobby.

"I stayed up all night working on the video," Nova said with a laugh.

I gave her shoulder a playful shove. "You didn't need to do that. We have plenty of time to get that out. I haven't even announced a timeline yet."

I already had enough songs for an album, all in the same vein of the music video. They were all dark and moody. This music video would make for the perfect launching point for the album.

"I already got a teaser edited. I made a version for YouTube and a mobile version for social media. I was going to show you over breakfast," Nova said as we left Night Owl Apartments. My heart pounded in my chest.

"I can't believe you did all of that already! Show me."

"Let's get to breakfast first. I thought we'd just go around the corner for some beignets," she laughed.

"Okay. Fine," I groaned as we moved into the courtyard in at the front of the building. "I should probably do an announcement that there's a teaser coming for social media anyway. You know, a kind of heads-up that something is getting ready to drop soon."

"Exactly," Nova said and led the way down the sidewalk. "It's a working brunch."

"Which means I'm paying," I told her, waving a finger at her when she opened her mouth to argue. "You did all that work and I haven't even paid you anything for it yet. Let me get the bill, especially if we are going to use that time to work."

"Okay, but you don't need to pay me anything for the video. I told you I've been itching to do something like this. You gave me the opportunity."

"Yes, but I will be paying you for it," I said as I fell in step next to her. "Wilted Rose Strings will be paying you."

The restaurant wasn't far and it seemed that we'd gotten there at the perfect time between the end of the brunch crowd and the start of the lunch rush. We grabbed a table near the entrance. and ordered coffees and beignets to share while Nova opened up her laptop. As soon as the waitress left our table, Nova turned the screen to me and offered her headphones. I put them on, the plush fabric muffling all sound in the restaurant. I hit play on the video.

It started with a shot of me from the back, walking down the upstairs hallway in the cloak. It cut to a shot of my legs below the knee peeking out from the cloak, the silver heels and prefect pedicure a stark contrast to the eerie cloaked figure that would soon be known as the frontwoman for Wilted Rose Strings. The final shot was a closeup of my hand holding the silver mask by the pool, the credits slowly fading onto the screen. The text was all gibberish, but I planned to change it for the release date of the full video. The teaser already had a snippet of the new song, the sexiest part that I hoped would be appealing for others to reuse on all the social media apps for their own creations.

"This is amazing!" I said and slid the laptop across the table.

Nova turned the laptop back to face her. "I know you said you wanted to do a kind of announcement that something was coming, but I think you should just drop this teaser with the release date of the full song. Shock factor."

"Maybe you're right," I said, looking up when our waitress approached with our coffees. "I think I just get ..." I didn't finish as the waitress stopped at our table, careful not to disturb the coffee art on the top of my mug as she sat it down. Nova asked to add an order of fruit to our bill before the woman left us in the silence.

Nova offered an encouraging smile and my stomach did somersaults. Would every new release feel like this? Would it ever get any easier? Less over-thinking, less anxiety? I'd always told myself that it was all just proof of how much I cared about what I had built, but a part of me wondered if it was doubt.

"It's stage fright," Nova said and lifted her mug from the table. "That's all it is. It gets to everyone. You want it to do well and it's scary to put yourself out there like that. It's normal to be nervous."

"I know that, but ... I'm being stupid," I groaned, pressing my fingers to my temples.

"You're just overthinking. There will be people who like it and people who don't. Some people you will never be able to make happy, but they don't matter because your music isn't for them anyway. Stick with your people and it'll be fine," Nova said and took a sip of her coffee, grimacing. "It's hot."

I looked down at the little leaf in the foam of my cup. It was what Angel would've told me. Maybe that was a part of it too, that Angel wasn't here to see all the behind-the-scenes before the video went live. The idea of waiting around, teasing the video was unnerving.

"What if we put the teaser out now and we drop the full music video tonight? Would that work? Is it all finalized?" I asked, looking up at Nova's surprised expression. She paused with her mug halfway to her lips for a second before lowering it to the table again.

"Um, yeah. It's finished. I just didn't think you'd want to release the whole thing so soon."

"Is it too soon? Maybe I should give it like another day between the teaser."

"Lily," Nova said with a laugh, reaching across the table to grab my hand. "That's the best part of owning your own business and being an independent artist. You do what you want. We can totally put the teaser out right now, blast it all over the place, and drop the full thing tonight."

"Yeah?" I asked, getting a nod in response. "Okay. Then, let's do that. No, better idea. Let's do that and then go out to celebrate. It will help me take my mind off things."

"Let's do it!"

I was glad I didn't have to explain what I was trying to avoid thinking about. Nova slid her coffee to one side of the table and opened her laptop again, already typing away as I sipped on my latte. While we adjusted the text on the credits, we decided that ten o'clock tonight would be the release time so that we could go out after and not worry about it. The pressure in my chest eased after we uploaded the video to YouTube. Nova got to work finalizing the mobile version, pausing only when our waitress returned with our food. I could barely eat as Nova finished working. I trusted her, so when she offered to do all the uploads herself I handed over my phone and forced myself to eat a beignet.

Nova sat back in her seat and looked up at me with a smile. "All done." She sat my phone on the table screen-side up and I caught sight of Angel's text for just a moment before the screen went dark. I almost reached for the phone. Everything was fine. He knew I just needed time to decompress.

"He just wanted to let you know that he's excited for the video tonight," Nova said.

I raised my hand, intending to reach for the phone and looping my fingers around the handle of my mug instead. I lifted it to my lips and drank, completely erasing the leaf in the foam. The warmth of the coffee was nice, but I knew that the caffeine would only add to the slight edge I felt. I lowered the mug with a sigh.

"I love him," I said.

"I know you do."

"It just—" I groaned in frustration. "I know why he did it. I know how much it bothers him what he has to do to stay alive, to stay safe for me, but it hurts that he lied."

"I know," Nova said, her frown deepening.

I popped the rest of my beignet into my mouth, the pastry not tasting nearly as sweet as before thanks to the change in subject.

"So, um," Nova adjusted in her seat and stabbed a fork into one of the beignets on our shared plate, moving it to her own. "You know a little bit about my family. What's yours like?"

She continued to fidget with her food, adding blueberries one at a time to her plate that told me the conversation had her just as uncomfortable as it had me.

"I've only met Bebe," I told her with a shrug. "I guess we never have really talked about our families, have we?"

Nova shook her head. "Not really. Well, you know that Bebe is really all I have. My mom died of cancer a while back. It was always just the three of us. I never knew my dad. I know his name was Jamal and that I took my mom's last name and not his. I could figure out more, but I don't care enough. He missed out and that's on him. My mom was great. Bebe is great. That's all that matters."

I could just hear my mom's judgements. *Nova was from a broken home. She had no father figure. He was probably a deadbeat who stepped out on them or was in prison.* Nova wasn't any of the stereotypes I grew up hearing though. Honestly, my family was the exact way rich people were so often portrayed.

I stabbed a strawberry from the fruit bowl and lifted it to my lips. "My parents mean well, but they are judgmental. I told them about my YouTube channel and how I was growing my business and they were supportive, but also not really, until they saw how big it was. My mom is worse about it than my dad. She feeds into the country club drama."

"What do they do for a living?" Nova put her fork down and plucked a whole strawberry from the bowl with her fingers.

"They both run businesses. My mom's makes more money, but it doesn't really matter. They both are over six-figure earners. Then there's the vineyard and the race horses. They do that together," I said, my stomach sinking when I saw the way Nova's eyes lit up.

"Jesus," she said under her breath. "So, you could put on one of those big hats and go to the Kentucky Derby, watch one of your horses race, and drink your family's wine while you're there?"

I shrugged. "If I wanted."

I wasn't going to tell her that that was exactly what my parents did each year.

She laughed in disbelief. "No disrespect, but they sound—"

"You're not wrong," I said and held my hands up in surrender. "They didn't like Angel at first, but they came around once we called them out on it. So, yeah, they are kinda the worst on the surface, but they can be humbled. That's more than some can say."

Nova sat the strawberry she was holding back on her plate. "They met him?"

In some ways, it was like I'd blocked the entire visit from my brain.

"Yeah. They met him," I said.

"And they didn't like him?" Nova laughed. "How? Angel is an old-school gentleman. He gives you the princess treatment."

I felt my cheeks heat. He was anything but a gentleman when we were behind closed doors together.

"It really came down to normal parent things. They just

worried he wasn't good enough for me. You know? They questioned his job, didn't like his long hair, thought he might be too old—"

"Angel had long hair?" Nova interrupted, laughing a second later. "Also, that's funny that they worried he was too old."

Yeah. The irony had not been lost on me either.

I shrugged. "Angel stood up for me. It pissed them off at first, but I think it showed them how serious we were and then they were able to see how kind he is and protective and ..."

I wasn't hungry anymore. I thought about the text sitting unread on my phone.

"Don't you dare," Nova said, raising an accusing finger to me.

"What? Why?"

"You need space to work through your thoughts and he deserves to stew in the guilt," Nova said and took the final beignet from our plate.

"So, I should just not respond?"

"That or give him a reason to come begging on his knees," she said with a grin, her cheeks flushed as she popped the entire pastry into her mouth.

I opened my mouth to ask what she meant before I thought about our night in the mansion. There was plenty of scandalous footage of me, footage that only Angel would know was actually me. Everyone else watching the music video tonight would wonder who the mysterious masked figure was, but Angel would know. He'd watch me descend those stairs in the lacy black teddy, see me straddling the cello in the gold corset, and watch me glide through the water in the sheer white nightgown ...

Nova let out a hum of satisfaction that only turned into a laugh when I looked up at her, my face burning with embarrassment. I quickly caught the eye of our waitress and she started our way. I was already fumbling to pull out my business debit card from my purse before she even reached us.

CHAPTER 28

"Do you want me to tell you when I post it?" Nova called from the living room.

"No!"

I came hobbling out of my bedroom with just one heel on, the other held firmly in my right hand. Nova sat on the couch with my laptop propped on her lap. She looked funny sitting there, dressed in a silver minidress and staring intently at the computer screen.

"Okay. I won't," she said and shut the laptop and stood up. "I scheduled it to go live, but I won't tell you what time. It'll be a surprise."

Surprise was exactly right.

"Are you ready? I need a drink," I said as I slipped my shoe on. I decided to be daring and wear the gold corset to the nightclub. I paired it with a leather miniskirt that I was sure I'd regret after hitting the dance floor. The fabric was structured, which I liked, but had a habit of riding up my thighs. I was a little worried about my ass peeking out the bottom, but I was more concerned with getting out of here and away from my laptop before I decided to abort the entire music video launch.

"I'm ready," Nova said, moving toward the door in her black dress. "I'll get an Uber," Nova said and moved toward the door.

I took a deep breath and followed her into the hall, locking my door and leading the way toward the elevator while she scrolled on her phone. I felt the pressure rise in my chest the entire ride to the lobby and then again as we sat in the back of the Uber. Thankfully, there wasn't a line to get into the club and after flashing our IDs we were able to walk straight to the bar.

"Want to start a tab?" the bartender asked.

"Two tequila shots," I told him and handed over my card. He looked a little taken aback, but smiled and nodded before turning for the large display of liquor along the wall.

"Would it help if I told you that the music video went live over an hour ago?" Nova asked.

God, it felt like my heart just shot through my chest.

"Oh God!" I gasped, glad when the bartender turned around with two shot glasses and a pair of limes. I took the glass from him and raised it to my lips, draining the whole thing before taking the lime.

"Would it make you feel better to know that your views are already double what your last video did in its first hour?" Nova asked.

"Another round, please?" I asked the bartender, turning my back on his amused expression to look over the crowded room. The club music pulsed through my feet, a deep bass that matched the racing of my heart.

"The comments are flooded with people wondering about the hooded figure," Nova said, tugging on my arm.

"Thank you," I told the bartender when he brought the next round. I almost hesitated before lifting the shot glass to my lips.

Almost.

"Let's celebrate!" I grimaced from the tart lime, tossing it into my empty shot glass before sliding the second glass toward Nova. "We should dance."

A smile spread on her face as she took the glass. I clapped my hands as she tipped her head back, drinking it all and reaching for the last lime.

"Let's dance," she agreed and pushed our glasses to the opposite side of the bar. I tugged her into the crowd, eager to forget about the music video and everything else from the week. I focused on the deep bass of the music, the way the crowd moved, the subtle buzz in my veins as the alcohol started to ease the tension ...

I let out a whoop, raising both of my arms and Nova followed my lead. A group of girls to our right started to cheer and soon we were all dancing together. I took Nova's hand and raised it above our heads, rocking my hips from side to side until she loosened up and danced along with me. Once the song was over, a few of the girls were pulled away by a couple of boys and the two that remained wished us a good night and headed for the bathroom together.

"Can we grab a table? I need a moment," Nova shouted over the club music.

I nodded and she took my hand, leading the way off the main dance floor and to a line of tables. There were several available in the crowded room, most people dancing. We took a table closest to the dance floor and Nova sank into a chair and leaned over to rub her feet immediately.

"You okay?" I asked.

She waved a hand at me. "Fine. Oh my God," she gasped. She straightened up with a broken piece of plastic between her index finger and thumb. She sat it on the table and that's when it was obvious what it was. "Eww! Someone's drink stirrer was stuck inside my heel!"

The swizzle stick was a florescent pink color with a little fleur-de-lis at the end. Nova scooted it to the side of the table. A group of guys brushed past me, one of them bumping into the edge of our table, and the stick vanished onto the sticky floor.

"Oh! I'm sorry," the guy who bumped the table said. He turned around to look at us, sending an apologetic look at me before looking at Nova, his eyes lingering on her.

"No worries. It's not like anything spilled," Nova said and motioned to our empty table.

"Yeah. I probably would've knocked them over and ruined the whole night," he said with a small laugh, nodding at one of the guys in his group before they started for the bar. He lingered by our table.

"Probably," Nova smiled. "It's too early in the night to be spilling stuff on my dress."

"How about I help you start the night right and get you a drink?" the man said, nodding toward the bar. "I promise I won't knock it over."

Nova's cheeks flushed when she glanced at me.

"You go ahead. I want to check on something," I told her, smiling. She rose from her seat and they started toward the bar, leaving me alone. My anxiety got the best of me and I opened YouTube before I could stop myself. The video already had a higher view count than anything else I'd released, the comments flooded with so much praise that I could hardly read the messages. I exited the app before my heart could explode with gratitude, noticing the notification of a text message right away.

Angel.

I know you wanted space and I fully intended to give it you, but ... WOW!

The text included a link to the YouTube video. My stomach immediately became a serious of tight knots that I wasn't sure how to unravel. Damn him. I couldn't summon the hurt I'd felt before. I was still mad at him, but I didn't *feel* mad anymore. I wanted to curl up in his lap. I wanted his arms around me. God, knowing how little I wore in that music video, I wanted him to strip the last of it off of me.

I looked up from my phone, taking in the crowd of dancers as

I let my mind wander. The group of girls were back on the floor, a boy wrapped around each one as they danced and twirled. The entire room was so packed with bodies that it was hard to make out who the arms and legs belonged to, where one group started and another ended, or who had dropped the glass beer bottle that shattered on the floor beside me.

My heart leaped into my throat. A man with a tray and dishrag was speaking to me, apologizing probably, but I couldn't hear him. It felt like I was being pulled through a tunnel, my vision blurring until I was standing in a different room. Nova was there, pressed against the wall by a dark-haired man. He bashed her head against the wall and she slid to the ground. The man moved in a blur, running straight for me. Angel appeared at my side, an arm extended in a shove that sent the dark-haired man flying across the room and into the wall next to Nova. Angel's eyes went wide in front of me, his mouth slack, and he looked down at the wood protruding through his chest. Before I could even brush his face, he fell apart, his body turning to ash in front of me and revealing Magdalena's smiling face as she held that bloody stake.

"I'm so sorry," the man said again, standing up from the floor with his tray full of shards of glass. He hurried off, leaving me to glance around the room.

Shit.

The light from my phone caught my attention, reminding me of Angel's text. My fingers moved furiously over the screen.

Where are you?

He was here. Nova was wearing her black dress in my vision. It looked like we were in some kind of back room or warehouse, something likely connected to the club. My phone vibrated.

Bullshit. I knew he was here. He knew that I knew. He was just being nice. I took a deep breath and opened up my photos, not needing to scroll very far to find the one I was looking for. I attached that photo of me in the luxurious mansion bedroom, posing in that lacy, black teddy and heels in such a way to make my body look curvier than it actually was. I sent the photo first and then typed out the message.

The screen lit up again, letting me know that he was typing a message. I was on my feet, ready to lure him toward the nearest exit. Instead, the message never came and the screen went dark. Panic rose into my chest, squeezing tight as I looked toward the bar for Nova. I found her with that guy and a drink in her hand, smiling at him like she was on the verge of having the best night.

I was about to ruin it.

I realized several of the other guys from his group were standing around them. I approached. I paused to decide how to approach when the one to Nova's right stepped aside. He was dressed in dark pants and a white T-shirt, a small hoop through one earlobe and a coy smile on his face as he turned to look at me.

"Are you the wingman?" he asked me. "Well, wingwoman? What do y'all call it?"

"I don't know. Yes. I don't know," I told him, stepping up to the bar and preparing to tap Nova's shoulder when she leaned closer to the man she was with.

"I don't think I'm going to have any luck here tonight," the guy to my right said. I turned to face him, ready to let him know that I wasn't interested when another idea struck me.

"What are you looking for?" I asked, perking up and turning away from Nova entirely so he could get a better look at me. He did, eyes roving over me in exactly the way I'd hoped. I took another small step toward him, already sure I could feel Angel's eyes on me.

"You're a total doll, but not my type," he said with an awkward laugh.

"Oh? What is your type?" I asked, resting my hand on his arm.

He smiled and took my hand, lacing his fingers with mine the way a friend might.

"Male," he said with a smile.

My stomach sank and the humor in his expression faded a little. He straightened up and took my other hand, setting our linked hands together on the counter and nodding for the bartender to come over.

"A drink for my friend," he told the bartender, waiting for me to answer.

"Rum and coke," I said past the lump in my throat.

"What's wrong? It's some guy, isn't it? What did he do, doll?" The man brushed my hair behind my ears. Maybe my plan wasn't entirely a wash.

"I was hoping to make my boyfriend jealous. He's watching and he deserves it," I told him, relief easing the tension in my shoulders when I saw his smile return.

"Oh! Well, you may not be my type, but I am a girl's girl and I can always play the part," the guy said and leaned in, wrapping an arm around my back. He pulled me to his side by my hip, flashing me a smile before he lowered his lips to my ear. "Do you see him?"

No. I didn't need to see him to know he was there. He'd seen the photo I sent. Disappointment was starting to take root in my gut the longer I stood there. The bartender returned with my drink, setting it down in front of me. I reached out to slide it closer when an arm reached between the man and I, making me step aside.

Angel took my drink from the bar and lifted it to his lips, taking a long drink.

"That was my date's drink, man," the guy next to me said, an arm slinking around my waist again.

Angel pinned me with his playful eyes before handing the drink to me. "I know there's plenty of fish in the sea, but I think you went fishing in the wrong pond, Mouse."

"Are you jealous?" I asked, lifting the glass to my lips and take a long drink for a little courage.

He only smiled wider as I leaned against my new friend. "I would be if he were straight." He turned to the man and said, "I don't mean that as an insult. I saw you dancing with another guy earlier. You have the looks to pull anyone here tonight, except for my girlfriend."

The man sent me an apologetic look and pulled away from me, lifting his nearly empty glass from the bar and pressing it to mine. "We tried, doll. You come and find me if you need anything."

"Thanks," I said, turning back to Angel as the man started back to join his friends at the other side of the bar. Nova had scooted another seat over, not at all aware that Angel was here, let alone me. I was sure she'd never noticed me approach or my entire act just now. I had just raised my hand to tap on her shoulder when Angel stepped closer, pulling me to his chest by my ass.

"What happened to a little space? I thought you were busy," I said, letting him take my hand that I'd extended toward Nova. He pressed his lips to my knuckles before placing it against his chest.

"I will always drop everything to hear you moan my name, Mouse," he said, eyes dark with intent. I was having a hard time focusing on the entire reason for coming over here, for asking that man to help get Angel's attention ...

"I knew it would get your attention," I said.

"Oh, you got my attention, Mouse," he scoffed, squeezing my ass and leaning closer so he could whisper in my ear. "Letting that man touch what's mine, that picture, your text ... You said you're always mine to take home. I can't stand to be away from you any longer and when I get you home, you'll pay for the way you teased me tonight."

He dragged his lips from my ear, along my chin, capturing my lips and claiming them as his. He gave my bottom lip a little bite, just hard enough to sting before he pulled back. I whimpered against his mouth, but not in the normal way. Tears pricked my eyes, blurring my vision as his hands moved to my face.

"What's wrong?" he asked.

"I needed you here because I had a vision. We need to get out of here. *You* need to get out of here," I said, trying to shove him away. He stood firm, not moving an inch away.

"What vision?" he asked, glancing at Nova's turned back.

"They're here. I don't know which ones, but Magdalena—"

He tugged on Nova's arm before I could finish. She turned, eyes widening and mouth parting when she noticed him. She sent me a questioning look as she climbed off her stool.

"We have to get out of here," I told her. "Right now."

"Um, okay," she said, taking my hand.

At least one of them had some urgency. Angel was busy scanning the room, looking for the vampire trio as I pulled them both toward the main entrance.

"No. The back," he said, practically knocking me over when he changed directions. I had to adjust my grip on Nova as we dove back into the crowd.

"Lily!" she gasped, her nails scraping my palm. I looked away from Angel just in time to see her tugged roughly from behind. She didn't even scream as she was pulled in the crowd, her look of terror the last thing I saw before she vanished.

CHAPTER 29

"F uck!"

Angel tugged me close to his side, gripping my bicep as though afraid I'd be snatched away too.

"Where is she?" I asked, my heart racing so fast that my chest hurt. Before I was ready, Angel pulled me along, pushing through the last of the crowd and pausing. Just ahead, staring at us from the crack in a door, was Magdalena. She flashed a flirty smile before slipping inside.

The door hadn't even shut before Angel caught it, practically dragging me inside the room. It was a large storeroom filled with metal shelves of plastic cups and extra liquor bottles. There was a loud crash and Angel groaned. I let out a scream as I was shoved away, my back bashing into one of the shelves the same moment I saw the shards of glass and vodka rain down over Angel's head.

He moved so fast that it was impossible to see what was happening. He'd whirled around to face the young man, a dark-haired vampire who looked no older than he did.

Alonzo.

Angel sent him flying backward, smashing into the end of a metal shelf that then slid all the way to the front wall. Angel launched himself at him, his giant black wings spread wide and his torso longer, less human. Alonzo opened his mouth wide, fangs ready, a pair of wings launching themselves from his back at the moment Angel's body connected with his.

"Lily!"

I turned to see Nova kneeling on the ground, a hand extended toward Magdalena. There was a flash of light and Magdalena was sent flying toward the opposite wall, a metal roll-up door crumpled around her like a piece of tin foil. She landed on her feet, dodging Nova's next spell. All the air shot from my lungs, stealing my scream when I realized that Magdalena had me in her arms. She fell, sending me sprawling onto the concrete and sliding knees first into one of the metal shelves.

Stars burst before my eyes from the pain, the scream bubbling forth just as I saw the shadow of the shelves closing in. Before I could be crushed, Angel appeared feet in front of me, holding the metal shelves up as glass bottles of liquor shattered on the floor around me. The smell burned my nose and made my eyes water as I looked up at him, dark wings spread wide and shirt ripped apart as his body had grown larger.

"Go!"

I did, ignoring the sting when I cut my palm on a shard of glass as I crawled from under the shelves. They came crashing down when Alonzo tackled Angel around the middle, both of them vanishing beneath the large shelf.

"Over here!" Nova yelled, pulling my attention to the back of the warehouse.

I started to run, glancing over my shoulder to make sure Magdalena was behind me and instead I ran straight into her chest. It was like running into a wall. My body screamed in protest and before I could crumple, she held me up by both my arms, my feet rising off the floor.

"Let her go!" Nova screamed, raising her arms.

Magdalena whirled around and I felt Nova's spell smash into my back, pain radiating from the spot up my back and down into my legs until my entire body was searing with pain. I didn't know

I'd screamed until I heard it echo off the walls. Someone ripped me away from her, a pair of strong, but gentle arms. Angel tucked me tightly to his chest with a deep growl.

"All these centuries and you've finally found a mate?" Magdalena said with a laugh. "What poor timing on your part."

"Leave her alone!" Angel snarled, setting me on my feet and tucking me behind his large wing so I couldn't see her anymore. I looked for Nova and when I saw her, my stomach dropped. Alonzo had her pressed to his chest, an arm locked around her neck as she struggled. I ran toward them, my hands locking on Alonzo's wing before he noticed me coming.

"Lily!" Angel yelled as I pulled on the wing and twisted it between my hands. Alonzo let out a pained cry and let go of Nova, but she wasn't able to move quick enough. He snatched her from behind, whirling her around and holding her aloft as he ran to the wall in a blur of speed. Nova let out a cry when her back connected with the wall and then went silent when he shoved her against it again, knocking her unconscious.

I felt sick as I recognized the scene. A sour taste filled my mouth and I struggled to focus as the sick feeling settled into my stomach. Alonzo turned from the wall, his eyes set on me. Angel was at my side just a second later, both men colliding. Angel shoved Alonzo, sending him across the room and into the wall beside Nova.

Before he could turn to face me like I knew he would, I ducked beneath Angel's wings. My feet slipped on the wet floor and I fell against a couple bottles of vodka that had rolled away from the nearest upturned shelf, somehow still intact despite the carnage around us. The one I'd fallen on rolled into a smear of blood that must've dripped from Angel's left wing, more blood dripping onto the bottle when it finally stopped at his feet.

Angel's eyes widened when I took the bottle by the neck and smashed it on the floor between us. He let out a scream in protest when I lifted the jagged edge of glass and raked it across my arm, gritting my teeth against the pain. Blood immediately flowed hot down my forearm. I looked up in time to see Magdalena hesitate just feet in front of us, the broken end of a chair leg aimed at Angel's chest.

Angel brushed past me to snatch the chair leg from her hands, tossing it against the roll-up door with enough force to cut through it and leave a gaping hole near the bottom. He threw Magdalana next, lifting her into the air like he was a professional wrestler in the ring and throwing her at the roll-up door next, forcing the door to pop off the track overhead.

Angel had me cradled at his chest and when I looked up, we were across the room next to Nova. The roll-up door landed with a bang against the floor and I saw two dark figures run into the alley.

"W-What happened?" Nova asked with a groan, a hand going to the back of her head.

"Both of you," Angel said and pulled Nova and I closer, her to his left side and me to his right. "Hold on tight."

I wrapped my arms around his neck and Nova held onto my forearms from the other side. My hair whooshed around me and then the smell of the dumpsters in the alley was replaced by the smell of seafood from the restaurant on the corner. Angel groaned in my ear as we flew, straining against whatever injury he'd sustained in the fight. We were in the air for just minutes before he landed on a rooftop, immediately lowering us to the ground and turning to face me with wide, worried eyes.

"I'm fine. It's okay," I told him, looking past him at Nova who had her head between her knees.

"The fuck you are," he snarled, drawing my attention back to him when he reached for my arm. I pulled it closer to my chest, not able to contain the gasp of pain that escaped between my teeth.

"Don't do anything. Give me a minute," Nova said.

Angel whipped around to face her, his mouth open as though ready to unleash a string of insults. Neither of us spoke. Nova wasn't just trying to cope with her head injury. She was bent over with her hands at the back of her head, healing herself. She finished murmuring, sitting up with a deep exhale a moment later. She looked anxiously at Angel, her eyes going from his face to his left wing. I followed her gaze, realizing that the blood wasn't from his wing at all. There was a deep cut along his shoulder that allowed the blood to run onto the webbing of his wing. The rest of his vampire features had faded away, but he was still provoked enough for the wings to remain draped protectively around us.

"Heal her," he growled, grabbing her arm.

Nova tugged free, shooting him a look of warning as she crawled closer to me. My corset clung to my forearm when I pulled it away. I heard Angel inhale with a quick hiss. He wasn't normally so affected by my blood, but there was a lot of it. I felt oddly numb, not concerned like I should probably be by how soaked my top was. The gold fabric was dark now and I could see beads of blood glide down my stomach in the places that were nothing but mesh. My leather skirt rode up high on my thighs, blood smeared across them and down to my knees.

"Heal her!"

Nova startled, accidentally pressing her fingers against the gash along my arm and making me cry out. Angel clapped a hand over my mouth, muffling my scream and pulling me to his chest. My heart was racing and my vision blurred. I felt the reality sink in like a brick in a harbor, towing me deeper into the cool darkness.

"It's deep enough that it will take a little time," Nova said, the words coming out quickly as she leaned over my arm. She began whispering again. At first it was a dull throb and then my arm itched, the sensation only growing worse. Angel held my bicep when I lifted my other arm to scratch, promising me that Nova was nearly finished. I could tell when she had. The itching went away and when I looked down, the cut was gone and only the smears of dried blood remained.

"Shit," Angel sighed.

"My vision," I said, sitting up and pausing as my head spun.

"You had a vision?" Nova asked, rising to her feet.

"She saw the attack," Angel said, his hands sliding around my waist.

"And I changed the future, so you're welcome," I said and

pushed his hands away. I stood up and nearly fell over, stumbling into Nova before Angel scooped me into his arms.

"We need to clean up before someone sees us," Angel said, carrying me through the door of the roof, Nova following after.

"I can walk," I said, raising a hand to slap his chest and resting it against my throbbing forehead instead. We walked down the final set of steps and through a door that opened into the end of a grand hallway. There were doors on both sides, keycard readers mounted above each gilded door handle.

"You sliced open your own arm. I doubt you can walk a straight line after that, magic or no magic," Angel scoffed as he stopped outside a door, the card reader beeping before he carried me into the large suite.

This time I did slap him.

Hard.

Across the face.

It didn't matter. It didn't hurt him. It wasn't meant to hurt him. Not really.

He sat me on my feet next to the little table beneath the small chandelier. I braced myself against the tabletop as I faced him, Nova standing so close to the door I was surprised she hadn't gone back into the hall to avoid the coming fight.

Angel's jaw tightened, almost intimidating as he looked back at me, not saying a word as he let me have my moment. God, he always made me feel small in the best of ways, like a deer about to be devoured by a mountain lion. But I would not be small, not tonight.

"I cut myself as a distraction because I saw what was going to happen," I said, pointing a finger at his chest. "Magdalena would've put that stake through your chest if I'd stayed put. I won't be locked away in my fate again like I was in that cellar. I won't let anyone else save me when I can save myself. I won't let anyone hurt you when I can stop it either."

"I'm a vampire," Angel snorted.

"I don't give a fuck!" I said and pushed on his chest, only feeling more unsteady. He grabbed onto my arm to keep me upright and once I was, I pulled free. My cheeks burned with embarrassment when I saw the humor in his face. "I'm a seer and I know she would've killed you, so shut up."

His smile dimmed, but not nearly enough to calm the irritation burning in my gut. I kept my eyes trained on him, crossed my arms and avoiding the temptation to look away or shift my stance when he stared right back with that challenging look that reminded me who was really in charge here. I hated him for it and ached for it all the same.

A retching sound broke my focus. Nova was bent over the trash can in the kitchenette. My stomach turned when she made that choaking sound again, finally looking up at us as she wiped the corners of her mouth.

"Healing takes a lot of energy and I've never done it for an injury as bad as that before," she said and groaned. "Do you have Aspirin?"

"In the plastic bag," Angel said and nodded toward the sitting area. His suitcase sat open on one of the two armchairs; his clothes were still neatly folded inside. Nova didn't have to moved them to tug the plastic shopping bag free, dumping out several bottles of pills and an assortment of bandages and wraps. I noticed a box of tampons slip off the coffee table and onto the floor.

I felt his fingers brush my hand and I pulled away before he could slip his hand in mine. I went for the bedroom on the opposite side of the suite, going past the king-size bed that sat untouched and into the large bathroom. I pulled a clean towel from the stack beneath the sink and turned to face him. Angel leaned in the doorway, watching me carefully.

"I need to clean up," I said, tossing the towel onto the counter and crossing my arms. He let out a deep sigh, the rip in his shirt from the cut on his shoulders sliding down to reveal that he'd healed throughout our argument. "Alone," I added when he didn't move.

He scoffed and straightened up. Instead of leaving the room, he pulled the door shut and went to the large bathtub next to the shower and turned on the faucet. "You can't barely walk in a straight line."

"You can wait outside."

"I won't have you passing out and drowning."

"You're a vampire," I said, taking the same tone he had in the main room. "I'm sure you'll hear it if I do."

Satisfaction settled in my chest, easing some of the annoyance as I saw the way his muscles tensed. He paused with his hand on the faucet for a moment before he dipped his fingers in the shallow water to test the temperature. He rose to full height and turned to face me, looking calmer than I was sure he felt.

"I can tell Nova that you'd rather have her come sit with you," he said and started for the door. He had it halfway opened when I stopped him.

"Stop," I said with a groan. He did, turning to send me a questioning gaze. "I don't want Nova."

"Do you want me to stay with you?" he asked in that way that told me he expected a real answer, a yes or no, not the wishy-washy half-truths I had prepared. It was easier to shrug him off, but I knew anything other than a yes would have him out the door to get Nova.

"Yes," I said, waiting until he shut the door to continue. "What I really want is to kick your ass."

"I know, Mouse," he said with a nod. "And I'll happily take whatever punishment you want to inflict on me because I deserve it. But I want to clean the horrors from the night off of you first. Please?"

He did deserve it, but what I really wanted was to curl up in his arms after. My eyes burned and I turned away from him, watching the tub fill as I unzipped my skirt and let the leather fall around my ankles. I took calming breaths as I unzipped the corset top, realizing when I reached the end of the fabric that the top was still held together between my shoulders by a single hook. I tried to reach it, my fingers brushing the metal as that tightness began to grow in my chest. Just as I worried my breathing would become unmanageable, Angel's fingers brushed my hair over one shoulder. He unhooked the top and it fell away, glancing off the tub and landing at my feet.

Angel left me to turn off the faucet, leaving us to stand in the silence. I sucked in a deep breath and slipped my thong off my hips, letting it join the rest of my ruined outfit on the floor as I stepped toward the tub. I nearly fell into the water when I raised my leg over the edge.

"Careful," Angel said, holding one of my arms and my waist as I climbed into the tub and sank into the warm water. He lowered himself to the ground beside the tub, his hand still clasped around mine.

"I am still so mad at you," I said, my voice catching in my throat.

"I'm glad to hear it because I'm not sure I will ever forgive myself," he said in a whisper, kissing the back of my hand and resting his chin on the porcelain. We sat in silence for a moment. I looked away from him and at the water instead, pulling my hand free from his so I could dip my arms in the water. I sank a little more so the warm water rose almost to my chin, my wet hair sticking to my collarbone.

"I understand why you did it," I said.

He sucked in a deep breath. "It doesn't matter why I did it. It matters that I did."

"And it doesn't matter that I'm mad at you and that I want to slap you across the face again because I still love you and I want you to hold me," I said, leaning my head on the edge up the tub and looking up at him. He'd sat back from the tub, his knees pulled to his chest and he stared back at me. He looked conflicted, so much emotion there in his eyes that it made my chest tighten.

"I was trying to protect you," he said, resting his arms on his knees. "Night Owl Apartments was supposed to be your safe haven, a place for you to explore your abilities and learn to control your visions. It was supposed to be a place you were safe from harm and my choice ruined that. I didn't just take that from you, I allowed it to be given to one of the people who hurt you."

"You don't deserve to feel unsafe either," I said and sat

straighter, the water barely high enough to cover my breasts. "You don't deserve it. You could feed from me. Nova can heal me after, so it won't be like you're hurting me—"

"No," Angel said firmly and stood up from the tile floor. I worried he might leave as he turned his back on me. He went to the counter and took a plastic cup from a basket of wrapped soaps and folded washcloths. He returned to me and knelt down by my head, dipping the plastic cup into the water and then pouring it over my head. I sat quietly as he saturated my hair and squeezed a dollop of shampoo into his palm.

"I will never lie to you like that again. I swear," Angel said as he massaged the shampoo into my hair.

I turned around to face him, leaning my hands on the edge of the tub so I could kiss him. He brushed a soap bubble from my cheek when I pulled back to look at him, happy to see he was smiling.

"I love you," I said and kissed the end of his nose.

"I'd feel better if you slapped me again," he said with a laugh, brushing more soap from my hairline. "I love you too."

"I will slap you again if you don't stop worrying about me. I'm a big girl. I can take care of myself," I said, smiling as a bubble transferred from my hair to his. I blew at it and watched as it floated behind him before Angel's smiling face obscured my view.

"I will never stop worrying about you, Mouse," he said, laughing in disbelief. "Now, turn around so I can rinse the shampoo from your hair."

I did, closing my eyes and relaxing at his touch.

CHAPTER 30

Nova was asleep on the couch, her shoes discarded near the coffee table and a throw blanket pulled so far over her head that all I could see was her forehead. Angel's suitcase had been halfway unpacked while I bathed, Nova's black dress lying in a heap on the floor beside it.

Angel rounded the couch for the suitcase, looking through the mess of fabric before pulling out a T-shirt and turning to face me. "Nova must've taken the sweatpants."

I tightened the towel around me and crossed the room to take the shirt from him. "It's fine."

I went back into the bedroom. I heard the door shut behind me a moment later and it was quiet. Despite Angel bathing me just minutes ago, I felt more naked than before as I felt his eyes on my bare back.

"So, that photo ..."

Heat flooded my core and face. I took a deep breath and let the towel fall around my ankles. I didn't turn around. Not yet.

"I knew you had to be watching me. I knew the photo would bring you out of hiding so I could get you to safety," I told him and pulled the T-shirt on. By the time I stuck my arms through the sleeves he was just inches behind me. I could sense him even though he wasn't touching me, feeling the tickle of his breath at my neck.

"You're such a tease," he chuckled.

The shirt began to stick to my skin around the neck and shoulders, my damp hair leaving wet spots where it was lying against my chest. I turned around, standing just inches away from that onery smirk.

"I bet you did a lot of canvasing while we were apart. It's obvious you didn't spend much time here," I said, thinking about his packed suitcase in the main room.

He groaned. "You found more interesting ways to keep occupied. I'd rather talk about that."

My stomach twisted at the thought of the music video, but not because of my new look. I knew it would do well. The teaser had done well—so much better than any I'd posted before—and I didn't want to think about how my video was performing. It was a mix of excitement and anxiety, like two snakes twisting together in my stomach. It must have been obvious, because chills ran over my skin when Angel placed a finger under my chin and raised my eyes to his.

"It came together really fast," I said, resisting the urge to look away from him and only feeling my face heat more. "Literally overnight."

His finger traced my jawline. "Did wardrobe come together that quickly or have you been keeping secrets, Mouse?"

I laced my fingers with his, removing his hand from my face. "Does it make you jealous that the internet got to see me in all that lingerie before you?" I teased.

He smirked and raised his other hand to brush my wet hair behind my ear. I took a step back, leaving his hand suspended in the air in a moment of surprise before he raised an eyebrow, as though challenging me further.

"The internet saw Wilted Rose Strings in lingerie," he said and took a step toward me, stopping when I took another step back. "I get Lily Thompson, *my* good girl, in lingerie. I promise you, it's the rest of the world who should be jealous."

"So, you weren't jealous for even a second when that guy put his arm around me at the club?" I asked, placing my hands on my hips. I saw a hint of annoyance glint in his eye and I wasn't sure if he actually had been jealous or if he was just eager to touch me.

"I told you I saw him with another guy," Angel said, keeping his voice playful despite the tension in his jaw and shoulders. "I knew he was gay before I ever saw him slide closer to you."

"Who's to say he wasn't bisexual?" I asked, taking a seat on the edge of the bed.

"You already had my attention when you sent me that photo. All this teasing tonight—I thought you wanted *me* to take control, Mouse. I'm the dominant. You're my good girl," he said.

I'd been so caught up in his gaze, those dark, predatory eyes, that I hadn't noticed him closing the space between us. My body ached, begging me to part my legs and make space for him.

"Is that what this is?" I asked innocently, pointing between us before pushing my hair behind me to show off the wet front of my shirt. His eyes fell to the soaked spots, his mouth parting with desire. I almost laughed. He was so distracted by the sight of me that his always-in-control persona slipped until he looked up at my face and I felt the heat rush to my cheeks and my stomach fill with butterflies.

No. I wouldn't back down so easily this time.

"You've been a naughty little thing tonight, Mouse," he scoffed, rubbing the back of his head.

I pushed myself back farther onto the bed, leaning back on my hands and setting my feet on the footboard. "And who gets to punish you when *you're* being naughty?"

He stood a little straighter, clearly intrigued. I could see that he finally discovered the rules of my game, but that subtle smirk told me he was still very much in charge. I could feel it between us, that pulse between my legs begging me to offer myself to him.

"Is that what this is? My punishment, Mouse?" he asked with a smirk.

"If you play nice, I'll go easy on you. So, put your back against the wall," I said, unable to sit still after I uttered my pathetic attempt at an order. "Please?"

He chuckled and backed to the wall, leaning against it with his hands by his sides. "My girl always gets what she wants," he said and pinned me with a warning gaze. "And what she deserves."

God. The threat was there as though he was reminding me just how much power he had over me, just how easy it would be to pin me to the mattress. I ignored the thought and parted my legs, watching the humor leave his expression the farther apart I spread them. I stopped just before he could really stare, pressing my thighs together as I twisted the hem of his shirt on my thighs.

My body heated for a new reason, making it easier to raise my eyes to his as I lifted the T-shirt, sliding it up to my waist so I could slip a hand beneath the fabric and palm my breast. He let out a deep groan and straightened up.

"No," I told him, the words sounding so firm that it took me by surprise as well. He froze, jaw tightening. "Your back stays against that wall or I stop."

Chills of pleasure ran over my skin when I saw the corners of his lips twitch. Like a dog left to sit on his haunches, he leaned back against the wall to wait for his treat. God, it only made it all that much hotter. I couldn't suppress my giggle as I arched my back on the bed and let my hand wander beneath the shirt again, watching the way he shifted against that wall.

I pushed the T-shirt farther, exposing my chest. I kept one hand on my left breast, letting the other trace down to my hip and then over my thigh. I spread my legs again, this time tipping my hips upward to allow him the perfect view as my fingers found my center.

He sucked in a deep breath and moved a hand to the front of his jeans, popping the button and sliding down the zipper before I could stop him.

"No touching," I said, my fingers stilling despite how close I was. The look of frustration on his face was worth it though—that alone put me so close to the edge that I had to slow my strokes to keep from losing myself too early. I wanted to tease him as long as I could get away with it, to punish him in the only way my little human self could.

He groaned as he lowered his hands to his sides anyway, his fingers tracing patterns on the wall behind him as though it might take his mind off the growing bulge at the front of his pants. I continued my show, urging that wave higher and higher, almost to the point of breaking before I slowed my movements to start all over again. It was starting to feel like too much even for me, but a look at Angel's tight expression and the way he squirmed was all the motivation I needed to keep at my game.

"Fuck, I bet you taste like honey," Angel said, his voice low, almost a growl. It sent shivers through my body.

"Are you going to beg?" I laughed.

I had to look away when that challenging look returned, dark eyes threatening to pin me in place and make me his.

"Is that what you want, Mouse?" he asked with the hum of a laugh. "You want me on my knees?"

A whimper escaped before I could stop it.

"Finished already?" he asked, making me remember what I was doing. My hands had stilled against my skin. I looked straight up at him as they retraced their paths, my right hand down my stomach toward my center and my left over the swell of my breast. His lips pulled into a smirk that had my heart racing.

"I'm just starting," I teased, coaxing that wave closer and closer. "I won't stop at one. That would be letting you off too easy."

"That's my girl, never stops chasing what she wants," he said, leaning against the wall and tipping his hips so his jeans slid further down his hips and revealed the curve of his abs. "How long do you plan on punishing me like this, denying me of your touch?"

God, the trance I was falling into ... Every nerve in my body was singing and it took all my self-control to slow my pace, keep myself perched just on the edge.

"Until you learn your lesson," I said in a breathy whisper. I made the mistake of looking up at him, watching as he licked his lips. He looked nearly ready to pounce, braced against that wall.

"I wish my hands were yours and I could feel how soft your skin is, how wet you are for me," he said with a moan that coaxed a small whimper past my lips before I could stop it. I gasped, moving my hand to my thigh to keep from losing myself.

He let out a growl, the sound that sent a jolt through my chest, that sound that usually came with a warning. I pressed my thighs together.

"Don't stop," he said roughly, smirking. "Unless you're done with your game."

"I don't plan on punishing you just once," I said, heat flooding my face as I thought about the last time.

Good things come in threes, Mouse...

"I think I might just punish you two, three times, maybe more," I giggled. The humor faded when I saw the way his body tensed. He moved a hand into his hair, pushing it back while the other gripped one end of his belt.

"No touching," I reminded him, the words sounding more like a question. Damn him.

"I'm imagining your hands sliding down your thighs," he said.

"Like this?" I asked, letting my fingers graze my skin on the way down my hips. I made sure to keep my eyes on his, struggling to keep in control as I let my fingers take over again.

"God, look at you," he moaned. "Making me watch while you come undone, the way you bite your lip as you get closer. All I can think about is biting that lip for you, moving your hands away and doing the work myself."

I stifled my whimper, but my legs were shaking and I couldn't stop it.

"That's it. Don't stop," Angel said over my soft cries. "One more, Mouse. Please? Don't let me off easy, I deserve it. Just one more."

Shit! Tears stung my eyes as I continued my pace, thinking of nothing but the lust in his eyes and those things he said.

"No. I can't. Please?"

"You will," Angel said, that deep tone back that sent an ache through my stomach and had my back arched and another whimper piercing the air between us. "That's my good girl."

"P-Please?" I asked between breaths, looking up at him. No longer leaning against the wall, he had his hands by his side and looked down at me with satisfaction. He'd won. He always knew how to twist this, put me back in my place where I felt so safe and desired. I couldn't even curse him for it because I wanted it just as much.

"You promised me three, Mouse," he said, raising his eyebrows.

I moaned, already poised and ready to give it to him, to show him that I always followed through. "Please touch me?"

He was between my legs so quickly that I gasped. His hands gripped my wrists, pinning my left to the mattress beneath me. He brought my right to his lips. He sucked on the end of my index and middle fingers, my fingers that I had dipped between my legs moments ago, before pinning my right hand to the bed. He moved my hands so they restrained by just one of his, leaving the other free to trace a path down my chest. He lowered his chest so his skin brushed mine, leaving soft kisses up my neck before he stopped at my ear.

"I should punish you for the way you teased me tonight," he growled, gripping my hip tight and making my heart leap in my chest. He let go of my hands so he could gather the hem of my T-shirt, raising it to my naval. "That wasn't very nice of you, was it?"

I stumbled over my words. "You don't play fair," I breathed.

"And I don't like your bratty behavior," he said, making me gasp when he ripped open the front of my shirt with a single tug, baring me. My legs tightened around him, wishing there was less fabric between us when the rough zipper of his jeans rubbed against me. "You tried making me jealous with another man." He grinned. I could tell that he was less jealous than he was amused that I'd tried.

"I'm yours," I said, sucking on my bottom lip only for him to pull it free with his thumb.

"And I'm yours, Mouse. Always. Forever," he said, cupping my face with one hand while he pushed his jeans and underwear down with the other. "Say it."

"I'm yours," I said again as he positioned himself between my legs. "Forever."

I gasped as he filled me. Rough. Deep.

"Mine," he growled.

Yes.

Always.

Forever.

CHAPTER 31

My stomach growled and just like that, I was officially awake. Angel wasn't in bed with me. From the smell of bacon and eggs, I was sure he was in the tiny kitchen just beyond the closed door. I sat up and a chill ran over my bare skin. I forgot that I was naked and reaching for the T-shirt at the foot of the bed, I remembered that he'd ripped apart the only clothing in the entire room.

It was immediately apparent how sore I was the moment I stood up and went for the bathroom. Thankfully, there was a robe hanging from a hook in the corner. I slipped it on and went to the main room.

Nova's eyes lingered on me for a moment, eyeing my robe before she looked up at my face. "Good morning."

"Good morning," I returned, noticing that she wasn't in Angel's clothes or the black dress she wore to the club. She had on a purple shirt with New Orleans across the front along with a matching pair of cotton shorts and a pair of flip-flops. I noticed a similar outfit, though mine was green, folded on the arm of the couch.

I looked at Angel as he divided the eggs onto two plates, the breakfast completed with bacon and English muffins. He smiled at me as he slid the plates across the counter to us. "You went out and got new clothes for us?"

"Just down to the lobby," he said and came around the counter to press a kiss to my temple. "There's a gift shop."

I debated eating first, but I felt a little embarrassed that I was in just a bathrobe. I took the clothes and hurried back into the bedroom, quickly pulling on the T-shirt and shorts. It was the same outfit as Nova's, just in green. We both totally looked like tourists. I went back into the main room to eat and I climbed onto the stool, ignoring the soreness, as I took a bite of English muffin.

"Poppy is putting pressure on the council to elect a new High Priestess," Nova said.

I glanced at Angel and saw the guilt written in his expression. Nova had already agreed to come with us. We had even looked at what the transfer process would look like for her to go to Yale. She was top of her class and her artwork was amazing. I was prepared to ask my parents for help too considering they are both Yale graduates. She didn't want to be the High Priestess. I think Bebe even knew this about her granddaughter and just forgot.

"Poppy can't be High Priestess," I said, looking at Angel for help. He gave me a little shrug. "You said she's corrupt and self-interested."

"She is. Her whole family has always operated that way. It's how she's even a council member," Nova scoffed, spearing an egg with her fork but not lifting it from the plate. "But even though Bebe isn't all there anymore, the coven still respects what she has to say and she picked me."

"Are there any other council members who would like the position? Maybe you could back someone and the fact that you were selected would provide some credibility," Angel said, leaning his elbows on the counter top.

Nova shook her head. "I don't know. James Hebert holds a lot of power on the council. He's known for playing the middle and being objective. He has lots of political friends in Louisiana, which could be a plus or a minus."

A politician could mean more safety for the coven. Safety seemed to be a huge concern for most of its members.

"Maybe you can throw his name out there for the sake of coven safety?" I asked, watching as Nova stared at the egg on her fork, twisting it around as though studying every inch of it. She sat the fork on the plate and pushed it aside.

"He's the only one I think I trust," she said with a sigh. "He doesn't like Poppy either, so that's worth something."

"Yes, it is," Angel said, taking her plate from the counter and emptying the scraps into the trashcan. He sat the dish in the sink and turned to look at me, worry settling in his eyes. "Speaking of safety —"

"I don't want to stay at Night Owl Apartments anymore," I said, the words spilling out so fast that it took him a moment to register what they meant. He smiled in relief.

"You'll move here with me?"

"Yes," I told him and turned to Nova. "I don't mean anything by the coven or the apartment. I know you run the place and you do a great job of it—"

Nova waved her hands in front of her. "I know what you mean. You should be with Angel and as far away from that guardian bitch as you can get. She's in Poppy's pocket and that's bad news."

"The second I get the chance I'm tossing her in that gate and getting rid of her for good. The Shadowlands can have her," Angel said, moving around the counter to stand by my side. "Can you move out today, right now?"

"Yes. Please. I don't want to be there without you." I looked to Nova, who had hopped down from her bar stool and was gathering her things from the couch.

"I'll help," she called out as she extricated her phone from between the couch cushions. "Have you seen my keys? Where did we park?"

I was already ahead of her, navigating the app on my phone to get a car. "We walked. I'll get us a ride."

"No, I'll drive you," Angel said, giving my thigh a squeeze. "You can pack your things in the back. I'll be right outside if you need me."

He wasn't allowed inside the building, not that a few hundred witches and warlocks would stop him if it came to that.

"Okay. Where did you park?" I asked him.

He must have used his vampire speed because he was already at the front door with my purse in one hand. "I'm not far. Come on."

The black SUV was parked in the garage beneath the hotel. We didn't have to wait long for one of the attendants to bring it to the covered entrance. It was a short drive from there to Night Owl Apartments, where Angel parked the car out front despite a sign designating the block as pick-up and drop-off only.

"I don't have much, so we'll be down soon," I said, leaning across the center consol to kiss him. I climbed out of the car and followed Nova to the front door. I heard her groan when we walked into the lobby, noticing Poppy standing behind the counter. She looked intrigued, almost like she wanted to approach us, but we kept on walking. Thankfully, the elevator opened as soon as Nova pushed the button and we were able to ride all the way to our floor without stopping.

"I'm going to grab the spellbooks," she said and went to her apartment door. "I'm going to shrink them so I can keep them on me at all times. I think they're too important to just leave around."

"Good idea," I said as I tugged the skeleton key free from my purse. "I just need to pack my suitcase."

I opened the door and walked into the large space. There were dishes sitting in the sink from our snack before we went to the club last night. All our concept notes for the music video were still scattered over the living room coffee table. I gathered them into a neat pile and tucked them inside a notebook.

Before I got any further, I dialed my mom's number and put

my phone on speaker. I finished packing my laptop bag before she even picked up.

"Lily! How's New Orleans?" I could hear her calling for my dad. "You should've told us you had a trip planned."

"It was kind of a last-minute thing. Angel surprised me," I said and lifted the phone from the coffee table so I could go into the bedroom. I moved my suitcase from the corner of the room onto the bed and sat my phone down so I could start gathering my clothes from the dresser.

"Hey, Lilypad," my dad said. I couldn't help but smile at the nickname. "Did he put a ring on your finger?" I heard my mom screaming in the background, a mix of outrage and excitement.

"No! No, it's not that kind of trip," I quickly yelled, bending over to pick up a shirt I'd dropped from the shock of the question. My mom was still yelling in the background, my dad trying to relay the message to her. "Mom!"

"Okay! I heard you. No proposal," she said in defense. "That's for the best, because there's hardly any time to plan a party to celebrate. I wanted to talk to you about that anyway. We're going to miss you for Thanksgiving this year. There's the horse race, of course, but we decided to go and visit some friends. You know, make a few connections, enjoy the season ..."

"There's a man I'm hoping to make a business deal with," my dad declared proudly.

Of course, there was. Always working, my parents.

"That's fine. We'll just stay in New York then," I said, tucking the last of my underwear into a side pocket in my suitcase.

"So, you're sure there won't be a proposal before then? We want you both home for Christmas, but if there's something before then we don't want to miss it," Mom said.

I gave up on keeping things organized and just tossed my bras into the suitcase, my fingers finding the ruby pendant at my neck. "No proposal. Angel is kind of ... Old fashioned isn't the right word for it, but he's traditional. You would know if he was proposing."

"Good man," Dad said, ignoring my mom's chiding in the background.

"Well, I guess there is something about tradition ... Please, tell me you'll have a big Catholic wedding. I really do think it might attract attention if you didn't," Mom said.

Any hope for keeping my clothes wrinkle-free went out the window with that comment and I started to toss the last of my clothes into the suitcase without a care of how they landed.

"There's no proposal and not one coming that I'm aware of. Angel would tell you guys first. Anyway, that's not why I called," I said, squishing my heels on top of the pile of clothes before slamming the suitcase shut. "I just wanted to let you guys know that things have been good. New Orleans has been a lot of fun and we're leaving to come home in a few days. I'll text you when we get on the road."

"Oh. Well, I'm glad." It was obvious my mom was disappointed that there wasn't more news. If I didn't have any drama to occupy her, I could always guarantee she would find some to share with me. Sure enough, to my dad's dismay judging from his groan, she launched into a story about a new lifeguard at the club who let the teenagers do whatever they wanted. I tuned her out as I worked to zip my suitcase shut, knowing it would've been an easier task if I had taken more care with packing it.

"Okay. Um, Mom?" I started, interrupting her as she detailed how anyone over seventeen was avoiding the pool because this lifeguard refused to tell the teens off. "I have to go. Angel and I have plans and I don't want to be late."

"Tell him we said hello! We'll get a round of golf the next time he's here," Dad called from the background,

"I love you both," I said, my finger hovering over the button to end the call, letting them both say their final goodbyes before I hung up. I let out a deep sigh that turned to a groan when I remembered that I'd forgotten to pack all my toiletries.

After another twenty minutes of packing and searching the apartment to make sure nothing was missed, I gathered my laptop bag and rolled the suitcase behind me into the hallway. At first, I thought maybe it was just all the natural light from the apartment that made seeing in the hallway difficult, but a look down at the elevator told me that the hallway was actually darker than normal. The sconces outside Nova's and my apartments had gone out while I'd been packing. Her door was slightly open for me. I thought she would've come to my apartment to offer her help. Surely it didn't take that long to find and shrink the four spellbooks.

Chills raced up my spine when I realized why this felt so strange, why the dark walls looked familiar. I let go of my suitcase and let my laptop bag fall to the floor beside it, whirling around to face the end of the hallway. I was frozen in place, angry that my powers hadn't warned me this time and terrified of what I knew would come next.

The figure was bathed in darkness as it reached for that silver cane at his hip just like he had in my vision. Before I could scream, he was in front of me, fear stealing all the air from my lungs. I turned to run, only to feel that cane come down around me, pulling my back to his chest.

He whispered in my ear, "Don't be afraid, Lily."

CHAPTER 32

He was gone a second later, just the ghost of a laugh left behind that propelled me into Nova's apartment. I slammed the door shut and turned the lock, scanning the room for Nova.

"Nova!" I yelled, taking just a few steps into the room when the redhead came out of the bedroom. A muffled sound to my left drew my attention and I turned to see Nova lying on the ground, her arms and legs tied and duct tape over her mouth.

"I'm glad we finally get some time to talk, just us girls."

I looked back at Olivia Saxon. More muffled cries came from Nova and when I looked at her, she was shaking her head. Tears rolled down her face and onto the hardwood floor beneath her.

"You remember my powers, don't you?" Olivia said, pulling my attention back to her. "I know everything. I already knew your boyfriend was after the cure for vampirism. I knew about the guardian blood. I didn't know about the hand of the maker until I touched your friend. It makes sense why your boyfriend has been tailing us now."

"You're with *them*?" I asked, trying to sort through why the hell a guardian would team up with a trio of vampires. Why would they team up with her?

"Angel hunted us down for a reason. He got rid of my brother for a reason. He only kept me alive because I benefitted him, but even I knew it was a matter of time before it wasn't worth the return to keep me alive," she said, taking a step closer to Nova. "The vampires found me after they tracked Angel to the warehouse. We talked and decided that maybe there was a way we could all get what we want. So, they left me in the warehouse while they learned more about what you two were doing here. That witch finding me was just the perfect opportunity. I was invited into the building. It made setting the trap easy."

Nova started screaming again past her gag and this time, I could tell it was a message. I followed her eyes toward the living area, only looking when Olivia turned her attention on Nova.

"Shut up!" Olivia gripped Nova's hair and gave her a shake, giving me enough time to look over the living space and see the small squares sitting on the floor beneath the coffee table. They were no larger than sticky notes, thicker though.

The spellbooks.

"Found them," Olivia said in a sing-song tone, dropping Nova and looking toward the living room.

I reached across the counter for the knife block, pulling free the first one I could grab, a paring knife, and launching it across the room at her. Olivia gasped, straightening up with wide eyes. I froze as she looked down at the knife buried in her shoulder, not moving until Nova began screaming again.

I ran for the coffee table, reaching for the books just as Olivia latched onto my ankle. With a yank, my hand missed the edge of the coffee table and my forehead bashed into it instead. My vision blurred as I blindly reached for the books, letting out a scream when my head was pulled back by my hair.

"Bitch!"

I screamed again as she sliced along my cheek with that knife. I abandoned my effort to reach the books and rolled onto my back instead, Olivia fighting to pin me down. She groaned in frustration when I dragged my nails down her face, leaving behind two long scratches that dripped blood onto my face. It was just enough of a distraction that she was able to slap me across the face, hard enough to gain the advantage.

"Do what I say, or I will cut you," she said, the tip of the knife poised just beneath my chin.

I already knew what they wanted. I was just bait, a way to get Angel wherever they wanted him. It was Paul all over again, telling me to be a good girl and follow directions. All it got me was locked away in their estate and then locked in the wine cellar.

"You already did," I said and punched her side.

I felt the sting of the knife as it cut my chin before it fell to the floor. I rolled onto my side, both of our hands fumbling for the handle. I yelled when she pulled my hair, feeling pieces of it snap as I tried elbowing her away.

"Give up!" Olivia screamed and shoved my head into the leg of the coffee table. The table slid into the couch and my hand was pulled away from the knife, allowing her to pick it up again. "Let's make things even."

She turned the knife point-down shoving my shoulder to the floor. Before she could stab me, I grabbed the leg of the coffee table and pulled it toward us. The knife lodged in the table top and I shoved it away before she could pull it free, sending it skittering across the floor toward the bedroom. I reached for it with my foot, but was distracted when I felt something slice into my left arm.

"I came prepared, bitch," Olivia said, twisting her dagger in her hand. She brought the point down toward my head, my hands on hers the only reason she hadn't taken out my left eye. I gave up on reaching for the paring knife on the floor and I gave it a weak kick instead, hoping it slid close enough for Nova.

"He's going to kill you," I said through my teeth, my arms vibrating from the effort to keep the dagger from plunging. "If they don't do it first."

Olivia laughed, a sound that came out little more than a growl. "He'll be too busy burying you."

Something changed as I looked back at her. She had the same blue eyes he had, even smiled in that same sinister way he did when she was mad. I'd always known Olivia to be calm, calculated, but she was every bit Paul Saxon's sister now and it made anger burn in my stomach.

"Fuck you!"

I spat in her face. It distracted her just enough that I was able to slap the dagger away before I punched her in the nose. My fingers popped from the force and blood dripped onto my shirt before I could shove her off. I rolled on top of her, pinning her hand that held the dagger to the floor while I punched her in the face with the other.

After several blows, I was able to pull the dagger free and point the tip at her. My heart hammered in my chest and I could feel my whole body shaking from the adrenaline as I raised the dagger above me and screamed, plunging it over and over into her chest. I didn't stop until blood coated her shirt, sticking to her skin and pooling around us. I dropped the dagger into the pool, falling over Olivia's legs as I tried to scoot away.

"Little warrior," a man said in a thick Spanish accent. It had me frozen in place.

I let out a gasp as the world blurred around me and my back smashed into something hard. My feet were off the ground and a man who looked near sixty was holding me up by my biceps. His red eyes roved over my body before they settled on my face, a smirk spreading.

"Lily Thompson," he said, his smile fading a little when his eyes landed on the pendant resting against my chest. "My name is Francisco de Palencia. I believe you met my son, Alonzo." Francisco said something in Spanish. Alonzo and Magdalena were standing near Nova. Alonzo walked toward us, nudging Olivia's boot as he passed. He stopped next to his father, a nearly identical smirk pulling across his face as he looked at me.

"Angel's little whore," he said, with a laugh. I was sure they could all hear my hummingbird-heart as he took my hand, raising my trembling fingers to his lips. I held my breath as he kissed my knuckles, keeping his eyes locked on mine. Suddenly he was inches away. I screamed as pain shot through my left arm from my wrist, his teeth deep in my flesh. I gasped as that familiar warmth spread through my arm, easing the pain and sending me into a stupor. I felt weak, sleepy. It was like climbing into a warm bed with fluffy blankets, sliding against Angel's bare chest and falling asleep in his arms ...

The sensation was gone in seconds and I was left with my hand still raised, a halfmoon bite mark on my forearm dripping blood onto the floor. Francisco spoke in Spanish again to his son, an order that Alonzo ignored with the shake of his head.

"I want him to see that I've had her," he said and raised a hand to brush a tear from my cheek. "Maybe I'll leave a few more marks before he joins us." He roughly patted the side of my face before he turned and walked back to Magdalena. She didn't seem impressed by the show, a scowl on her face that didn't fade until Alonzo kissed her full in the mouth, transferring my blood from his lips to hers. She licked the last smear of it off his chin before she knelt down next to Nova who immediately started screaming with terror, her voice still too muffled to be heard past the apartment door.

"Leave the witch. Take the girl," Francisco said, nodding toward Olivia's limp body as he lowered me to the ground.

I could hardly stand, shaking so violently that I couldn't fight as Francisco withdrew a pair of handcuffs from his back pocket. He clicked one in place around my left forearm, making me cry out when it rubbed against the bite mark. He fastened them behind my back and then withdrew a piece of black fabric.

I was immediately transported back in time. I could see nothing, but I heard the crunch of gravel, felt those rough hands as he carried me.

I told you to be a good girl, Lovely.

"No. No. Please!" I begged as he unfolded the pillowcase. Magdalena appeared at his side, nothing but a whirl of color, and shoved me roughly against the wall. She slapped a piece of duct tape over my mouth, keeping her hand there.

"Make this easy for us or we will make it hard for you," she said and lowered her hand.

My eyes met Nova's when Magdalena moved aside. She'd moved her bound hands from behind her back to her front, her arms and legs pulled close to her as she lay on the floor. After a glance at the vampires, she lifted her shirt, revealing the handle of that paring knife I'd kicked her way earlier. Relief made my body go slack and I nearly tripped when Francisco led me away from the wall and toward the window in the living room.

"Such a mess you made, Lily," Alonzo laughed as he carried Olivia across his shoulders and joined the three of us near the window. With an effortless kick, he shattered the large window and before the pieces had even settled against the floor, Francisco pulled me into his arms and we were airborne.

CHAPTER 33

I was spared the blindfold, left to watch as the neighborhood I'd come to know slipped away into the distance below. I couldn't be sure how fast we were moving or how far away we'd flown before the three vampires landed in an area surrounded by warehouses, empty semi-trucks, and lots of chain-link fencing armed with barbed wire around the top. We were near the water. I only knew because the air reeked of fish and that didn't go away when I was taken inside one of the warehouses.

We went into a large room that must have been a fish processing plant at some point. Old conveyer belts stretched across the room. There was a mural of a catfish along the back wall, paint peeling off in several places. The vampires began speaking in Spanish, exchanging a few words before we stopped walking.

"You. Here," Francisco said to me.

I had no other choice. I walked to him and he moved me toward the nearest conveyor belt. He unlocked the cuff around my right wrist and tightened it around the metal leg of the conveyor belt, forcing me to sit on the floor. I jumped when Alonzo tossed Olivia's limp body onto the conveyor belt above me. I wondered how long it would take before her body would reanimate and I would face her again.

"Angel will be here soon," Magdalena said, combing through her hair with the three fingers of her right hand. "That girl had a knife. She probably cut herself free and went straight to him after we left."

I wasn't sure if I should be relieved or terrified. I knew this was a trap set for him, not me. He was strong, strong enough to fight off Paul and Olivia before, but it would be four against one and three of them were vampires at least as old as he was.

I was distracted as the vampires spoke in Spanish again. What-ever Alonzo said had piqued the others' interest. He smiled and looked at me before facing his father again.

"She has powers," he scoffed. "I could taste it in her blood."

Francisco made his way toward me, adjusting his grip on his cane as he knelt down. My skin stung as he ripped the duct tape free, letting it flutter to the floor before he straightened up and placed the end of his cane under my chin. He raised my face so I looked up at him, red eyes studying me.

"What are you?" he asked curiously. I didn't speak right away and he drew the cane back, making me flinch and brace for the blow that never came. When I looked again I saw that he'd handed the cane to Alonzo. He braced his hands on the conveyor belt above me, lowering himself so he was just a few inches away from my face.

"She was with those other witches," Magdalena said.

"No." Francisco shook his head. "There's a calmness around her. Do you remember the way that woman in Italy felt?"

Alonzo and Magdalena exchanged looks of surprise before looking back at me.

"A seer?" Alonzo asked. "Where did Angel find you, pretty girl?"

"You've played with your food enough, son," Francisco said and straightened up, sending Alonzo a look of warning as he took his cane back from him.

"But they always taste so much better when they're scared," Alonzo said in a mocking tone.

There was a gasp above me and Olivia thrashed against the conveyor belt. She froze when she saw the trio, looked around the room, and then smiled when she saw me sitting beneath her. She hopped down from the conveyor belt, revealing her blood-soaked shirt and pants.

"Just in time," Magdalena told her and nodded toward the exit. "I hear wings."

"He wouldn't be stupid enough to come alone, would he?" Alonzo laughed.

Olivia pointed to me. "For her, yes."

I hoped she wasn't right. Maybe he had Nova with him. She'd used her magic against them once before. We managed to escape the club, maybe we could do it again. They were silent, listening to sounds too low for my human ears to pick up. Alonzo laughed, shaking his head in disbelief.

A bang startled me, the metal door across the room flying off the hinges and shooting across the floor toward us. Alonzo stopped it with his foot, leaving a deep dent in the thick metal. Angel burst into the room, several feet taller than normal and with large wings stretched behind him. His shirt was ripped at one shoulder low enough that he shredded it the rest of the way and tossed the fabric to the side as he walked. He let out a yell that echoed around the room, Spanish insults that made Alonzo take a few steps forward before Francisco stretched his cane in front of him.

"En inglés, cuñado," Alonzo teased, and pointed to me on the floor.

Angel let another round of Spanish insults fly as he walked, coming to a stop just feet away from Alonzo. "I haven't been your brother-in-law since you tossed your sister into her grave."

"You mean, since *you* killed her," Alonzo said, suddenly just as tall as Angel. He pulled his shirt from over his head before his wings could sprout, handing the fabric to Magdalena who tossed it aside without a care.

In seconds, Angel was out of arm's reach, Magdalena's hands pressed against his chest. She gave him another shove that sent him skidding several feet. Angel took another step forward and stopped, his eyes going to me and the color leaving his face.

"I roughed up your bitch a little," Alonzo said from next to me. I gasped when he lifted my left arm to show off the bite mark. "Don't worry. I'll take care of it."

The moment Alonzo's tongue made contact with my skin Angel was airborne. A boom echoed through the room, the concrete floor shaking. Francisco and Magdalena had both attacked, pinning Angel to the floor before pulling him into a kneeling position.

"See? Perfect," Alonzo said, showing my now healed arm to him.

"Just let her go. She doesn't deserve this violence. This has nothing to do with her," Angel said, attempting to tug his arms free from Magdalena and Francisco.

"Your little seer here can take care of herself," Alonzo laughed.

"Bitch got lucky," Olivia sneered and spat on the floor between us. "And I've done my part. Goodbye."

"Not yet," Francisco said, stopping her. "You wanted them gone. I'm a man of my word. I want you to see it for yourself."

I felt sick, looking away from Francisco's smiling face and straight at Angel. He held my gaze, something in his eyes pleading with me. I took a deep breath and then another, trying to calm my nerves. He nodded, prompting me to continue the ritual. I needed to clear my head. I needed to empty my mind the way I did for lessons with Nova.

Pain shot up my right arm and I screamed. Angel thrashed against Magdalena and Francisco as Alonzo bit down harder, sucking my blood and sending me deeper into that strange floaty space in my mind, almost like falling into one of my visions.

"I'm a seer! I'm a seer! What do you want to know?" I screamed.

The silence in the warehouse made my skin prickle with goosebumps.

"Lily," Angel said, shaking his head. "Don't."

Alonzo let go of my arm and I drew it close to my chest, feeling the warm blood seep into my shirt.

"She's a seer. She can't see things that have already happened," Magdalena said, looking from Francisco to Alonzo.

"I can," Olivia said. Fear cut through me. "I can see everything about a person with one touch."

"But that takes all the fun out of this," Alonzo said.

"I know that they're looking for the cure for vampirism. They got the first ingredient for the spell: blood of power. They have guardian blood. They came here to find the witch with the rest of the spell. That witch you left back at the apartment, she's the key. They need the hand of the maker, which I assume is one of you," Olivia said. She watched them all carefully and sure enough, Francisco and Magdalena both looked at Alonzo.

"Does she know where your family's fortune is?" Francisco asked, tapping Angel's bare chest with his cane.

"No," Angel said. "I told you this doesn't involve her. She doesn't know anything about that part of my life."

"That's a lie," Olivia laughed, coming to stand next to me. She leaned back against the conveyor belt. "He told her about Maria."

All three de Palencia vampires stiffened. She was right. Angel told me he'd left the money at his grandfather's estate. He didn't say where though. I screamed when Alonzo gripped my arm, digging his fingers into the bite mark.

"You've touched him before. Do you know where it is?" Francisco asked her.

Olvia's smile dimmed a little. "I take in so much information that it's hard to remember anything aside from what I'm looking for, especially from someone with centuries of experiences," she said, eyeing Angel. "But, I can find out easy enough."

She crossed the room, Angel's jaw tensing as she got closer.

"Wait," Alonzo said, holding a hand out to her. He laughed, like whatever he'd just thought about was the funniest thing he'd ever heard. "You touch him. Find out where he left the family fortune. But don't tell anyone, except for her." He pointed at me.

"What?" Magdalena asked. "Let's just get the information, kill them, and be done."

"No. Better idea," Alonzo said, holding up an index finger for them all to wait. "Go on. Touch him and go tell Lily."

Olivia hesitated for a moment before taking the final two steps to Angel and putting a hand on top of his head. Angel let out a string of curses as Olivia stood there. She finally turned and started back across the space to me, smiling.

"Why not just tell us?" Magdalena asked.

"Because Angel only knows where he left it hundreds of years ago. Spain is very different now. Our own hometown no longer exists on a map. We ransacked his grandfather's house and the home he shared with Maria. Angel will remember where he left the money, but Lily will know where it will be in the future."

Fuck.

Magdalena smiled and Francisco let out a booming laugh.

"Tell her where he left it, girl," Francisco said, prompting Olivia to continue across the room to me. My heart slammed against my ribcage as she knelt in front of me, my vision blurring as I went lightheaded. She lowered her lips to my ear, her voice so low that even I could barely hear her.

"It's at his grandfather's estate, one mile from where the house sat, buried beneath a stable." Olivia straightened up, giving me a view of the fear in Angel's eyes. He shook his head, begging me to keep quiet.

"Now," Francisco said, letting go of Angel's arm so Alonzo could take his place. He moved into the space between Angel and me, looking directly at me as he sat the end of his cane on the floor. Using the heel of his foot, he snapped it in half, tossing the handle and scooping up the remaining wooden cane, eyeing the jagged end before he looked back at me.

"You're a seer," he said, repeating my words from earlier with a deep laugh. "Tell us where that money is now."

CHAPTER 34

Francisco surged forward with vampire speed, putting him inches away from Angel when he said, "I hope your pretty little mate knows how to use her powers."

"I buried it under the stable. That's where I left it," Angel said, not at all concerned with the jagged end of the cane that Francisco had resting against his chest. "Leave her alone. Let her go. This isn't about her."

"It is now," Francisco said. "A lot has changed since you left and we haven't been to our homeland since we tore apart your family's home. We can't even be sure where it is anymore, but your precious girl is the only one who can tell us exactly where that money is."

"Please," Angel begged. "Let her go."

"You won't get off so easily," Francisco said before turning to address me. "If you can't use your abilities to see where the fortune is, I will kill you. I can always find another seer to get that money. If you can use your abilities to tell me where that money is, then I will kill Angel."

Ice shot through my veins.

"Lily," Angel said, pulling me out of my despair for the only shot at hope we had left. "You can do this."

I looked up at Francisco and his smug expression. "You got what you want. Just go find another seer, someone more experienced," I told him, screaming when he raised his right hand to show a set of claws at the end of his fingers. "No! Please!"

Angel managed to stifle his yell as Francisco dragged his claws across his chest, leaving deep enough cuts to send a steady flow of blood down Angel's chest.

"Stop! Please, stop!" The handcuff was cutting into my wrist as I tugged against it.

Francisco placed another cut on Angel's right cheek before slamming his fist into his nose, the crunching sound making my stomach turn. Angel raised his head in time to take another blow to the face and then another to the gut.

"Please! I can't focus! I can't see anything when you're hurting him!"

Francisco turned away from Angel and dropped the cane, letting it clatter to the floor before he stepped over it to reach me. He brushed my hair behind my ear and then I was tossed into the leg of the conveyor belt by the force of his slap. I saw stars; my cheek stung.

"Don't touch her!" Angel barked, silencing the room again. "She said she'll do it. She needs to focus. Let her focus."

"You better hope she can do it," Francisco said and bent down next to me. He uncuffed me from the leg of the conveyor belt and then gripped the hair at the top of my head. I whimpered as he dragged me across the room, giving me a final shove into Angel's bloody chest.

"It's okay, Mouse. It will be okay," he said as I cupped his face, trying to brush away the blood leaking from his nose. "You can do this."

"We're going to find the cure. We have to find the cure and get married and have a family. I want you to be mortal. I want to carry your child, start a new life," I sobbed.

"I've already lived a long life, Mouse," he said, leaning his forehead against mine. "You have barely gotten your start in this world. I won't let anyone take that from you. Just this one thing, that's all you have to do and you're free. Just a little bit of focus, Mouse. Please, do this for me. Just one more thing for me."

"I don't know. I can't summon the vision on my own that well. I can barely do it with a trigger. I don't know that—"

"Look at me!"

That deep voice felt like a shot through my core. It was the commanding voice that was reserved for just us, that tone that always melted me in place. I looked past all the gore and into his eyes, focusing on that stern gaze.

"Eyes on me. Don't you dare look away. You keep your eyes on me, Mouse," he said.

"Yes."

"Put your hands on me," he said, waiting until I laid my palms against his chest to speak again. "Deep breath. Come on."

I did, focusing on the feeling of his chest rising and falling. I matched my breathing to his.

"Close your eyes and go there. Think of me in that countryside, that stupid boy rebelling against his grandfather, that man who didn't feel deserving of what he left behind. Just go there, Mouse. Do it for me. Please," he said, his voice soft, so raw that I couldn't help but fall into that memory all over again, remembering what he told me of the time he stole that horse and all the things he said. The way his grandfather understood him, was more concerned about that grieving boy than his prize horse.

Of course, Angel would bury the last thing he had of his family there. That stable mattered more than anything to his grandfather. It was where Angel finally confronted his life and all the loss he'd endured. I could imagine him burying a chest filled with that fortune in the earth, the vision taking shape from there.

My eyes were focused on that spot where I imagined Angel burying the money, but there wasn't a field around it anymore. There wasn't even any grass or a barn. There were rows of dirt and I immediately saw the whole scene because I knew what those rows were. It was a vineyard, not nearly as large as my family's, but large enough to have at least twelve rows that stretched several yards back from the mansion. That spot that I kept my eyes on, making it the focal point of my mind, the scene only grew more and more vivid ...

Angel's family fortune was buried just feet down that third row in the vineyard, right between the third and fourth row.

I opened my eyes, meeting Angel's hopeful gaze, but I didn't get to say a word before Alonzo and Magdalena began screaming. The world was a blur of color and wind around me for a moment. I was tucked against Angel's chest. He lowered me to the ground and stood up, moving into place behind a line of witches.

Nova left formation to help me to my feet.

"How did you get them?" I asked her, eyeing the witches. James Hebert and one of the other women from the council stood just feet away, both dressed in loungewear, like Nova had interrupted their casual weekend plans. There were three more I didn't recognize who stood on the other side of Bebe.

"Angel knew we'd need help," Nova said, stopping next to Angel. "I'll explain it later."

Bebe stood center, both arms raised. Alonzo and Magdalena stopped screaming when she lowered her arms, both crumpling to the floor as they struggled to gain their strength.

"For weeks you have tormented the innocent people of this city," Bebe said, her voice booming through the room. "You targeted an innocent young seer who wanted nothing but help, help for herself and for the man she loves. You used her against him, a man who rejects his nature for the sake of all that's good. You planted that guardian bitch in our coven and she let you inside our walls."

Francisco ignored his son and Magdalena, walking past them. "Don't act like your witchcraft is so innocent."

"You attacked my granddaughter!"

"Yes, twice, I believe," he answered, not at all phased when Alonzo began screaming again just feet away. He didn't even look at his son, his eyes locked on Bebe until she ended the spell.

"Demon bat from Hell!" Bebe shouted and shot sparks at Francisco's feet when he took another step forward.

He laughed, taking a step toward his son as he struggled to get to his feet. Francisco patted Alonzo on the back. "We are undying, death reincarnate, sent to wander the earth," he said with a shrug. "We're vampires. Not even Hell would accept us."

I was nearly knocked over from the force of Angel's wings. He launched himself over the line of witches, landing on top of Alonzo. A scream pierced the air and my heart stopped before I realized it wasn't Angel's. Magdalena reached the fighting pair first, tossing Angel off and sending him skidding into the conveyor belt to the left.

Blood poured onto the floor from Alonzo's arm, making the floor slick enough that he nearly slipped in it as he got to his feet to face us.

"Destroy them!" Bebe yelled.

All of the witches raised their arms for attack, but they were seconds too late. Alonzo, Magdalena, and Francisco were all gone. Olivia stood in the empty space before us, her face draining of color.

She ran, making it only a few feet before Nova's spell hit her and she fell to the concrete floor. She struggled, but it was like her ankles and wrists were bound by invisible chains.

"Fucking witches," she grumbled.

Bebe pointed a finger at her and her mouth opened and closed, but no noise came out.

Angel walked back to us, wiping the fresh blood around his mouth as he shrank to his normal size and his wings receded into his back. He stopped in front of Bebe. "I can tell you where that gate is, the one I dropped her brother into." He wrapped an arm around my waist and pulled me to his side. "Lily has been through enough tonight. I'd like to get her someplace safe as soon as I can."

Bebe nodded and motioned for two of the closest warlocks to join us before addressing Angel again. "Go back to Night Owl Apartments with Nova. She can explain what's happened. You're safe there, *all* of you." Bebe placed a hand on Angel's shoulder for a moment before turning to relay instructions to the warlocks. Angel kissed my temple before joining them, leaving me to go to Nova.

"Are you okay?" I asked.

She shrugged, offering a weak smile. "Well, I wasn't kidnapped."

I pulled her into a hug. "I was so worried Olivia would steal the spellbooks."

"No one touched them. They're in my pockets now," Nova said when she pulled away.

I thought about the cure in that spellbook and the hex concealing the full instructions from us. Without that book, there would be no way for Angel to become mortal again. I looked at him as he talked with Bebe and the warlocks, the way his wounds had faded but the blood remained. It was just the same for Olivia as she lay on the ground, blood saturating the front of her clothes. I had done that. I killed her back in the apartment and I did it to protect my future with Angel. But protecting the future didn't mean we had to leave the past behind. We would have to embrace it.

"Nova," I started and turned back to her. "Before you guys got here, I saw something—"

"We'll talk back at the apartment," she said, nodding toward Angel as he joined us again.

He let out a deep sigh and pulled me to his chest, kissing my forehead before kissing my lips. I didn't care that we had an audience. I deepened the kiss, held his face to mine, thanked whatever supernatural forces were at play that allowed me to have him despite everything.

He broke the kiss and looked up at Nova. "Hang on tight. It's a bit of a trip back home."

She groaned. "I hate traveling like this. Can't we just take a car?"

"Just close your eyes," I told her with a laugh as she tightened her arms around us. "We'll be there before you know it."

It wasn't my first trip like this and I was sure it wouldn't be my last.

CHAPTER 35

When we got to Night Owl Apartments, Nova immediately led us down the hall into the employee lounge. I sat down on the couch, Angel sitting next to me.

"Let me take care of that," he said, pointing to the bite mark on my right arm. The venom had run its course and it no longer hurt. I held out my arm to him and he gently lifted it to his mouth, sealing the bite with his tongue. By the time he was done, the puncture wounds were already slowly knitting together.

"Anyone need healing?" Nova asked, setting a tray on the coffee table. There was a full pitcher of water and three empty glasses. Angel filled one of the glasses and sat it in front of me.

"Here," he said before continuing to inspect me for injuries.

I ignored him, dipping one of the napkins from the tray into the cup and raising it to his face.

"Lily," he admonished, moving my hand away before I could get near the dried blood on his chin. I slapped his hand away and swiped at the blood anyway, folding the napkin in half and dipping it in the glass again.

He groaned as the water turned pink, but didn't protest when I turned to continue cleaning him. "All of my injuries are healed. A little blood won't hurt me and it's impossible for me to exhaust myself. I can go months without food or water, you on the other hand ..."

"I think I'll survive another five minutes," I teased, finally clearing away the blood around his mouth so I could see that onery smirk.

"Hang on," Nova said, already crossing the room for the bar cart in the corner. "I'll get you a towel."

Angel brushed my hair away from my face, lightly touching the bruise on my cheek. I tried not to wince. "Can you stop fussing over me for once?" I teased, brushing his hand away.

"Never," he said.

I took the towel from Nova and dipped it in the water. Angel sat still while I wiped away the blood, the towel stained beyond saving by the time I was finished with his chest. Nova used her powers to set it aflame, wrinkling her nose until it had turned to ash between her fingers.

"Were the witches easy to convince?" Angel asked her. He poured another glass of water and sat it in front of me. I rolled my eyes, but lifted it to my lips. I could be amenable.

"Bebe was, of course," Nova said from across the coffee table. "It didn't take much at all to gather a group. Hebert was one of the first to volunteer. Honestly, it was the drive to the warehouse that took the longest."

"What about Poppy?" I asked. There was silence. The anger practically radiated off Angel.

"Well, she was there. She was defensive, saying she didn't know about the other vampires," Nova said.

"You believe that?" Angel asked roughly.

Nova adjusted in her seat anxiously and nodded. "Bebe compelled her. It's a spell reserved only for people suspected of being traitors. She was telling the truth. She had no idea. She believed the worst of you from the beginning and thought she found proof. She was honest in her apology."

"Apology," Angel scoffed, shaking his head.

"She was removed from the council on the spot," Nova interjected, looking from me to Angel. "And because she was removed, she can't be elected back into office. So, James Hebert will be the new High Priest of the coven. Poppy can't keep her nose out of stuff, so I think I'll give her my job over apartment operations. She'll be really good at managing tenants and it will keep her busy enough that hopefully she won't miss being on the council that much. It makes it easier for everyone."

"That sounds great," I told her. "And you said that you got the spellbooks after I was taken, so we are still on track for the cure."

Nova smiled and started to empty her pockets. She sat all four tiny books onto the table and looked at each before identifying which had the spell for the cure. She waved a hand over it and it grew to its original size.

"Better than on track," Angel said. We watched as he stood up and pulled a severed hand from his back pocket. My stomach rolled and I thought I might be sick before I realized what he had done.

"Hand of the maker," Nova gasped as he placed Alonzo's hand on the coffee table.

"That's why you attacked," I said.

He nodded. "I knew they were moments from getting away. The witches would be too much for them. It's too important. They wouldn't stick around, not after what they learned about the cure from Olivia. They'd know I'd be looking for Alonzo."

I was stunned and so was Nova from the looks of her. She had a hard time getting her question out, drumming her hands over the cover of the spellbook like it would help her think.

"So, um, do you have the dagger?" she asked.

Angel pulled the dagger from his waistband and sat it down next to the hand. We all stared at the two objects for a moment. I could tell that Nova was deep in thought. She started to drum her fingers over the cover of the spellbook again. Finally, she stopped and sat back.

"Okay," she said in an exhale. "I'm ready."

"I trust you," Angel said firmly, no hint of worry in his voice like the first time she'd performed the spell.

"You can do this, Nova," I said.

She nodded and opened the book, finding the page for the cure. She gripped the hilt of the dagger and closed her eyes. She began murmuring. I recognized some of the words from the last time. Her voice began to shake, growing louder as she neared the end of the spell. She opened her eyes and sucked in a deep breath, stabbing the tip of the dagger into the middle of the hand.

The tip sank deep into the coffee table where the hand had vanished. My heart sank like a stone in a river. Angel's hand tightened on my knee and before I could ask if the spell had worked, I saw the dark ink spread on the page of the spellbook.

Blood of power.
Hand of the maker.
Bone of family.

I read the message three times before I understood what it meant. Was it even possible to find any of his family members? Would there be anything left of them? Angel's hand was still on my knee. I sat mine on top of his when I realized it was trembling.

"Do you, um, have any descendants?" Nova asked.

Angel shook his head. "Just me."

The room was quiet. We sat for a long moment like that, all of us staring at those three lines in the spellbook until Nova shut it with a thump. Angel slid his hand out from beneath mine and stood up.

"I'll go gather your things," he said and kissed the top of my head. "We should get home. The semester starts in just a few days."

"I'll help you," I said, rising from the couch and taking a few steps before he stopped me.

"No. You survived that attack upstairs. You shouldn't have to see the aftermath."

He left the room and neither Nova nor I spoke for a long time. I drank the last of my water and sat down across from her, watching as she shrank the spellbook and packed all four away in her pockets again.

"What did you want to tell me before we left the warehouse?" she asked.

"What?" It took a moment before it dawned on me. The vision. The vineyard. The mansion. Angel burying that chest.

"You said you saw something?"

"Oh. Right," I said, chewing on my bottom lip. "I saw Angel at home, in Spain."

Nova gasped. "It all makes sense now," she said and lifted the dagger from the table. "His family is in Spain. Of course, we'd have to go there for the cure."

Well, she wasn't wrong. She just didn't know that there were more there than just bones.

"Yeah. Makes sense," I agreed, taking the dagger and standing up. "Let's go wait for Angel in the lobby."

"I'm sorry about your studio," Nova said and sat the final item from the extra bedroom, a stack of acoustic panels, on the living room coffee table. My cello was set up in the corner next to a line of other recording equipment.

"It's okay. I'll just rent a space when we're ready to record again. It'll be better anyway," I told her, looking toward the kitchen when Angel popped the cork out of a wine bottle. He poured three glasses. He didn't drink often—vampire and all— but he lifted the glass to his lips and took a sip before gathering all three between his hands and crossing the living room to join us on the couch.

"All moved in?" he asked Nova.

She took a glass from him and raised it in a toast. "Yes. Finally."

We pressed out glasses together.

"We were just looking at Wilted Rose Strings online," Nova said.

I felt sick. Shit. I was still in shock and talking about it didn't make it any better. I wanted to run away and celebrate all at the same time and I wasn't really sure why. I was self-sabotaging, probably. Definitely self-sabotaging.

"Lily?" Angel asked, setting his wine glass on the table and scooting closer to me. "What's wrong?"

"Nothing," I said and shook my head, trying to blink away the tears.

"Is everything going well? When I last checked, people all over the internet were talking about you, especially the new persona. Your video is ranked on YouTube."

"No. It's going well. I don't know. It's just..."

He brushed my hair from my face. Nova only smiled wider, getting an annoyed stare from Angel.

"What is it?" he asked her before looking back at me.

"I'm almost up to twenty-thousand dollars," I whispered.

He smiled, brushing away a tear. "That's great. I'm sure next year you'll double it. You're too talented not to."

I covered my face with my hands and they both laughed. He tugged my hands away and set them in my lap.

"No, I'm almost up to twenty-thousand this month," I told him.

He looked to Nova who only laughed harder, nearly spilling her wine onto the couch.

"I made ten-thousand last month," I said. I reached for my glass only for Angel to pull me into a hug first. "It's not all in one place. It's social media, Spotify, YouTube, other creator programs—"

"Lily, it's amazing!" Angel pulled away from the hug. "You're amazing."

My face hurt. The entire room felt hot, especially as he looked at me in awe.

"Okay," I said, kicking Nova to stop her from laughing so hard. "I don't want to talk about it anymore. I want to just … do normal college girl things." Even as I said the words I knew how ridiculous it was. Nova snorted into her wine glass, but at least she wasn't laughing anymore.

"Classes start next week," Angel said.

"Monday," I corrected. It was technically just a few days away. We got home from New Orleans with just enough time for me to prepare.

Nova clapped her hands together. "And I got into Yale, believe it or not, so I start Monday too and I am excited. Lily gave me a tour when we went to get books yesterday."

"Don't say it like that," I told her, reaching past Angel to swat her leg. "Your art is so good." I would never tell her about the favor I asked of my parents. I wasn't lying when I told her that she was a great artist. Yale had also thought so and was happy to have her in the program. I was worried my parents would resort to donating more money than they already did to the university, but it turned out that the recommendation of two high-profile alums was more than enough for the program to accept one more transfer student.

"Okay. Fine. I'm just excited that everything came together the way it did," she said and took another sip from her glass.

"I'm going to put my laptop on the charger," I said, taking my laptop from the coffee table and grabbing my wine glass. My heart didn't slow until I sat my laptop on my desk and pulled out my phone. I downed the last of my wine as I waited for my mom to pick up.

"Mom," I said, going toward the bedroom door. I made sure Angel saw me on the phone before I shut the door.

"Dad's here too. I have you on speaker," she said, my dad calling out a greeting from the background.

"What did you guys think? It's gorgeous, isn't it?" I asked, my stomach aching with guilt.

"Oh, it's beautiful!" my mom said, drawing out the words. "I told your dad that we should keep it for ourselves. The estate has been in the family a long time, you know it's paid off. We don't own any other properties. You could expand our vineyard and the business."

"Donna," my dad chided in the background. I heard static on the line, and my parents whispering before a deep breath came through the line. "All right, Lilypad. You never ask us for anything."

"I asked about Nova—"

"You never ask for anything for yourself," he corrected, ignoring my mom in the background. It sounded a little like she was bargaining with him and it made me anxious that my whole plan was asking for too much. God, I was a spoiled brat and I was a selfish one for even asking this. I stared at the log-in page for my laptop, wondering if I should just shut it and forget the whole thing.

"Dad, I know it's crazy—"

"I want you to listen to what I have to say first, Lilypad," he said.

I bit my lip as I logged into my computer, the listing coming up immediately. "Okay."

"I talked to my guy—my accountant. I talked with my accountant. We looked at your trust fund again. Everything is fine and you can afford it, especially with the information you provided us from your business. It's really not a matter of the money, Lilypad. Our concern is you and why you want to do this," he said.

I knew they would ask, but part of me wish they would live up to the stereotype and act like one million dollars was chump change. It was, for them. The moment I graduated college and gained access to my trust fund I would become a millionaire. That was just from the trust fund alone, not the multi-six-figures I was projected to make in just another few months. I'd doubled my income from my YouTube every month since I started it and I was overwhelmed with the influencer side of things on social media.

And my mom was right about one thing, the one thing they'd wanted to do once my dad decided to retire from his business career.

Expand their winery.

"The vineyard is perfect and it's one of the oldest in the country," I said.

"Lily Thompson, you've never shown interest in taking over the family business," my dad said firmly, making me feel more like I was in a board room than my bedroom. "Which is why I have to ask and why you better tell me the truth, young lady. Why are you asking that your trust purchase this property in Spain?"

This was humiliating. Still though, this was so important. We needed this. It was the only way we could get in that vineyard.

"It's the only thing left of his family, Dad," I said, my voice thick with emotion. I closed my eyes and tried to take a deep breath, relief coming just second later in the form of two words.

"Okay then."

I felt like Jell-O. I sank into the desk chair and stared at the photos of the Spanish estate, the view of the mountains, the two-story mansion, the pool overlooking the vineyard …

"Okay?" I asked.

"Yes. Okay. I'll tell the realtor to move forward with the purchase. Your mother and I would like to buy the vineyard. I assumed you would accept that, but if you really want a vineyard—"

"No, Dad. You and Mom can expand. You can have the vineyard," I said through my tears.

"So, that will change things a little. Your trust will purchase the house then. When you said the estate was in Spain, we both had our suspicions that Angel was involved."

"Please, don't tell him. It's a surprise," I said, hearing my mom gasp. "And no, it's not a proposal. Not yet. No, we didn't get secretly married. No, we aren't running off to Spain together. I just want to give him his family's land, you know, whenever it all happens?"

In any other circumstance, this would feel like a stupid risk.

Maybe buying your boyfriend's family home was a stupid risk, but it was too perfect.

"How romantic," my mom cooed in the background.

"We won't spill the beans to anyone. Right, Donna?" my dad said, his tone thick with accusation.

My mom gasped. "Don't look at me like that. I won't tell a soul."

I could hardly contain my excitement. I gave them the updates since we got back from New Orleans, let them know that I was prepared for the start of the semester, and then we ended the call. I knew it would take some time. I would be sitting on this secret for a while, but it would be worth it in the end. I was sure.

I knew we would visit that vineyard in the future, because I saw it in my vision back at the warehouse. Maybe Angel could have more than just the cure. Maybe he could take back what belonged to his family, what he had lost centuries ago.

I went to the bathroom to splash a little water on my face. I tucked my phone in my pocket and opened the bedroom door. Angel finished emptying the last of the wine bottle into Nova's glass before standing up. He wrapped his arms around my waist and pressed his lips to mine for just a moment, leaving me wanting more.

"Better, Mouse?" he asked, his lips brushing mine, teasing me.

"Better than ever," I said and rose onto my toes to kiss him.

ACKNOWLEDGMENTS

There are so many people who have helped me along this journey as an author, but especially the Curse of Wings series. First, I need to thank all of my friends for their support and encouragement. Jill, you have been amazing and so helpful. Thank you for reading all of my books and pointing out all the mistakes. I mean it, it helps so much and I'm a better author for it. Whitney, thank you for encouraging me on the rough days and reminding me of my goals. Being an author can get lonely and you both always know how to make me feel a little less alone.

I am so thankful for my family for their support. My husband has always encouraged me to chase my dreams, even during the messy days of getting started as a published author. Alex, you have always been by my side and I can't thank you enough for your support and reassurance. I love you so much. I'm thankful for our son for reminding me, especially on those super busy and stressful days, that it's important to do things just for fun and the joy of creating something new.

Of course, all of this couldn't have happened without the help of my amazing editor Lucia Ferrara. I have worked with Lucia on all but one of my books and it is always such a great experience. Lucia, I have learned so much from your feedback. You are always a lot of fun to work with and I look forward to sending my books to you every time I finish them. I'm always excited to see what you think. Thank you for helping make my books the best they can be.

I write all of my books for the love of writing and storytelling, but I am so incredibly thankful for the readers. Thank you for reading this book and any book I've written. It means so much to me.

ABOUT THE AUTHOR

Amy Prokopis is a fiction author from Oklahoma who writes paranormal romance and romantasy books. She graduated from Oklahoma State University with a bachelor's degree in English and a minor in German before obtaining a master's degree in school counseling. Besides writing, Amy enjoys distance running and spending time with her husband, their son, and their Havanese, June.

ALSO BY AMY PROKOPIS

Visit my website to subscribe to my newsletter!

www.amyprokopis.com

Follow me on social media!

A girl on the run for her life.
A boy searching for a better future.
Two nations on the brink of war.

Guardians of the sixth gate.
Complete the circle.
Find your match.

He's a 500-year-old vampire looking for the cure.

She's a college girl with a traumatic past.

She has all the answers he's looking for.

She just doesn't know it yet.

Winter Romance
with a witchy twist!

Enter the Trial for Marriage.
Win her own hand.
Usurp the throne.
Free the Light Realm.

www.ingramcontent.com/pod-product-compliance
Lightning Source LLC
Chambersburg PA
CBHW071412300726
48976CB00006B/2071